MALIQUE'S QUEST

By Giselle Lumas

Also by Giselle Lumas

Romance:

Tug of Love
Melody's Blues
Truth or Dare: A Love Story
A Holiday Bet
Alida's Way
Her Forgotten Halo
Captain of My Heart
The Captain's Son

Young Adult Romance:

Sandy Times

Young Adult Fiction:

Journal of a Cymbal Player

Children's Book:

THE SUPERHERO WHO SAVED CHRISTMAS (Co-author Tyler Lumas)

Collection of Romantic Short Stories:

Love Stories Short and Sweet: Some with a Little Tart

Visit the author's website at www.gisellelumas.com.
Email the author at gigilumas@att.net.

This is a work of fiction. Names, characters, and incidents
are products of the author's imagination or are used
fictitiously and are not to be construed as real.

DEDICATION

For my kids. I love you.

CHAPTER ONE

On a sunny April Saturday afternoon, Malique Laveaux
zoomed on his skateboard with a racing heartbeat and
jumbled nerves. He won the skating competition fair and
square, so why was he now running or rather skating for his
life? Probably because of the four guys chasing after him
and possibly something to do with the fifty dollars, he
snatched out of Ricardo's hand. Despite his rush of
adrenalin, he grinned from the memory. The shock and
disbelief on Ricardo's face was priceless.

Malique saw that the road he planned to take was, in
fact, a dead end. He skidded to a stop, pressed the back of
the skateboard with his right foot. The board flipped in the
air, and then he caught it. He threw the board over the
chain-linked fence, backed up a few feet then climbed over.
He picked up his board and decided to take the rest of the
way home on foot. He glanced behind him and noticed he
finally managed to lose the guys. Good. He needed to catch
his breath. He saw a little flower shop on Main Street close
to his school, so he slipped inside.

His breathing was heavy, and he was sweating. A
petite woman with curly brown hair and beautiful hazel
eyes with remarkable thick lashes was at the counter and
looked a little startled by his appearance.

He didn't blame her. What normal kid in Beach City,
California would wear an oversized gray trench coat, denim
shorts passed the knees, military boots, and a two-inch afro
and carrying a skateboard?

"Hello, may I help you?" The woman asked kindly.

Malique leaned against the counter, still fighting to
catch his breath. "Yes--- yes--- yes--- please mam---" deep
breath in, hold it, deep breath out. He briefly closed his
eyes. He heard his inner calming voice remind him again.

Take a deep breath in--- hold it for a moment--- deep breath out, repeat two more times. He did as his voice told him to and filled his body and spirit with calm. Finally, he spoke again, "May I have some water, please?"

"Sure," the lady said, "Lani!" The woman shouted. "Lani, come bring this young man a cup of water."

Malique could hear what sounded like a girl shout, "Fine." He listened to the stomping of feet going farther into the back of the store.

A girl with curlier hair than the lady at the counter appeared. The girl must have been about ten years old, brown hair with natural golden highlights, cat-like hazel eyes with a hint of gold in them, full lips, and an attitude that would undoubtedly scare any horrible monster away. The girl looked up at Malique and said, "Here." She shoved the glass of cold water at him.

He gratefully accepted the water, "Thank you." He then gulped it down.

The girl crossed her arms, then rolled her eyes before she abruptly turned and stalked out of the room.

"I'm sorry. You'll have to excuse my niece. She believes she is the ultimate princess and shouldn't have to serve anyone, ever. Of course, she is mistaken--- she isn't the ultimate princess. I am." The woman calmly explained, then smiled.

Malique wasn't sure if he should laugh since it seemed she was serious.

Her smile broadened as if reading his mind. "I'm kidding, of course," she admitted.

"Oh. Okay." Malique said with uncertainty.

Malique took a sip of water and felt the chilly water trickle down his throat.

"So, you are running from someone?"

Malique's light brown eyes widened. He took another sip of the water then nodded in agreement.

"Why?" The woman asked, resting her elbows on the countertop and leaning forward.

"I--- I--- I won a skateboarding bet fair and square, but the guy didn't want to pay me. He flashed the money in my face to taunt me, but he was an idiot. I reached out and grabbed it since it was rightfully mine and ran."

The woman laughed. "Oh, you remind me of my sister. She was so strong and would not allow anyone to pull a fast one on her, either."

Malique could see that the woman's eyes were getting misty. He started to feel uncomfortable. He didn't want to get stuck in the middle of some lady's sad memories. He had enough of his own old memories to deal with, and he was only fifteen.

He cleared his throat, then placed the glass on the countertop. "Thank you for the water, mam."

"Before you go---" the woman hesitated. He noticed something like a spark in her eye, "What is your name?"

"Malique," he said as he rushed out of the flower shop and hopped on the skateboard. He only had two more blocks to go until he reached his foster mom's house. Sasha would be angry with him for being thirty minutes late for dinner.

Sasha was in her kitchen, leaning over her stove. Malique walked up behind her and kissed her on the cheek. "Hi, mom."

"Mali, why are you late?" She asked in her naturally raspy, deep voice. He always felt the warmth in his heart whenever she called him Mali.

"I lost track of time. Sorry."

"Why do you smell like flowers?"

"No idea," Malique quickly changed the subject. "What are you making?"

"Spaghetti. Can you and Mel butter the bread, sprinkle the garlic seasoning on it--- then stick it in the oven for a few minutes?"

Malique knew Sasha wasn't asking but rather instructing.

"Mel!" Malique shouted.

Melanie Richards appeared in the kitchen doorway seconds later. Her straight waist-length black hair was pulled back in a messy ponytail. She put her hands on her hips. "You summoned me, oh mighty brother from another mother."

Malique rolled his eyes but still managed to smile, "Mom needs us to butter the rolls."

"Sure, as long as I get the end pieces."

He handed her a butter knife and said, "Whatever you wish, Princess."

After dinner, Melanie and Malique cleaned the kitchen then went to their separate rooms. Malique finished his homework then lay on his bed, tossing a ball up and down. His mind drifted to the woman and the girl from the flower shop. Something about them seemed familiar, almost as if he knew them before, but he knew that was impossible because he had never met them before in his life.

Maybe the woman was just reminding him of his birth mother. That must be it. The little girl is probably about the same age as his sister would have been had she survived the car crash.

He stopped tossing the ball and held it for a moment. He hadn't thought about the crash in years. Why would he start thinking about it now?

Malique felt hot. He sat up and took off his long sleeve t-shirt, denim shorts, and thick socks. He walked over to the full-length mirror that hung on the back of his bedroom door. He took a deep breath then glanced at himself in the mirror.

"Zebra," he said to the reflection in disgust. That's what the kids at the group home had called him. He didn't blame them. There truly wasn't any other way to describe his two-toned skin. He wondered what his real skin color was supposed to be. His entire body was a kaleidoscope of patterns, shades, and shapes: one elbow was darker than the other; one hand was darker than the other. He always wore long sleeve shirts to cover his arms. He wanted to be in shorts but was embarrassed by his legs, so opted for longer shorts passed his knees.

For some reason, tennis shoes were uncomfortable. Malique's feet were unusually sensitive, so he wore military work boots with thick socks. Most people viewed him as odd, but he didn't care. He felt comfortable and natural. It was bad enough he had to wear long-sleeve shirts. He refused to make any other sacrifice. His feet were protected- after all, it's what carried the rest of his body daily.

"Respect the feet always," a flash of a memory popped into his head of an older man sitting next to him with dark skin holding a thick cigar in his right hand. "If it's the only thing you remember from me, grandson, remember to respect the feet."

Malique glanced down at his feet. He reached for the foot scrub, nail clippers, and file. He didn't know why his grandfather was so adamant about keeping up his feet, but since it was the only few memories he recalled of his family, he consistently maintained his feet. He would soak them weekly, scrub and file them nightly.

Later that night, Malique saw images of his baby sister. She was only three months old, but her eyes were catlike with thick lashes, and hazel. He dreamt of the accident again. One moment he was sitting in the back seat of the car with his sister, the next the car was spinning out of control, rammed into something hard then flipped in a rolling motion at least three times then--- blackness.

He always woke when the blackness of the dream set in. He felt his heart ramming in his chest. The pain in his soul cracked, and the agony across his skin prickled with searing heat. It was always the same whenever the dream started. It didn't matter that his foster mom had given him a dream catcher to hang above his bed while he slept. She said the web of silk string would capture all the horrible dreams and turn them into something happy.

But the problem was it wasn't just a dream or a horrible nightmare; it was an awful, shocking, traumatic, and dramatic experience that he would never be able to erase from his brain. He tried not to think about it. He tried to redirect his thoughts just as his therapist had told him. He tried to think of his grandfather instead, but always, always the memory would take over.

Malique blinked and let his eyes roam to the green glow of the digital radio alarm clock on his nightstand. It was 3:13 AM. He had another three and a half hours to go before he had to get ready to start his day at Beach City High School. *Big whoop*, he thought with an enormous amount of sarcasm.

He didn't exactly enjoy serving time at the institute for the spoiled, wealthy upper-class kids who predominately lived in overpriced beach houses and drove Mercedes, BMW's or Audi's to school. He didn't need all of that. All he needed was his skateboard, radio, and yes, the Kindle his foster mom bought him for his birthday. The Kindle was one luxury he had--- Okay, and his generic MP3 player. His escape was reading and music.

Many kids didn't know Malique. He was pretty much a loner at school. That didn't mean he was lonely, though. He only felt isolated or disconnected when he was with an organized crowd where he didn't belong. Unfortunately, that pretty much described his entire experience at school.

At some point, he must have drifted off to sleep because he woke to the radio alarm blasting a Bruno Mars song. Unfortunately, today was anything but a lazy day.

Malique breezed through his school day up until his last period, which was P.E. Derrick, a six-foot, two hundred pound bully tried to humiliate Malique by ripping Malique's long sleeves off his shirt.

"What?" Malique shouted, "Are you trying to undress me for your own pleasure! Do you have the hots for me or something?" Malique shouted at Derrick in retaliation as loud as possible. Everyone in the gym turned to stare.

"No, you freak! I just want to remind everyone of what a freak you are with your zebra skin! You freak! Are you contagious?"

"That's right! I am a freak!" Malique shouted in the middle of the gym with his fists balled up tight. He visualized taking a swing at Derrick right across his left cheek with such force that he would be thrown across the gym then would slide down the wall with a crushing force. Instead of hitting him, Malique took a deep breath then continued to shout, "I was born with two-tone skin. There's nothing I can do about it--- just like you were born an asshole!"

"Hey!" the coach shouted before blowing a whistle loudly. "Malique," the coach pointed his thumb towards the gyms main exit, "principal's office now!"

Never would the coach send Derrick to the office. Nope. Not the prized quarterback for the school of the rich and privileged a-holes.

Malique skipped the showers, grabbed his stuff then headed for the principal's office. He didn't care how sweaty and odor offensive he might be. He was tired of the bull. He passed Vicky, the redhead at the principal's receptionist desk, to sit in the usual spot near the principal's office door. The door was open, so the principal knew when Malique took a seat.

"Malique, I wasn't expecting you to appear until Friday but already on a Monday?" Malique stood and followed the voice.

13

"Yes, Mr. Johnson. I guess I just couldn't wait to see you."

Mr. Johnson laughed. "Have a seat."

"Thanks."

"So--- profanity this time?"

Malique sighed, then answered, "Yep. I couldn't think of a better word to describe Derrick."

Mr. Johnson clasped his hands together and looked into Malique's light brown eyes. "Well, considering the coach is a close friend of Derrick's father. I'm not surprised he sent you instead of Derrick. Besides, you were the only one who used profanity."

"Do you even know what happened?" Malique asked, scratching his chin.

"Yes, I have eyes and ears everywhere and will often know what happened before you set foot into my office." Mr. Johnson couldn't hide his proud grin. He cleared his throat then said in a low voice, "Don't worry, Malique. I know you're a smart kid. Take the rest of the afternoon off. I'm not counting this against you. I'm watching the coach and Derrick." Mr. Johnson cleared his throat again then said more loudly so others outside his office could hear, "No more profanity. Choose your words carefully. You're dismissed."

Malique smirked, stood up from the leather chair then mumbled, "Yes, sir."

Malique skateboarded home with his backpack over one shoulder. As he was about to pass the flower shop, he heard a familiar female voice, "Hey! Shouldn't you be in school?"

Malique skidded to a stop then turned to see who was speaking. It was the ten-year-old girl from the other day who had given him the glass of water. She was standing in the doorway of the flower shop. "I could ask you the same question."

"Well, if you did ask, I would say it's none of your business, or I would tell you my auntie picked me up early to go to a doctor's appointment. We went already and just got back. So--- why aren't you in school?" She asked, tilting her head to the side.

"I am going with your first answer and say--- It's none of your business."

The girl narrowed her hazel eyes at him, crossed her arms, and tapped her right foot. Her thick, curly hair bounced whenever she moved her head. "Well, that's not fair," she whined. "I said that at first, but then I gave you the real answer. It would be polite if you gave me the real answer, wouldn't it?"

Malique tried to hide his grin. He imagined his little sister would probably do the same. He remembered his mom would cross her arms and tap her right foot whenever he got caught doing something wrong.

"Fine," Malique said, moving closer to her then spoke in a low voice, "between the two of us--- I was asked politely to leave school since I participated in a fight."

Her eyes widened, and she let out a gasp. "Wow---" she whispered, "you were in a fight?"

"Yep."

"You don't have any blood on you."

"Well, it wasn't a physical fight--- more of a verbal match. But it could have easily turned into a real fight."

She uncrossed her arms, then glanced over her shoulder to make sure no one was around. She whispered, "This is going to sound weird, but I had a dream about you---"

Malique raised his eyebrows, "Really?"

"Yep."

"What happened in the dream?"

The girl glanced over her shoulder into the shop and then over Malique's shoulder outside. She gulped then said, whispering, "We were on a sh---"

The girl was interrupted by her aunt, who said, "Well, hello, Malique, how are you?"

"He got into a fight at school and was asked politely to leave."

Malique wanted to get the focus off of himself, so he cleared his throat, then said, "Hey, don't you think it's a little rude to tell a stranger's business." He tilted his head, thought for a moment, then added, "Somehow, it seems unfair that you both know my name, but I don't know anything about the two of you."

The girl faked a shocked expression and dramatically put her right hand over her heart. "What lies are spoken in my aunt Sokie's flower shop!"

The woman grinned and rolled her eyes, "Oh, Malique, Lani has a flair for drama," her eyes twinkled, "just like my sister. She has a hobby in trouble and dramatic ways to get herself out of it."

Malique felt comfortable with the two of them. He strangely felt connected and wanted to know more about them. "So, Sokie and Lani?" He asked.

"Yep. See, you lied. You know a lot about us."

He frowned and asked, "Like what?"

"Our names, where we live--- where we work."

His eyebrows raised from surprise, "Wait--- you guys live here?"

"We aren't guys, and yes, we do," Lani answered.

"Stop giving Malique a hard time." Sokie gently placed a hand on Lani's shoulder.

Malique grinned and nudged Lani on the other shoulder, "Yeah, listen to your auntie. Stop giving me a hard time."

Lani shook her head, "It's too much fun. Hey, why don't you stay for dinner?"

"Oh," Sokie sounded off guard.

Malique waved his hand. "No, I better go home. My mom will know about the fight and will wonder why I haven't shown up at home yet. Maybe another time Lani."

Just as Malique was about to leave, the flower shop door opened, and the bell chimed. Malique turned to see a girl he occasionally saw around his school. "Clarissa, you're early today," Sokie said to the girl.

Clarissa flipped her brunette wavy hair over her right shoulder and dropped her over-loaded gray backpack onto the countertop. "Last period ended early." Clarissa glanced at Malique. She narrowed her eyes then tilted her head to her right side. Her hair swayed as she moved. Her eyes were such a bright blue Malique couldn't help staring. He'd always seen her from afar. They never had any of the same classes, and she hung out with the so-called popular kids at school.

"Hey," Clarissa said, she snapped her right hand then pointed at Malique, "I know you. You go to my school. What are you doing here?"

Lani bounced up and down and announced, "He's my new friend. He promised to have dinner with us tomorrow."

Sokie and Malique both started to correct her, but Clarissa said, "Cool," before they could get any other words into dispute.

Malique blinked in surprise. He would have thought someone as beautiful and fashionable as Clarissa wouldn't want to spend any time with him.

"I've always wanted to get to know you," Clarissa stuck her right hand out and said in a raspy voice, "I'm Clarissa Jones, but I guess you already figured that out. I work here a few days a week, and Lani baby sit's me every once in a while." She grinned, perfect sparkling white teeth with a dimple in her left cheek. Malique felt his heart skip a beat. He reached for her hand to shake it and prayed his hands weren't as sweaty as he thought they were.

17

Thankfully, if they were moist, Clarissa didn't make any indication of the fact. Instead, she grinned wider.

Everyone looked at Lani as she nodded excitedly and said, "Yep, I babysit her."

Sokie giggled.

Clarissa turned her attention back to Malique and slowly withdrew her hand. She blinked a few times rapidly then looked into his eyes. Her cheeks flushed a slight pink. She cleared her throat, then said, "So, what's your name?"

"He's Malique," Lani answered for him, still bouncing up and down, but now she was shifting from foot to foot.

"Um, Lani, why don't you help me carry these boxes upstairs?" Sokie suggested as she pointed to the boxes in the corner of the store, Malique hadn't noticed before.

Lani stomped her foot but took a couple of boxes. She followed Sokie to a room in the back of the shop.

Clarissa and Malique watched them disappear. Malique took a deep breath to calm his nerves. He shouldn't have anything to be nervous about. So what, Clarissa was beautiful, but they didn't know each other. So, nothing to worry about, right? "Um--- as Lani said--- I'm Malique, but you can call me Mali."

"So what grade are you in?" she asked as she walked behind the counter and reached for her backpack. She shoved her backpack into a hidden cubby behind the counter.

"I'm a sophomore. What about you?" Malique asked.

"Same here. I'm surprised we've never been in any classes together."

"Well, I guess we don't have the same interests or something." He wasn't going to mention that he was in predominately remedial classes, to his foster mother's disappointment. He just didn't see the point in taking advanced classes when he didn't plan on going to college. He planned to learn all he wanted to learn on his own through reading and personal experience. He wasn't sure

18

what he wanted to do after high school, but Malique figured he had a couple of years to figure it out.

"So, what are you interested in?" Clarissa asked, leaning over the counter, resting her chin in her right palm.

"Well--- I--- um---"

"Other than skateboarding and getting into fights with Derrick, I mean," she grinned.

"I--- um---" What was wrong with him?? His mind was useless. Why couldn't he talk to her?

She smiled. "You know--- you're kind of cute."

Malique's jaw dropped open from shock. No one ever told him that before. He scratched his head, then reached for his skateboard. He needed to go. "I better go." That's right; he needed to run.

Clarissa only grinned bigger.

What was wrong with her? He wondered. Before he could get away, though, Lani rushed back to them. Before he could stop her, she jumped into his arms and wrapped her arms tightly around him and gave him a big kiss on his cheek. He felt his heart tug towards the little girl. "Come back for dinner tomorrow, okay?" Lani asked, holding his face between her tiny hands and looking into his eyes. "Promise."

Malique sighed and said, "How can I say no to you?"

"And that is why she thinks she's the princess," Clarissa said.

"Yep," Sokie agreed.

Malique let Lani go then walked towards the door. His nerves were rattled. Not sure what to make of any of the females in the flower shop. He just knew it was beyond time to get out of there. He skateboarded his way home.

CHAPTER TWO

There was a message on the answering machine when Malique entered the kitchen. He knew in his gut that it would be his foster mom. He sighed then reluctantly clicked the play button. "Malique, you know when you get into trouble at school, I expect you to come straight home. If CSS hears about this, they can come by to check on you. I talked to the principal. We will talk about it later. Since you're home, make dinner tonight. It's a hamburger helper night. There are crackers in the cupboard. Help the other kids with their homework too. We can all watch a movie when I get off of work. Love you." The machine beeped. CSS (Child Social Services) were not his favorite people. He felt pretty confident, though, that he would stay with Sasha. He was fifteen now. He only had three years left. At least he hoped he'd stay. He liked it here.

There was another message on the machine that began to play. It sounded as though someone was having difficulty breathing. Malique wasn't sure if it was a male or female, but it seemed like someone old, "Don't let them see it. Don't---" then there was a click. Malique grabbed the cordless phone. He went through caller ID. There was a call from Sasha and a blocked number. Malique shook his head, then deleted the messages. He figured it was someone calling the wrong number.

He started thinking about the last message and thought the voice sounded vaguely familiar. He wasn't sure how, but it did. Now he wished he hadn't erased it so fast; he should have played it a few more times. Maybe it would have made him remember whatever it was that he was missing or forgot. *Hmm, don't let them see. See what? And who was them?*

20

Malique shook his head again. He needed to think about other things. He glanced at the clock. The other kids would be coming home soon. It was already almost four. Two of the kids would be coming back after soccer practice, and Melanie would be coming home after flute lessons. He decided to start making the hamburger helper, knowing that the three kids would like to eat as soon as they got home. While Malique was cocking, images of Clarissa popped into his head, the way she flipped her wavy brunette hair to the other side of her shoulder, her bright blue eyes burning into his. He felt dizzy just thinking about her. "Get a grip Malique," he chastised himself.

He'd never had a girlfriend. It might have something to do with his inability to communicate with girls. So, he couldn't maintain a decent conversation with them. How would he be able to ask anyone out on a date? How would he hold a girl's interest on a date if he couldn't talk to them? They couldn't just make out for the whole date, could they? Hmmm--- he started to wonder. He could make out with Clarissa for a while. He began to fantasize about what it would be like to kiss her. He imagined she'd be an excellent kisser since she seemed to hold hands with a different guy every week. So a week must be her limit for boyfriends, he guessed.

Then he felt a jolt of panic. What would he do if she ever wanted to kiss him??? He'd never kissed a girl before. Well, not anyone who wasn't a mom or sister figure anyway. How was he going to handle that? He was fifteen and had never been kissed. He was probably the last guy on campus who never kissed a girl. He had a hard time breathing suddenly.

Malique had to put the wooden spoon down he was holding to mix the hamburger helper, and had to raise both of his arms above his head in an attempt to catch his breath. Just as he was finally feeling enough air enter his lungs, Melody walked into the kitchen. "Hey Malique, oh,

21

yummy, hamburger helper. Woo hoo!" She dropped her flute case onto the table. Luckily, she hadn't noticed Malique's difficulty in catching his breath. Instead, she immediately started discussing her day at school.

Soon the twin eleven-year-old boys who were also foster kids to Sasha entered the house. They kicked off their cleats and shoved them underneath the coffee table in the living room. Malique could see them from the kitchen. They were both loaded with dirt and grass stains. He wondered if there were any dirt and grass left on the field. "Hey, you two take your showers before you eat. After we all eat, we all need to do our homework."

The twins groaned but did as they were told. They all adored Sasha and her daughter Melody. They all wanted to stay with Sasha, so they never gave each other any trouble. Sasha lived by the three strikes you're out rule. If any of them did anything serious three times, she would call CSS, and they would be removed. None of them ever witnessed Sasha calling CSS to complain, but none of them wanted to risk it either.

Around seven-thirty, that evening, Sasha returned home from working as a nurse at the local hospital. She would be off of work for the next couple of days, so she was in a perky mood. "So, how was everyone's day?" Sasha asked Melanie and Malique. They were all lounging in the family room. A reality show on one of the music video stations was on. They made a single general comment, "Fine," almost in unison.

Sasha gave each of them a kiss even though none of them sincerely acknowledged her. They were in the I'm-watching-a-show-I-really-wanna-watch zone. She waved a tired hand at all of them then carried herself to the kitchen. Moments later, Malique appeared.

"What? You aren't watching that reality show garbage?" Sasha asked.

"Well, kind of. I just wanted to tell you something before I forgot."

Sasha grabbed a dish from one of her top cabinets in her kitchen, scooped up some hamburger helper, plopped it on a plate then stuck it in the microwave for a minute and a half. "What's up?"

"Would you mind if I have dinner at a friend's house tomorrow? I know it's kind of last minute, but I thought it would be okay since you have the next couple of days off. Since their house is on the way home, I thought that would be double okay."

Sasha smiled a little, "Of course, you can go to your friend's house."

Malique grinned, "Thanks." He gave her a thumb's up.

"Just give me your friend's name and phone number in case something comes up, and I need to get in touch with you."

"Oh," Malique felt the happy bubble he had only moments ago begin to break. "I don't have their number."

"Their? As in more than one friend?"

Malique bit the side of his lip. Did he have to go through the interrogation? It wasn't as if he was going out on his first date or something. It was just dinner with Lani and Sokie. *Geesh!* He sighed. "Their names are Lani and Sokie. Lani is ten and lives with her Aunt Sokie. Sokie owns the flower shop on Main Street."

The microwave beeped. Sasha grabbed two potholders from one of the granite countertops then opened the microwave to pull out her dinner. She grabbed a fork from one of the drawers and sat at the oval oak table. Sasha pointed a finger up as a signal to Malique to pause for a moment. She wanted to take a bite of her dinner. She closed her eyes and let out a small groan. She chewed then swallowed. "You'd think this was a gourmet dish! Mmmm--- it tastes so good. I must be really hungry." She let out a little laugh. "I usually don't like hamburger helper."

23

Malique shifted from leg to leg. He wanted to talk about Lani and Sokie, not about hamburger helper. As if reading his mind, Sasha said, "Okay, so--- look up the name and phone number of Sokie's flower shop and give it to me. Actually, write it down and leave it on the refrigerator with one of the magnets. Okay?"

Malique grinned, "Okay."

"Who's Sokie?" Melanie asked

Malique tilted his head back and let out an exaggerated sigh. He lifted his hands above his head and asked no one specific, "Why me? Why all the questions?? Geez!"

Melanie looked at her mom for an answer to her question.

"She owns a flower shop on Main Street. She and her niece invited him to dinner tomorrow?"

"Hmm--- Interesting," Melanie said as she grabbed an apple then walked out of the kitchen.

Malique dropped his hands, then tilted his head to the side. "Why is it interesting?" Malique mumbled.

"Probably because you never go to dinner anywhere," Sasha answered. Changing the subject, she asked, "Did you do your homework?"

"Yep."

"Did the other kids do their homework?"

"Nope, the boys are doing it now in their rooms."

"I already did mine!" Melanie shouted from the family room.

"Does she have to hear everything?" Malique asked.

"Yes!" Melanie shouted.

The next day at school, Malique was putting his skateboard in his locker when Derrick walked by and gave him a little shove. Malique almost hit his head on the side of his locker. "Derrick! Stop messing with him!" Derrick turned around, and so did Malique. Clarissa approached them both, carrying a couple of books.

"Why do you care?" Derrick asked.

"He's a friend. Leave him alone."

Derrick narrowed his eyes and shook his head. "Whatever," he said, then stalked off.

Clarissa stood next to Malique. He closed his locker after pulling out a notebook and textbook. "I'll walk with you to your class," Clarissa said with a bright smile.

"Um--- I--- why?" Malique said awkwardly.

"Because I want to get to know you. That's what people sometimes do."

"But--- really--- why do you want to get to know me?" Malique frowned. He wasn't sure how to feel about a girl sticking up for him. He was used to Derrick and knew how to handle him. Her intervention would only make things worse.

"Malique, you've been here for the same amount of time I have, but we've never spoken. I like to get to know people, okay? Don't be so defensive."

"That's what I don't get. Why do you want to get to know me now? It's like you said, I've been here for just as long as you have and now suddenly you see me. I don't get it."

"Well, mostly because any friend of Lani and Sokie's is automatically a friend of mine. I also figured if you talk to me here at school, it might make dinner tonight a little less awkward for you."

"Wait, you're going to be there tonight?" Malique felt his heartbeat increase. He wondered if she could hear his heart slamming into the walls of his chest.

Her eyes were bright, and the dimple on her left cheek exposed as she smiled again, "Yes, of course." Just when he thought his heart couldn't beat any faster, it accelerated at the sight of her dimple. How could one person be so amazingly beautiful and be talking to him of all people?

Malique frowned.

"Why are you frowning?"

"I don't know," he answered honestly. "I mean--- I---"

Clarissa glanced at her cellphone. "We better get walking, or we will both be late for class. Where are you headed?"

"Science. What about you?"

"English, my favorite subject," Clarissa said with another smile and almost skipped as she walked.

They headed towards the Science building. Finally, Malique said, "You know--- why are you so perky? Like--- all the time?"

Clarissa said, "Why wouldn't I be? I woke up this morning and had an awesome breakfast. And now--- I'm here with you."

"Wow," Malique found himself smiling. "That was--- that was super cheesy." He chuckled.

She giggled too.

"It's true, though. I mean, it takes a lot to upset me. I just think no one should take life for granted, and each day a person wakes up, they should shout out a gigantic THANK YOU and start the day fresh."

Neither of them noticed other students staring and whispering as they walked together. When they reached the science building, Clarissa said, "I'll meet you in front of the cafeteria during lunch, okay?"

Malique's mouth dropped open. "I---"

"You know--- you do that a lot. Open your mouth and stutter," she laughed.

He took in a deep breath. "You sure you want to hang out with me like that? Wouldn't that drop you from the popular crowd or lower you on some sort of radar or something?"

"There is no such thing as popular," she waved with her hand. "See you at lunch." She turned then started jogging towards the English building.

Malique had a hard time focusing during his classes. His mind kept involuntarily drifting to Clarissa. The way the denim jeans wrapped around her legs snuggly and the way the bright blue shirt made her eyes a more dazzling blue. Then, of course, the waves in her hair were silky, and he wanted to run his hands through it.

At lunch, he grabbed and stuffed everything from his backpack into his locker then wandered over to the cafeteria. He shifted from leg to leg as he waited for Clarissa. He generally either slipped into the library or walked around the campus aimlessly. He rarely actually went to the cafeteria. A few people looked at him with questioning eyes. From the corner of his eyes, he saw hair flying around. He turned to see Clarissa running towards him. He couldn't help but smile.

"Sorry for making you wait," she said almost out of breath. She placed her right hand on his shoulder and held her stomach with her other hand. She took in a few breaths in and out. "I had to talk to Mr. Gatlin about my paper for psychology. He gave me a seventy-two out of a hundred. I aced that paper." She shook her head, "He's rereading it and will let me know tomorrow."

"You mean he's going to change the grade?" Malique asked, surprised.

"He'd better. I proved he was wrong--- he's having a hard time with a student being right and he's wrong."

"Hmmm---"

"What?" Clarissa asked. Finally, catching her breath, she removed her hand from his shoulder.

"It's just that I didn't know they could do that," he said.

"Do what?" Clarissa asked, confused.

"Change a grade," Malique explained.

"That's because you don't talk to people. If you tried to get to know other people--- other students--- teachers--- then you would know that."

27

Malique shook his head, then mimicked her with a high pitched voice, "If you talked to other people, you'd know." He shook his head again. "You're making me out to be someone who doesn't communicate with any other human being. Clarissa, I'm just saying I didn't know teachers were allowed to change grades," he explained in his regular voice.

"Oh, well, yes. Whenever a teacher tries to give me anything less than a ninety-five percent, I talk to them."

"So you mean, you've never received a grade lower than ninety-five percent?" he asked, amazed.

"No, I'm saying I've received plenty of grades lower than that, but I always talk the teacher out of it."

"Hmmm---"

She appeared to be getting bored with the conversation but explained quickly, "Both of my parents are attorneys, okay. I know how to argue my way out of anything. Can we go eat now?" She didn't wait for his answer but instead grabbed his hand and pulled him into the cafeteria.

Now, there were stares. Malique immediately felt uncomfortable. Everyone was looking at Clarissa, holding Malique's hand. Clarissa appeared to be clueless. If she wasn't, she chose to ignore the stares and continued to hold his hand until they reached the end of the line. They each picked up a tray. "Looks like its meatloaf and mashed potatoes today. Are you up for it?"

"It comes with a chocolate chip cookie so yep, I'm up for it," Malique said with a smile.

"You can't have the cookie until you eat all your lunch first."

"But the cookie is included with the lunch. I can eat the cookie first if I want to," Malique argued.

Clarissa put a hand over her heart and let out a gasp, "No! You can't do that. That's just out of order. My nanny would never approve."

"Wow," Malique shook his head.

"What?" She asked, handing her tray to the woman with the big spoon to plop a large gob of mashed potatoes onto her plate.

"Nanny? You have a nanny."

She sighed. "Yes, my parents are never at home. She's one of my best friends."

"So, do you ever cook or clean?"

They moved onto the meatloaf man who cut an inch thick piece of the meat and gently placed it on the plates. When they reached the cookies, Clarissa pointed to the biggest cookie and the cookie woman with thongs in her hand-picked it out and placed it on her plate.

"Of course I do."

Malique found that hard to believe and laughed.

"What?"

After Malique received the smallest cookie of the bunch, he followed Clarissa to a table where a few girls were sitting.

"I just find that hard to believe--- I mean--- I don't know if I would want someone else picking up my mess or any of my things, for that matter."

Clarissa shook her head in disagreement. When they were closer to the table, the three girls' eyes widened in surprise. Clarissa introduced Malique, "Angie," she pointed to a redhead with long curly hair, freckles, and green eyes. "Celeste," the dark-haired, seriously mean-looking girl with dark brown eyes. "---and Lisa," she pointed to a blue-eyed beauty with thick black hair who had a perfect double dimple smile. "This is Malique. He's going to sit with us today."

"Um, do you honestly think it's a good idea, C? My Derrick is going to be here any minute now," Celeste questioned.

"Yep, if Derrick has a problem with it, he can eat somewhere else," Clarissa said matter of factly, with a shrug of her shoulders. "I don't like him and wish he would stop eating with us."

Celeste gave Malique a dirty look and clenched her jaw.

"You guys can sit next to me," Lisa said perkily.

Both Malique and Clarissa placed their trays on the table at the same time. Then they sat down at the same time. Angie and Celeste exchanged glances, but Malique and Clarissa didn't notice.

"So anyway--- Malique here doesn't believe I know how to cook and clean. Can any of you ladies explain to him how I'm a world-class chef and borderline OCD when it comes to keeping stuff clean?"

Lisa laughed out loud and almost spat out the sandwich she was eating. "She's horrible! Clarissa can barely make mac n' cheese from the box! As for cleaning, she's a slob. She's lucky she has a housekeeper."

Clarissa's mouth dropped open. "You know, I should shovel a spoonful of mashed potatoes and fling it at you for that! I won't though--- only 'cause I'm hungry."

Angie chimed it, "Yep, I agree with Lisa. Sorry C."

Malique laughed.

"So---" Lisa asked, "why have you suddenly decided to grace us with your presence today Malique Laveaux?"

"Geez Lisa," Angie elbowed her, "Don't have to pry so soon. I was going to wait for us to be alone with Clarissa, then we could talk about him behind his back. You know?"

"Yes, I know, but I thought I'd try the more direct approach--- You know--- just dig right in and get to the nitty-gritty."

"Does anyone say nitty-gritty anymore?" Angie asked.

"Ladies---" Clarissa said, almost shouting. "Knock it off. Okay?"

"Well, explain."

Malique bit the side of his lip, not saying a word. He shrugged his shoulders, feeling out of place. He wanted to go to the library and somehow sneak his lunch in. Usually, he just walked in with his backpack and ate his lunch while he read a book in one of the small cubicles. He was starting to miss the safety and solitude of his cubicle right now.

"He's a friend of Lani and Sokie's, so I thought I'd get to know him. It's as simple as that."

"Hmm---" Lisa said.

Angie tilted her head to the side, "And why are you working at that flower shop anyway?"

Clarissa sighed as if she were tired of the same old story, "I told you guys this a thousand and one times before. I have to work if I want to get the new iPad. My parents are making me."

"But why? I mean, they can just get it for you today. It doesn't make sense to me," Angie said snobbishly.

"Look, not all parents spoil their kids. I have to pretty much work for everything I have."

"Oh, right--- like the maid, the nanny and the personal chef don't do anything for you," Angie said, with a hint of bitterness in her tone. Malique found the conversation fascinating. He would have said the same thing Angie did, but Angie just said it quicker before he did.

Clarissa frowned for the first time since he met her. Her face reddened. "Angie, you don't know me as well as you think you do. I would advise you to keep your mouth shut."

At that moment, Derrick and a couple of other guys from the football team approached the table. "So what, you and freak boy are an item now?"

"Derrick!" Clarissa shouted angrily. The whole table became silent, and all eyes were on Clarissa. "Well---" She stood up exasperated. "Malique--- let's sit outside. It's full of hot air over here, and I just can't be around it anymore."

Malique's mouth moved to the side. He knew there was probably something he was supposed to say, but his mind was blank. He didn't like being the center of attention. He always wanted to be invisible, so why try starting to be visible now. He stood and followed Clarissa as she stomped off. They found a table under a tree on the patio. The patio overlooked the center of the campus. Surprisingly, it was quiet. He guessed it was because no one else was on the patio.

Malique immediately relaxed. Clarissa was sitting across from him, and her face was still red. She ate all of her meatloaf and most of her mashed potatoes in silence. She took a sip of her bottled water then finally made eye contact with Malique. He felt his heart race again. How did she manage to do that to him with just a look?

"I'm sorry," she said in a low voice.

Malique took a sip of his water. "Why? You didn't do anything."

"Well, I know--- I mean--- I just know you wouldn't have had to deal with them if it weren't for me forcing you to eat with me."

Malique rolled his eyes. "Um--- you didn't force me to do anything. I wanted to eat lunch with you. If I didn't, I wouldn't have shown up."

Clarissa put her elbow on the table then her chin in her palm. "I didn't know they were going to be jerks. I mean, I knew Derrick would, but not my girls."

"Look, I'm sure they were only curious. They didn't mean anything by it."

"Yeah, well, I don't think I'm talking to them for a while. Will you have lunch with me tomorrow too?"

"Umm---"

"Please?" She asked.

"Sure."

"Thanks," she gave a small smile.

He wanted to know more about her. He found it fascinating that even though her parents were well off, she was working. He thought it must have been a sore subject, though, so would have to save it for another conversation another day.

"So, you have made a big impression on Lani," she said. Some of the brightness in her eyes was coming back, and she even gave a little grin.

"I don't know why. I ran into the shop one day on accident. Then she saw me yesterday on my way home and stopped me. She's something else."

"Yes, she is. She's extremely perceptive for a ten-year-old. She's also an extraordinarily good judge of character," Clarissa said proudly. "I've been babysitting her since she was seven. We're pretty close. She's like the baby sister I've always wanted."

Malique's expression saddened a little. Briefly, he thought of his baby sister. He was thinking of her a lot now.

"What's the matter?"

Malique shook his head, "Oh, nothing." The five-minute warning bell rang.

Clarissa looked disappointed. "Geesh! We barely finished lunch. All the drama in the caf took up so much time. I'm sorry."

Malique stood up. He shoved the water bottle under his arm and held the cookie between his teeth. He reached for Clarissa's tray. She passed it to him. He dumped the contents from each of the trays then placed them in the tray holder slots above the trash can. He took a bite of his cookie then held the water bottle. "So, what class do you have now?" Clarissa asked.

Malique grinned, "Art, my favorite. What about you?"

It was her turn to grin, "Dance, my favorite."

They walked towards the gym, where Clarissa's dance class was held in one of the smaller classrooms adjacent to the gym. "Hey, I thought you said English was your favorite."

"Ah--- Mali! You were paying attention!" She exclaimed. "I have two favorites--- English and dance." He felt his heart tickle when she called him by his nickname.

"Let me guess--- theater is also a favorite."

"I love going to the theater--- movie, plays, music--- you name it. Maybe we can go together someday," Clarissa offered.

"Maybe," Malique said with a wave goodbye. It was his turn to start jogging to his class.

After school, Malique hung around his locker a little longer than usual. He was hoping Clarissa would want to walk to the flower shop together. He'd let her ride his skateboard if she wanted to. After about ten minutes, Malique figured she must have left already. He'd have to find out where her locker was tomorrow. It would be nice to stop by and say hi to her.

Dinner at the flower shop wasn't supposed to be until seven since the flower shop closed at six-thirty. So that meant he had three and a half hours to kill. He decided to go home for a few hours to work on his homework. Melanie was on the phone when he walked in. "Oh, hold on a sec. One of my brothers just came home." She covered the mouthpiece on the phone, then asked Malique, "What are you doing home? I thought you are supposed to have dinner with friends?"

"Do you need to know everything?" He dropped his backpack on the carpet next to the coffee table.

Melanie was lounging on the brown leather couch with her socked covered feet on the coffee table. He pushed them off the table then sat next to her. He stood up briefly to fling off his trench coat, tossed it on the love seat then sat back down.

"Why ask? You know I do," she answered.

"It's not until seven."

"Oh," then she went back to talking to her friend.

Malique tuned her out. He put his arms behind his head and closed his eyes. He hadn't realized how tired he was until he sat on the couch. His breathing began to slow, and he dozed off briefly. He heard a clear, crisp male voice in his head say, "They are coming soon. Be ready."

Malique sat up straight and looked around, blinking his eyes. Melanie was still on the phone. "Did--- did you--- did you hear that?" Malique asked Melanie.

Melanie frowned, placed her friend on hold, and asked, annoyed, "What?"

"Someone--- I--- did you hear someone else say something here in the room?"

"Uh--- no," Melanie said in her annoying sisterly way.

Malique shook his head, trying to clear it. It couldn't have been a dream. He didn't fall into a deep sleep or anything. He scratched his chin and felt a little stubble. He wondered if he should shave before going to the flower shop. It wasn't as if he had a ton of hairs on his face--- just a few random stubbles sprouting here and there. He wished he had a dad he could ask. He thought of his grandpa. What would he say? He guessed he would say shave off whatever stubble you do have. *Be presentable for the ladies. Always be presentable.*

CHAPTER THREE

Malique arrived at the flower shop just as Sokie was turning the blue neon CLOSED sign-on. She unlocked the door and held it open while he walked in. She caught a whiff of his aftershave. "Well, well, well--- don't you smell nice for a change?" She locked the door again once he made it inside the store.

He laughed. "I thought I'd take a shower before dinner. You and Lani always seem to run into me when I'm sweaty and smelly."

She nodded in agreement. "Well, thank you. It will make eating dinner pleasant." She patted him on the back. "Clarissa and Lani are already upstairs, and they better have the table set and ready. There are chips we can munch on until the lasagna is ready to come out of the oven."

"Oh, one of my favorites. Is it homemade?"

"Well, it depends on what you mean by homemade. I made it to the store, and I took it out of the box and put it in the oven." She laughed. "Follow me," she waved and walked passed him. They walked passed a few refrigerators holding flowers in vases then to the back room he had seen Lani disappear into several times. They walked behind a curtain to what appeared to be a small storage area for supplies and a locked door. Sokie opened the door and gestured him to go first. Malique found a staircase and began his climb. The closer he got to the top of the stairs, the more he could hear Lani and Clarissa arguing.

"Lani, you're putting too much dip on your chips. There won't be any left for Malique when he gets here."

"Malique doesn't like dip. He won't care," Lani explained in a sensible tone.

"How do you know that?"

"I don't know. I just do," Lani said in an exasperated tone.

Malique finally made it to the top of the stairs and entered a rather large living room with tan carpet, oak coffee table, light brown couch, and a love seat, each covered with a white crocheted blanket. There was also a rocking chair in the corner of the room and a flat-screen television mounted on the wall. The kitchen was off to the right. It was half the size of the living room with a small four seated round oak table. A big bowl of French onion dip was in the middle of the table, and a Ruffles bag of chips was directly in front of Lani. "Lani, no more until after dinner," Sokie reprimanded.

Lani finished chewing the chip that was already in her mouth then crossed her arms. "That's not fair. Why do I have to be the only one who can't have chips and dip?"

"Because you are the only one that will get so full of junk food, you won't eat any of your dinner." Sokie held up her finger before Lani could say anything further. "Ah, ah, ah--- not another word."

Lani crossed her arms tighter and pouted with her lower lip sticking out a lot more than her upper lip dramatically. Malique grinned. "Tell you what; I won't have any chips either. I will wait for you. Okay?" He offered to Lani.

She uncrossed her arms, then said, "Okay."

"Besides, you're right. I don't like dip." He loved salsa but not regular dip. He wondered how she knew that.

Clarissa gave Lani an amazed look.

Malique took a seat next to Clarissa. "I was going to ask you if you wanted to walk here together after school."

"Oh, I'm sorry," Clarissa said as she grabbed the chip bag from Lani's reach and put it in her lap. She grabbed a chip and popped the whole thing in her mouth. She chewed, swallowed, then explained. "I guess I should have offered you a ride here but figured you'd probably want to go home for a few hours. We had a ton of orders to fill. It's been a busy day."

"Yes, it's been busy," Sokie agreed and sat in the only remaining seat between Malique and Lani. "It's a good thing, but it can get pretty exhausting. I'm so lucky to have Clarissa helping me out."

"Oh, you drive?" Malique asked.

"Shhhhh---" Clarissa said with her right index finger to her lip. "No, I don't have a license, but I've known how to drive ever since I was twelve. My nanny showed me how. She said she learned how at a young age, and since I was exceedingly mature for my age, she thought I should learn. My parents are never around, so I drive all the time."

"Wow," was all Malique managed to say since it was the only thing he could come up with. To think he was going to offer her a ride on his skateboard. He mentally banged his head on a wall, over and over again. He glanced at Sokie and Clarissa. They were still exchanging flower arrangement ideas for a demanding customer.

Sokie and Clarissa stopped talking. Sokie glanced at Lani curiously then at Malique. "Hmm," Sokie said. Malique wondered what Sokie was thinking about.

"C, don't you think you should stop eating all of the chips? There won't be any left for after dinner for Malique and me," Lani whined.

"Mali, and you will have plenty to munch on after dinner."

"Mali?" Sokie asked with a confused expression on her face. "Who's Mali?"

"Oh, it's my nickname," Malique explained.

Lani crossed her arms and started to pout again. "So Clarissa can call you Mali, but we can't?" She appeared to be genuinely hurt but the discovery.

Malique rubbed the sides of his temples. "Lani, you and Sokie can call me Mali anytime. I just never got around to telling you both."

"But she knew, and I knew you longer," Lani's face was getting red. Malique didn't understand why she was getting so upset. Big deal, Clarissa knew his nickname first.

"Lani, that's enough. Clarissa and Malique go to school together so they will probably see each other a lot more."

"Well," Lani continued pouting, "that's not fair." Her arms were still crossed, and she was still frowning at Malique.

"Why is it not fair?" Malique asked, a little annoyed.

"We are supposed to be closer. We have a lot more to talk about. You shouldn't be hanging around Clarissa more than me."

Clarissa leaned over to Malique and said in a whisper. "I think she has a crush on you. You're her first." Malique was shocked.

The timer on the stove went off. Sokie stood and grabbed a couple of potholders from one of the kitchen countertops. She opened the oven to check on the lasagna. "Mmm--- it's ready! We will let it cool for a few minutes, and then we can all dig in."

Lani remained silent for the duration of dinner.

Clarissa shared a few of her ideas for the upcoming Halloween season for floral arrangements. "Do people order flowers for Halloween?" Malique asked.

"People order flowers all the time, especially when there is love in the air. We will start getting advanced orders for Thanksgiving less than a week after Halloween. Christmas is the busiest next to Valentine's Day, of course."

"Maybe I should consider going into the floral business," Malique said softly.

"Hey, that's something I haven't asked you yet," Clarissa said. "Do you work? What are you planning to do after high school? Are you going to go to college? What are you thinking about majoring in?"

Malique started to feel uneasy. He could barely handle being asked one question, but to be bombarded with multiple questions at one time was nerve-wracking. To top that off, the questions had to be something he was uncertain of--- the future. He didn't like thinking about the future. Going into the future would only remove him farther from his past. Being farther from his past meant he would be farther and farther away from his mom, sister, and grandfather.

"Hello---," Clarissa said.

"Oh, sorry," Malique said to Clarissa. "I got lost in thought for a second. No, I don't work yet. My mom won't let me. She wants me to focus on my school work and wants me to be available whenever she needs me to watch my brothers and sister."

"Oh," Sokie sounded disappointed. "You have brothers and a sister?"

"Yes, one very loud and opinionated sister and two jocks for brothers."

"Well, that must be fun. I always wanted a brother or sister," Clarissa said.

"Yeah, me too," Lani said, "but we have each other. Right C?"

Clarissa smiled, then agreed with a simple, "Yep."

"Neither of you are missing anything. Having siblings aren't what they are cracked up to be. They get into your stuff. They get into your business--- it's not pretty."

Sokie laughed a hearty laugh. "Oh yes, I remember my sister would always want to wear my clothes, date my boyfriends, make my friends hers--- very annoying."

"My mom used to try to steal your boyfriends?" Lani asked, genuinely curious.

"Oh yes---"

"What about my dad? Was he your boyfriend?"

Sokie rolled her eyes, "Heck, no."

Clarissa almost choked on the chip she was eating, from laughter.

"Wow," Malique said with a giggle, "that was a little harsh."

Sokie sighed heavily, "He was--- how should I put it---"

"A dork?" Clarissa offered.

Sokie shook her head in disagreement.

"Muy intelligente? Mucho machismo?" Clarissa tried again.

"What's with the Espanol?" Malique asked.

"Figured it might sound better--- or--- something," Clarissa said before popping another chip in her mouth.

Lani snatched the bag of chips out of Clarissa's hands with a massive frown on her face. "My dad wasn't a dork. He wasn't mucho intelligente either, or whatever you said--- stop bad-mouthing my daddy when you didn't even know him!"

Sokie bit the side of her mouth then said, "Honey, she was complimenting your dad in Spanish--- kind of. Anyway, your dad was a complicated man, and someday I will tell you more. I just don't think right now is the time."

"You promise?" Lani asked.

Sokie nodded in agreement.

"Pinky promise me," Lani was still holding the chips in her left arm but stuck out her right pinky, holding it over the table. Sokie reached out with her right hand, sticking her pinky out. The two encircled their pinkies.

"I pinky promise to tell you all that I know about your father in the future when the time is right." Then Sokie reached across the table and kissed Lani on the lips. She also quickly grabbed the chips out of Lani's arm before she realized what was happening.

"Hey---" Lani said.

"Let's eat some real food," Sokie said.

After dinner, Sokie surprised everyone with a batch of brownies and vanilla ice cream for dessert. Lani smacked her lips as she finished up the last of her ice cream. "Thank you, Aunt Sokie. That was so good!"

Sokie began gathering all of the dishes from the table then kissed Lani on the top of her curly head. "You're welcome, Lani."

"Oh, wait," Clarissa held up her hand to stop Sokie before picking up any more dishes. "Mali and I will clean up. Right Mali?" She asked, looking at Malique.

"Oh--- right--- It's only fair."

Malique stood, grabbed the dishes from Sokie's hands then followed Clarissa into the kitchen.

"Well--- I guess I cannot argue with that demand. Thank you both," Sokie said before sitting back down at the table.

Malique washed the dishes while Clarissa put them away. They worked in comfortable silence. Lani and Sokie went into the small family room and started watching television. By the time Malique and Clarissa were done, Lani's head was resting on Sokie's lap, and her eyes were closed.

"Well, I guess we should get going since Princess Lani is asleep," Clarissa said.

"I'm not asleep. I was just resting my eyes," Lani sat up quickly with her eyes wide open.

Clarissa yawned. "I still need to go--- I'm sleepy. I'll see you tomorrow, though."

"Oh, I thought you had the day off."

"Nah, I think I will come in anyway. You don't have to pay. I just need something to do."

Sokie shrugged her shoulders. "Okay, but I will pay you if you end up working. Thank you."

"Guess I will be going too. Thank you for dinner and dessert it was delicious," Malique said with a smile.

Malique grabbed his skateboard then walked with Clarissa down the stair to the entrance of the flower shop. They each gave both Sokie and Lani a hug goodbye.

"Mali, I will give you a ride home. I don't want you to skateboard home in the dark. Weirdo's are out there."

"You don't have to. I can take care of myself."

"Well, I'm going to anyway," Clarissa insisted. She pulled her keys out of her oversized handbag then clicked her remote. The alarm beeped on a bright yellow Volkswagen Beetle. "Hop in."

Malique shrugged his shoulders then hopped into the car; he kept his skateboard on his lap as he buckled up. "Thanks," he said as Clarissa buckled herself in.

"At least now I can see where you live--- More to know about you."

"Oh--- great---" Malique murmured sarcastically.

"So--- you never mention your dad. Why is that?"

Malique cleared his throat. "I never knew him. He left right after my little sister was born. I don't remember much about him. If I remember right, he was never home even when my mom and dad were together."

"Do you know anything about him?"

"No, not really. I don't want to know anymore. I mean, you would think my dad would have come for me after the accident--- But---" Malique stopped himself. He hadn't meant to bring up the accident.

Clarissa still hadn't started the car. They were still sitting in front of the flower shop. "Accident? What accident?"

Malique groaned. He didn't want to talk about it. In fact, he didn't want to talk period. "On second thought---" He touched the handle of the passenger door then said, "I think I will just skate home."

Before he could unlock the door, though, Clarissa quickly turned the ignition then pulled away from the curb. "Too late," she grinned.

Malique shook his head from exasperation.

"Look, you don't have to tell me tonight if you don't want to talk about it, but friends tell friends everything."

"No, they don't," Malique said, with a little bit of a high pitched voice and shaking his head vigorously.

Clarissa rolled her eyes. "Well, we will."

"No, we won't."

Clarissa laughed. "Geez--- You're ridiculous. You know that?"

Malique smiled despite his agitation.

"So, tell me where you live."

"Crap--- do I have to?"

She lightly punched him on his left shoulder.

"Fine, just turn right at the next street. The third corner--- make another right."

"So, what are your plans for the weekend?"

"My sister will be playing in her school's concert this weekend--- other than that; I will probably just go skateboarding or something."

"Oh--- Okay. Well, if you want to do something, just call me. I'll give you my phone number when we get to your house."

A few moments later, Malique pointed to his house. It was a single story with red brick surrounding the front of the house, with a white security screen on the front door. He was about to leave, but she stopped him, "Wait, can you pass me the notepad and pen from the glove box?" She pointed to the glove box in front of him.

"Sure," he opened the glove box, and sure enough, there was a pen and small notepad. He passed it to her. Clarissa scribbled her name, email address, and phone number, then drew a smiley face and a flower and gave it to him.

He took it and said, "Okay, thank you." He hopped out of the car before she asked any more questions or made anymore demands. He waved then rushed to the door to get inside.

CHAPTER FOUR

Saturday morning was peaceful. Sasha had taken Malique's foster brothers to a football game. Melanie had left early in the morning to go to her school to help set up and prepare for the concert she would be performing in. So, Malique mostly had the whole house to himself for the first few hours of the day. He planned to spend the day playing video games in his pajamas. Nothing exciting--- at least that was the plan--- until the doorbell rang. Knowing that he was the only one in the house, he knew he would have to answer the door. He groaned, put down his video game controller then headed toward the front door. He didn't care that his afro was flat on one side and puffy on the other. It was HIS Saturday, and his day to relax--- not impress. He looked through the peephole just as his foster mom always told him to. He didn't recognize the older gentleman on the other side. But the stranger looked--- What would the right word be--- educated or--- worldly. So he opened the door.

The man let out a heavy sigh of--- What?? Relief maybe. The man stuck out his right hand and introduced himself. "Hi, you must be Malique. I'm Professor Chapman from Los Angeles University. How are you?"

Malique glanced at the man's outstretched hand then up his arm to his chest. Professor Chapman was wearing a light brown corduroy jacket with brown patches at the elbows, a soft blue button-up shirt, blue jeans, and loafers with a pair of white socks. Malique smirked, accepted his hand, and gave him what he thought was a manly handshake. "Kind of dressed stereotypically, aren't you? I mean--- like--- you're overdressed for the part."

Professor Chapman laughed a fake laugh. "Well, it was always a dream of mine to become a professor, and I've always wanted to dress the part. I even bought myself a pipe, but I don't smoke it." He chuckled, this time genuinely. He shoved his glasses further up his nose. His blue eyes looked into Malique's.

"So, how do you know my name, and why are you here?" Malique asked, crossing his arms in front of his chest.

"Well, honestly, I've been searching for you. I was a friend of your mom's."

Malique immediately uncrossed his arms. "You're a friend of my mom's? You know, Sasha?"

Mr. Chapman appeared confused, but then he shook his head as if to clear his thinking. "What? Oh, no--- not your foster mom. I was friends with your real mom--- Monique."

Malique felt his heart begin racing. He felt the tension rise in his throat; it was a feeling he tended to get just before he needed to have a good cry. Hearing someone else speak his mother's name after so many years of not hearing it touched something profound inside of him. "How--- how do you know my mom?"

"We went to college for a while. I dated her roommate for a long time. Mo was one of my best friends. I was sorry to hear about her passing. We were email buddies, and suddenly one day, I just stopped receiving emails from her. So I asked around and just found out a year ago about the accident. So I've been searching for you and your sister ever since."

"Oh, well," Malique felt that sudden sinking feeling of sadness weighing down on his heart. "My sister died in the crash too."

Mr. Chapman had a stunned look on his face. Then shook his head vigorously. His light brown hair covered his eyes momentarily; he used one of his large hands to shift the hair away from his eyes. "Oh, no," he said excitedly, "she didn't. I looked at the police records. I--- okay--- I shouldn't have said that. But--- listen--- Never mind, how I know--- but your sister is alive. The car seat was thrown out of the car, and she was missing for a few hours, but they found her alongside the road. She was fortunate. Anyway, they placed her in a home. I'm trying to find her as well."

Malique's entire body relaxed. He didn't know what to say. He felt an unusual feeling overwhelm him. His sister was alive! He had always hoped but squashed the hope because he didn't want to get hurt again. But, here and now, this complete stranger was telling him she was actually alive. Well, was Mr. Chapman a stranger? Maybe to him but not to his mom--- Maybe---

"Do you mind if I come inside? I could certainly use some heat and a chair for sitting in for a little while."

"I'm sorry, I know you say you knew my mom, and you knew about the accident, but I don't know you. My mom would kill me if she found out that I let a stranger in her house---"

"Okay, I understand," Mr. Chapman said disappointedly. He paused for a moment then took out his wallet from a back pocket in his jeans. The professor took out a business card. "I've got an idea," he handed Malique the card, "here is my business card. My phone number and email are on there. Google me and hey--- google your mom. There should be pictures of us together somewhere--- I think you can even download pictures from our college yearbook at the University's website. You will see we were best buds back then. Call me when you're ready to talk. I have lots of information I can provide---" Mr. Chapman licked his lips then bit down on his bottom lip for a moment. He looked into Malique's eyes. Mr. Chapman's eyes were watery; he placed his right hand on Malique's shoulder. "There are some things you need to know. Okay?"

Malique hesitantly accepted the card. "Okay," he agreed.

Mr. Chapman removed his hand from Malique's shoulder but outstretched it for a shake. "It was a pleasure to find and meet you, Malique, finally."

"Um--- thank you?"

Mr. Chapman chuckled. "Okay, hope to see you soon." Mr. Chapman waved, then turned and walked down the porch steps. Malique closed the door, locked it then leaned against it. He stared down at the card. It read Mr. Evan Chapman, Professor of History, Los Angeles University. It also had the University's logo embedded in the card in gold scripting. He knew his mom attended the same University. He didn't remember her talking much about her roommate, much less anyone by the name of Evan. He sighed. There was only one thing he could do--- To take Mr. Chapman's advice and google--- But--- He needed a computer to do that.

He would either have to go to the library or wait until school on Monday. Malique rubbed his hands through his hair. He was suddenly feeling antsy. He wanted answers now and couldn't see himself waiting until Monday. He thought for a minute. Sasha had a laptop, but he wouldn't be able to use it until she got home. Then she would end up asking him questions about why he was using it. Then she'd probably get her feelings hurt if she knew he was researching about his mom. Just then, he heard another knock on the door.

He turned around and looked through the peek hole. On the other side was someone with dark wavy long hair--- His heart skipped a beat. "Clarissa?" He asked to no one. She knocked on the door again.

Now, he wished he'd taken his shower and wasn't still in his pajamas. He put his head down, then shook it. Why was she so--- so--- Interested in him? Well, she would just have to accept his messy side. He cleared his throat, then pulled open the door.

"Well, good afternoon, sleepyhead," Clarissa said and pushed on the door to let herself in.

He tried to hide his irritation but asked, "What the heck??"

She laughed. "Well, I would have called you to let you know I was coming over with bagels if you gave me your phone number. You know--- you need to work on your social skills. When someone, especially a girl, gives you their phone number, it's only polite for you to give them your number--- You know?"

"Well--- Maybe--- well--- Psst--- maybe I didn't want your number. Maybe I didn't want to give you mine."

"Obviously. That's why I'm here."

He let out a breath of exasperation. "Clarissa---"

She held up the bag of bagels. "So you have six different bagels to choose from. I wasn't sure what type you liked, so I picked a few of my favorites. Plus, I have a little container of pure cream cheese that we can share. I hope you have milk or orange juice 'cause I didn't think to buy any."

"Um--- I---"

She looked around the house and saw the kitchen beyond the family room. As she walked toward the kitchen, she passed the bag of bagels to him and removed her jacket. She placed her coat on the back of one of the chairs, then pulled the chair out and sat down. She curled her right leg under her left then pretty much sat on her foot.

"Well--- Gee--- make yourself at home," Malique said sarcastically.

"Go ahead--- pick one out, then I'll pick mine," Clarissa said perkily.

On cue, his stomach growled--- which only made him more annoyed.

"How did you know I would be here? I told you I was going to my sister's concert and skateboarding."

"Well, I know the concert at the junior high school isn't supposed to start until later today. I figured if you were skateboarding, you wouldn't be too far from your house--- so I just took a chance. Glad I did, right? Now you have a free lunch."

"Breakfast---" Malique said grumpily.

"It's eleven-thirty--- give me a break."

"Fine--- brunch." He smiled.

Clarissa stared at him for a moment.

"Um--- what?" Malique asked, feeling uncomfortable.

"I love it when you smile."

"Stop being cheesy," Malique said, rolling his eyes.

She giggled. "Speaking of cheese--- get the cream cheese out of the bag--- Grab a knife--- pick a bagel already. I'm hungry."

He put the bag on the table in front of her. Then walked over to the oak cabinets and pulled out two glasses. "We have apple juice, orange juice, and milk--- which do you want?"

"Oh--- I'll take apple. I love apple juice."

He placed the glasses on the table, filled one with apple and the other with orange juice. "You pick which bagel you want first--- ladies first." Malique insisted.

"Why, thank you, sir. I appreciate it." She grabbed the cinnamon and raisin one.

"Just don't pick the cinnamon and raisin one--- or blueberry or jalapeno and cheese--- or garlic," Malique said.

Clarissa put her hands on her hips, "Knock it off! I'm taking the cinnamon and raisin."

"Let me guess, it's your favorite," he teased.

She took a bite of the bagel. She nodded in agreement as she chewed.

He looked in the bag and grabbed the blueberry bagel then sat next to her.

The sun was shining on top of the oak table. As Malique used the plastic knife to spread the cream cheese on top of his bagel, the sun highlighted some of the shapes on his hand. He was glad that he was wearing his long-sleeved pajamas so that Clarissa couldn't see his arms. He noticed Clarissa was staring at his hands from the corner of his eyes. He was accustomed to people staring, but something about the way Clarissa was looking at him made his stomach do summersaults.

"So, where are you planning on skateboarding?" Clarissa asked.

Malique took a bite of his bagel and thought for a moment. He didn't want to skateboard today--- He wanted to get to a computer to research. Then the thought occurred to him. "Hey C, do you have a computer? With the internet?"

Clarissa stopped chewing and tilted her head to the side. "I do. I have my laptop in my backpack. It's in the car. Why? What's up?"

Malique started to regret asking--- he should have known there would be questions---but at least he didn't have to worry about hurting her feelings. "I need to Google someone."

"Oh--- really? Who?"

He took another bite of his bagel and chewed then took a sip of his orange juice. He debated how much he should tell her. He wondered if she needed to know any of it. "A professor named Evan Chapman and someone named Monique."

"Hmmm---" Clarissa finished her bagel, then sipped some more of her apple juice. "A professor--- from where?"

Malique scratched behind his neck a little nervously, "Los Angeles University."

"Who is he, and who's Monique?"

"You aren't going to just let me use your computer without a gazillion questions, are you?"

"Nope--- not until you answer all of my questions."

"So basically you're holding your laptop for ransom?" He asked, annoyed.

"Yep," she said honestly.

Malique finished his bagel then held his hands up as his sign of surrender. "Fine--- Gees--- C. Okay, how much do I need to tell you?"

"Finish telling me about the accident you mentioned last night then tell me who Professor Evan Chapman is--- then tell me who Monique is? Is she a girlfriend?"

"What? No---" Malique put his elbows on the table then rubbed his face in his hands from the frustration. "Fine--- okay."

"Okay? Okay, as in you will tell me?"

"Yes--- Geees--- He rubbed his face again. "When I was five, my mom was driving my sister and me somewhere. Where--- I don't remember. I just remember it was raining super hard, and I don't think my mom wanted to take us with her, but she had no choice. Anyway, I was sitting in the back seat with my sister. She was in her infant car seat in the middle seat, and I was to the right of her. While my mom was driving, we were sideswiped--- the car was spinning and flipping. I blacked out. When I woke up, I was in a hospital. I was told my mom and sister died. There's a gap of time I don't remember---"

"But---" Clarissa's face seemed paler than normal, "but---" she pointed her index finger at the table--- "You said you have twin brothers and a sister---"

"Foster family," Malique explained.

Clarissa took another sip of apple juice then blinked a few times, "Oh--- I--- I didn't know--- I'm so sorry."

"Why are you, sorry? That's what I hate--- People telling me they are sorry, and they didn't do anything." Malique rubbed the back of his neck and closed his eyes.

"It's just that people don't know what else to say. They feel bad for you and what you went through Mali. Don't be offended by it. People care."

Malique opened his eyes and fought not to roll them at her. "You have a lot more faith in people than I do."

"Yes, I do," she said matter of factly. She took another sip of apple juice then encouraged him to continue talking. "So who is this Professor Chapman and who is Monique."

"See--- That's why I need to Google. I need to find out more about him. He just showed up a few minutes before you came over. He said he was best friends with my biological mom. Monique was my mom's name. He said he just found out about the accident a year ago. He said he was looking for my sister and me. When I told him that my sister died in the accident, he said, no, she didn't. He said he looked at the police report and found out she survived. He said he has a lot to tell me."

"Wow!" Clarissa sat back suddenly as if she was struck by something. "That's incredible! You--- you have to find her."

Malique nodded in agreement. "Yes. But I think I first need to find out if Professor Chapman truly was best friends with my mom, and I need to know if he's reliable and honest. I can't just take his word for it."

"I agree." She stood up and shuffled through her purse for her keys. "Why don't you take a shower, get dressed? I will go get the laptop from the car and start searching the internet."

"What makes you think I need a shower?" Malique frowned.

"Please--- You have total bed head right now, and you're in your pj's. Cute, by the way." Malique rolled his eyes.

"You know--- you need to stop rolling your eyes at me. Especially since you're using me for my laptop right now."

He rolled his eyes again. "Fine, I'm going to take a shower--- but don't start digging too deep without me. I don't want to miss any information, okay?"

"Yeah, okay--- whatever--- go take your shower," Clarissa said.

Malique disappeared down the hall to his room then into the bathroom. When Clarissa heard the water turn on, she went to her car for the laptop.

Fifteen minutes later, Malique wandered back into the kitchen. He was wearing long denim shorts, a long-sleeve gray thermal shirt, and his predictable military boots with thick white socks. Clarissa heard the clump, clump of the boots as he re-entered the kitchen. He was running a giant comb through his hair. He had curly ringlets throughout his hair. "So, did you find anything?"

"Not yet. I'm on the University website now and just found where they keep their yearbooks. Do you know what year your mom graduated from college?"

"Well, she had me a year or so after she graduated, so it must have been 1995, 1996 or 97?"

"Hmm---" Malique stood behind her. She was sitting at the kitchen table again. She was clicking on several links then found the 1995 yearbook. What was your mom's maiden name?"

"Alexander."

She searched for the professor and his mother--- nothing appeared. She clicked on 1996 with the same results. Finally, for 1997, though, a picture of Evan Chapman with glasses popped up on the screen. The professor was on the yearbook committee for that year. When Clarissa typed in his mom's name, an image of a beautiful light-skinned black woman appeared on the screen. She had curly hair and perfect teeth, dimples in each cheek, hazel eyes with thick lashes. She had no make-up except for glossy lips. "Wow," Clarissa said quietly, "she was so beautiful."

Malique felt a lump in his throat. "Yep," he agreed quietly.

"Let's see if she was in any clubs or on any committees."

"Okay," Malique said, still standing behind her and watching as she clicked away on the computer.

Clarissa tapped on the screen, "It looks like she was an editor of the school newspaper and in the history club."

"She liked history?"

"And journalism--- apparently."

"Let's check the school newspaper archives and see if they have anything else," Malique suggested.

"Okay," she said. Malique leaned in closer to see the screen more clearly. His face was right next to Clarissa's. So close, he could smell the shampoo in her hair. Coconut and lime, maybe? Her cheek was right next to his. He felt butterflies in his stomach. He quickly stood up. Then nervously reached for the chair next to her and decided to scoot a chair next to her rather than leaning in and being so close to her. She hadn't even noticed how flustered he became.

"Oh--- look!" She said excitedly and began pointing at the screen again. "Here's a picture of your mom and Evan. They are kissing each other."

"What? Kissing!"

"Oh, relax--- it looks like it was during a New Year's celebration. Friends do kiss each other, you know?"

"No, they don't," Malique said crabbily.

Clarissa looked at him then, with a twinkle in her eyes. "We will."

Malique froze for a moment, not knowing what to say.

She giggled then went back to focusing on the computer. She tapped her fingers to the keys and kept searching for more. Malique's brain stopped working momentarily. He daydreamed about kissing Clarissa. He wondered if they would--- And if it would be a real kiss or just a quick, friendly kiss. He asked himself which kind did he prefer? He wanted a real kiss. He seriously doubted that was something he would ever get from any girl, especially from Clarissa. "Hey, here's another picture of the two of them together. It looks like they were at a museum or something, but---" She tapped at the screen--- "Look--- there is someone else with them--- is that maybe your dad?"

He leaned in closer. His face was so close to the monitor. "That might be him, but he's so far away and blurred--- you know? Does it say who is in the picture?" He asked.

"Nope," she answered.

"But your mom is holding both of their hands---, so it looks like Professor Chapman was telling the truth. He was a good friend of your mom's."

Malique sat back in the chair. "Yep, I guess so."

"So, what are you going to do?" Clarissa asked curiously.

"I guess I will go meet him. I think I will wait until next weekend, though."

"Geesh--- that long? I would call him back today if I were you and insist on meeting him tomorrow."

"No--- I don't want to seem too eager. Besides, I can wait," Malique said. The truth was he needed some time to digest the fact that his sister was supposedly still alive, and suddenly he had someone who could tell him more about his parents. It was a lot to digest.

"Well, I will keep looking for more information tonight and print out pictures and whatever else I might find. I can give them to you on Monday at school," Clarissa volunteered. She began closing programs on the computer then started to shut it down.

Malique sat there watching her. When she closed her laptop, she turned to look at him.

"Thank you, C."

She blinked her blue eyes. She smiled a little--- enough to show the dimple. He felt the thudding of his heart and knew she had to hear it.

She reached for his left hand. "Anything to help a friend."

She released his hand, then stood up. She stuffed her laptop back into her backpack and said, "Enjoy the rest of the bagels. I'll see you on Monday."

She started to walk toward the door. Malique stood up and said, "Oh, wait--- you forgot your jacket."

He grabbed her jacket then rushed to meet her by the door. He handed her the coat. She bundled the coat under one arm and looked up at Malique. He was standing so close to her. Before he realized what was happening, she moved in closer. She tilted her head, stood on her tippy toes, and kissed him on the lips. He blinked. He didn't want a friend kiss. Without any further thought, he reached out with both hands on her waist and pulled her in. She gently dropped her backpack and jacket. She wrapped her arms around his neck and kissed him again. But this time, they each opened their mouths and allowed their tongues to slow dance around each other. Malique let out a tiny moan, Clarissa did the same. Malique could no longer think--- all he could do was feel the incredible sensations inside of him and across his skin. He felt goosebumps across his skin, and he felt something enveloping his heart--- it was as if he was thawing after being frozen and untouched for so long.

Almost as suddenly as it had started--- it ended. Clarissa pulled away. She rested her head on his chest for a moment. "Wow!" She whispered breathlessly. Malique held her for as long as she allowed him to. He was sure she'd never want to see him again.

She finally pulled away, cleared her throat, then grabbed her belongings again. "I'd better go," she said.

He only nodded. He was afraid to speak. He opened the door for her. He walked her outside, watched her get into her yellow Beetle, and waved to her as she drove away.

If it was possible to smile and frown at the same time--- Malique was sure he would be doing it right now. He didn't know how to feel. He had just kissed the most beautiful girl from school. It was the most amazing experience in his life. He wanted to do it again. He wanted to do it longer. He also never wanted to do it again, either--- because she was the most beautiful girl at school! What if he kissed her wrong? What if that was the worst kiss for her? He'd be an even bigger laughing stock at school than he already was. What was he thinking when he kissed her?? Oh, right--- That was the problem--- he wasn't thinking!

CHAPTER FIVE

On Monday morning, Malique decided to avoid Clarissa until he was brave enough to face her--- which could be never. Until then, he decided that he would return to his routine of lunch and breaks in the library in the security of his cubicle. He knew he made the right decision when after third period, Cassidy Walker visited him by his locker. He was a six-foot-eight basketball player who was also one of Clarissa's ex-boyfriends. He was needless to say, tall. He was also muscular, tanned with dark curly hair and brown eyes. He was chewing gum, leaning up against Malique's locker and obviously waiting for him.

"Hey, Malique," Cassidy said in his deep voice.

Malique was stunned Cassidy knew his name. "Hey," Malique responded in what he hoped to be a confident deep voice.

"Look, I know you've been spending a lot of time with Clarissa. Just letting you know--- I'm not okay with it."

Malique frowned. He could feel his blood begin to boil. "It's okay. You don't have to be okay with it." Malique surprised himself. He wondered where that came from.

Cassidy's jaw clenched, and his fist balled up. "I don't want you seeing her anymore."

"Too bad. If Clarissa wants to see me, she can. It's not up to you. Now, can you move so I can get my books out?"

"No, not until you tell me you will leave her alone," Cassidy said stubbornly.

"Look, Cassidy, I need to get to class. Just because you have insecurities, doesn't mean you need to block my locker and cause me to be late. Dude, you can have any girl you want. Why are you obsessing over Clarissa?"

Cassidy lunged toward Malique, lifted his hands as if he were about to wrap them around Malique's throat. Just then, a history teacher who also happened to be a physical education teacher stood behind Malique. "Malique, is everything okay? Cassidy, don't you have to get to class?"

Malique's eyes were wide. He'd never been more grateful to see a teacher. "Yes, everything is fine."

Cassidy leaned in closer to Malique and looked down on him with menacing eyes. "You better back off C," Cassidy threatened in a low voice then walked away without acknowledging the teacher.

For the rest of the day, Malique successfully avoided Clarissa. He told himself that it had nothing to do with Cassidy's threats but more to do with him not ready to face her. What did the kiss mean? Was it just any other kiss for her? It meant a lot to him. He cherished it. He wanted to bottle it up and keep it as a lifelong memory to take out and observe again later in the future. The visit from Cassidy, though, reminded him of just how many dates she had. How many other guys on campus had obsessions with her? How many other guys liked her or even loved her? He didn't need any drama. He just wanted to survive high school and get on with his life.

Later that day, when he was home, he finished his homework and sat on his bed, his back leaned against the headboard. He had taken out the Professor's business card and was now staring at it and contemplating calling him when the phone rang. He ignored the phone since he heard feet running across the living room floor. He listened to the mumble of Melanie's voice then the sound of feet running down the hall. Seconds later, Melanie burst into his room. "Someone named Clarissa is on the phone for you."

"Can you tell her I'm not here? Tell her I'm skateboarding and won't be back for a while."

Melanie sighed and rolled her eyes. "Fine. Whatever." She ran back down the hall.

Malique continued to look at the business card, flipping it around idly. He supposed it was time to call the Professor. He had to call him sometime, might as well call him now.

Melanie walked back into his room. "Hey, wanna play video games with me?"

He scratched his chin and said, "Sure. Are you done with your homework?"

"Yes, are you?"

He rolled his eyes, "Yes."

Melanie motioned him to get up and out of his room. "Well, let's play then--- come on. Hurry up before the boys wanna play something."

Malique rose from the bed and followed Melanie to the living room. "Can you set it up? You can pick the game. I gotta make a quick call."

"Fine," Melanie said. "First, you don't want to take a call, and now you gotta make one--- Whatever."

Malique ignored her but picked up the phone in the living room and nervously dialed the number on the card. He took calming breaths as he waited for someone to pick up the phone on the other end. On the third ring, the professor answered, "Professor Chapman, how can I help you?"

Malique cleared his throat. "Um--- Hi--- this is Malique."

"So glad you called Malique, how are you?" He could hear the smile in the professor's voice.

"I'm fine--- um--- I was wondering if you still wanted to meet with me."

"Of course, when and where would be good for you?"

"How about Saturday? Um--- at the coffee shop on Main Street?" The coffee shop was on the same street as the flower shop, but about half a block further down and across the street from it.

"Sure, sounds good. Would ten o'clock a.m. work for you?"

"Yes," Malique answered.

"Okay, see you then. And oh, it's my treat, okay?" Professor Chapman said.

"Okay," Malique said.

Clarissa called every day, at least twice a day. Malique successfully avoided her all week. He also managed to avoid both Derrick and Cassidy. In his eyes, it was a fantastic week. But on Friday evening, he began to feel nervous about his upcoming meeting with Professor Chapman. What did the professor have to tell him? How far away was his sister? Then he realized he'd have to at least pass the flower shop on Saturday on his way to and from the coffee shop. That would mean he might run into Clarissa. He didn't think it through when he suggested the coffee shop. He supposed he could just ride his skateboard across the street and watch out for her Beetle. Still, he didn't want to have to worry about running into her.

At eight on Saturday morning, Sasha stuck her head in Malique's room, "Mali, I'm taking the boys to their game. Do you want to go? Mel is going."

He was lying on his stomach, drool was on his pillow, and his right arm was hanging off the bed. He felt he could have slept another hour or so but blinked his eyes open. He sat up, yawned, then stretched. His afro was shaped like a cone on top of his head. He scratched his chest. "I'm sorry, what'd do say?" He yawned again. He caught a whiff of his own breath and made a face.

Sasha giggled. "You are always a sight to see in the morning." She laughed again.

"Gee--- thanks."

"Anyway, I said--- I'm taking the boys to their game. Do you want to go with us? Mel is going?"

"Oh, heck no," he said with a little laugh.

She giggled again. "Okay, just be sure to lock up if you go anywhere. And don't get into any trouble. I love you." She walked into his room and kissed him on the forehead.

"Love you too, Mom," he said.

Mel rushed into his room. "You brat--- you're not going?!" She was wearing blue jeans and a white t-shirt. Her hair was pulled back into a neat ponytail and braid. "Then why do I have to go?" She crossed her arms and tapped her foot.

"Because I said so," Sasha said as she turned and walked out of the room.

Mel stomped her foot, turned, and followed Sasha. Malique grinned. These were the moments when he loved being the older brother. He had privileges that Mel didn't.

At nine forty-five, that same morning, Malique grabbed his skateboard and the keys. He locked up the house, plopped the keys in his pocket, and began his skateboard journey to the coffee shop. He was wearing his favorite pair of long denim shorts, gray tank top with a black and gray long sleeve plaid shirt. As he skated, the back of his shirt flowed behind him. His military boots clunked against the concrete as he pushed his board for a faster speed. As he approached the flower shop, his eyes shifted up and down the street. Thankfully, he didn't see Clarissa's car. He still crossed the road as an extra precaution, besides he'd have to cross the street anyway to get into the coffee shop.

He glanced at his watch. He made good time. He had five minutes to spare. He flipped up his board, caught it, then walked into the coffee shop. He glanced around and didn't see the professor. Good. It would give him a little time to relax his nerves and calm his breathing from the skateboard ride. He decided to wait for the professor at a small table inside the shop near the front window facing the door so he could see when the professor arrived. He didn't have to wait long; a few short seconds after he sat down, the professor walked in. Malique watched as Professor Chapman glanced around the shop until they finally made eye contact. Today the professor was wearing a white dress shirt and blue denim jeans.

Professor Chapman approached the table with his right hand outstretched. Malique stood, accepted his hand, and shook it firmly. "Malique, so glad you decided to meet me."

"Me too, I guess," Malique said, trying to hide his nervousness. He wondered if maybe he should have told Sasha about this meeting. Perhaps he should have told her all about Professor Chapman. At least then someone would know where he was and who with. Suddenly, his stomach did flip-flops. What if this man wanted to do harm? He tried to squash his fears, but it was a constant battle as he stood there.

The professor frowned a little, "So you still don't trust me. I don't blame you. I'm still a stranger to you. But--- well--- let me get us something to eat and drink. What would you like?" The professor put his hands on his hips with an expression of determination on his face.

"Um---" Malique rarely, if ever, went to coffee shops. The only reason he suggested it was that it just sounded like a good public place to meet that was close by. He scratched his right cheek and glanced at the menu mounted on the wall. Then his eyes went to the display case that held all of the baked goods and breakfast sandwiches. Finally, he shrugged his shoulders but said, "I guess I'll have a medium hot chocolate and a slice of banana nut bread."

Professor Chapman grinned and waved his pointed index finger at Malique, "That was one of your mom's favorites--- Banana nut bread."

Malique tilted his head to the side. "Really?" He asked, amazed.

"Yes," Professor Chapman said, "Okay, hot chocolate and a slice of banana nut bread coming up." The professor turned and immediately stood in line to place their order.

Malique sat back down and looked out the window. He could see the flower shop from where he was sitting. He still didn't see Clarissa's car. He felt a little bit of disappointment rise inside of him. But, for the most part, he was still relieved. He just might not see her today. Feeling a little disappointed, he leaned back in his chair and tried to talk himself into believing that he should feel relieved not to see her. It didn't work. He mostly felt disappointed.

A few moments later, Professor Chapman returned to the table, holding a receipt and a brown bag. He placed the bag on the table, "Reach in and grab your bread. The muffin is mine." He grinned. "I'll be right back with our drinks." He walked over to the counter and waited with his arms crossed.

Malique opened the bag and reached in to grab the bread. It was still warm, and it was a nice thick slice. The scent of bananas and nuts wafted to his nose and immediately affected his stomach. He rubbed his belly in appreciation. As much as he wanted to bite into the bread, he decided he'd wait for his drink and for Professor Chapman to return to the table. He didn't want to be rude or disrespectful.

Professor Chapman returned with a drink in each of his hands. "Oh, you didn't have to wait for me. Dig in," he urged.

"Thank you," Malique said. He took a bite of the bread and groaned.

"Been a while since you had banana nut bread?"

"Yep," Malique responded after he swallowed his first bite. He closed his eyes momentarily, and he heard a female voice, "Mali, don't eat it all--- save some for me, okay?" It was so clear and loud that he stopped chewing, and his eyes flew open. He looked around.

"Are you okay?" Professor Chapman asked.

Malique blinked then continued to chew and swallow what was already in his mouth. "Who--- Did you hear someone call me?"

Professor tilted his head and looked concerned. "No," he said simply.

"I thought---" Malique shook his head.

The professor took a sip of his coffee and began to unwrap his muffin. "So, tell me--- has that been happening a lot lately?"

"What?"

"Voices?" The professor was serious, but he was asking in a casual and laid-back tone.

Malique weighed his options. He could lie to the professor and tell him no, but what if the professor knew something. What if the professor knew who the voices were or why he was hearing them? He decided to tell the truth. If the professor decided to lock him up for mental instability then--- oh, well--- the truth was the better way to go. "I--- well--- every once in a while."

"Is it a male or a female?"

Malique was hesitant to respond. He needed answers, so he figured he might as well talk to the professor. "Both--- I mean---not at the same time--- but every once in awhile, I will hear a male voice and sometimes a female."

"Hmmm--- Interesting." The professor reached into his front left pocket of his dress shirt and took out a small spiral notepad and pen. Malique hadn't noticed it before. The professor immediately flipped the notebook open and scribbled something down.

Malique thought it strange and wondered what he was jotting down and why.

"Tell me--- I notice that you are wearing long sleeves and military boots. I don't see many kids wearing what you are--- is there a reason?"

Malique felt drained. Suddenly, he felt as if he was being set up for something. Malique wasn't hungry anymore, and he stood up, getting ready to ride his skateboard home.

"No, Malique, sit---, please. I just need to know---" Professor put down his coffee and stood, as well. He shook his head. "Maybe, I'm doing this all wrong."

"You think?" Malique asked sarcastically. He felt twinges of anger bursting inside of him.

"Okay, you want to ask me questions first--- Sit---, please. I just have a lot of questions that I've wanted to ask you too. We need each other, Malique. Please---" He gestured to Malique's seat again, "Please--- sit down."

Malique took a deep breath--- his eyes went up to the ceiling as if trying to find the answer to whether or not he should stay. His eyes went towards the window and caught a glimpse of what appeared to be Clarissa's car pulling up in front of the flower shop. His blood flow increased. He swallowed and sat down reluctantly. Moments later, though, the car pulled away.

"So--- what do you want to know from me?"

"Well--- how do you meet my mom?"

The professor grinned widely, "Mo was in one of my English classes in our freshman year in college. She sat right next to me. On the first day of class, we went out for coffee. We hung out with each other every school day and almost every weekend while we were in school together."

"So, did you know my dad too?"

The professor's eyes changed to something dark for a moment then seemed to tone down a bit--- as if from force. He frowned but said, "Yes. We were friends. Your mom was crazy about him. The way she would look at him sometimes would hurt me. I mean--- I wished---" The professor paused and put his head down for a moment. He cleared his throat. "I'm not going to lie to you, Malique. I was very much in love with your mother. I always hoped that she would forget about your father and choose me instead. But, I think she just knew me too well. Sometimes when you know someone too well--- you just don't think of them in the romantic sense, I guess. She knew when I was lying--- she knew I loved women. She knew I probably wouldn't be faithful to her, but I always still hoped---"

Malique felt a little uncomfortable and shifted in his seat. There was a lot of sadness in the professor's eyes. He was silent for quite some time, but finally, he took a deep breath in, exhaled, then said, "Malique," the professor cleared his throat, "I think I'm done for the day too. We still have lots to talk about. Why don't we meet again soon?" The professor scratched his forehead.

Malique felt a little disappointed that they couldn't finish talking today, but yet he was relieved. He didn't expect to feel so drained--- so emotionally exhausted. They hadn't even talked for very long. Malique nodded. He glanced out the window and saw that Clarissa still hadn't returned to the flower shop.

"I'm sorry. I guess we are both a little disappointed, but I think it's draining for both of us. We both are emotional, but we do have a lot to discuss. Maybe it's best that since this is the first official meeting, we meet for just a short while--- a small dose. You understand and agree, right?" Professor Chapman asked.

"Yeah, sure. I get it. Just call me when you're ready to meet again."

"Likewise," the professor nodded and reached out to shake Malique's hand.

Malique quickly put the rest of his bread in the bag and grabbed his drink. He waved goodbye one more time to the professor. When he was outside, he hopped on his skateboard and was about to make the journey back home. Just as his foot touched his board, a yellow Beetle pulled up next to the curb right in front of him. His heart rammed into his chest.

CHAPTER SIX

Clarissa glared at Malique from inside her Beetle. She rolled down the window. "Hop in," she demanded, obviously not asking. The look on her face challenged Malique to argue with her. For a moment, he contemplated skating away, but the look on her face made him think she might try to run him down with her car. But did he really want to get in a car when she looked that angry? Not really.

He bent down so he could get a better look at her, "Um--- why? Where are you going?"

"Just get in the car," she said agitatedly.

He shook his head no. As he did so, his afro moved from side to side.

Professor Chapman walked out of the coffee shop and saw Malique slouching down, talking to Clarissa. "Malique, everything okay?"

Clarissa's eyes squinted then her eyebrows met each other into a scowl. "Is that Professor Chapman? You met him and didn't tell me??" Her voice was a high pitched squeal.

"I---" Malique wondered where and in what book did it say that he had to tell Clarissa anything? Why would she get mad about anything going on in his life? He looked away from Clarissa to look at Professor Chapman, "Um--- Yeah, everything is ok. Just talking to--- Just---"

Clarissa put her car in park, turned the ignition off and stepped out of the vehicle. She ignored Malique and walked around her car to the sidewalk. She was decked out in faded light blue denim jeans with a hole on the left knee and a white t-shirt. She had more curls in her hair than usual. It was loose and free--- wild. Clarissa held her keys in her left hand and stuck out her right. "Malique has horrible social skills. Actually, I think it's more like--- absolutely no social skills what so ever. If we waited for him to introduce us, we would never be introduced." She cleared her throat, then said, "I'm Clarissa Jones. I go to school with Malique."

Professor Chapman grinned and shook her hand, "Well, it's a pleasure to meet you, Clarissa. I'm Professor Chapman. I'm just getting acquainted--- or rather re-acquainted with Malique--- It depends how you look at it. His mother and I used to be best friends in college. Well, I will leave the two of you alone now. I hope to be talking to you again soon, Malique."

Malique nodded. Clarissa and Malique watched Professor Chapman walk away and get into a silver Lexus. Then they watched him drive away.

Clarissa leaned against her Beetle with her arms crossed. She crossed her feet and was staring down at the cracks in the sidewalk. "You know--- Malique. You suck."

Malique's mouth moved to the left side of his face, and then he bit his bottom lip. What was he supposed to say or do?

"You aren't even going to say anything?" She asked in her high, pitched squealing voice again. She looked up at him.

"What do you want me to say? What am I supposed to say?"

"We kissed. And it wasn't just a little friendly kiss either--- It was--- it--- You know what?" She shook her head, then mumbled, "Forget it."

She walked back to the driver's side of her car then started it before he could think to stop her. She did a U-turn then parked her car across the street at the flower shop. He watched as she got out of the car, slammed the door with her gigantic purse on her shoulder then clicked her alarm on. She stomped into the flower shop.

Malique swallowed and stared at the flower shop for a few minutes. He was rubbing his neck, still trying to figure out what he should do when Lani stepped out of the shop. Her hair was loose in wild spiral curls. She was in blue jeans and a long sleeve cotton shirt. She looked up, and down the street, then her eyes landed on the coffee shop and eventually made eye contact with him. She frowned and waved him over. She didn't wait for a response just turned around and went back into the shop.

Malique wondered if all females believed they could boss him around and tell him where to go. Rather than risk Lani also being mad at him, he decided to follow her orders and go into the flower shop. He skillfully skateboarded while he held his drink in one hand and the bag of his banana nut bread in the other. After crossing the street, he skidded to a stop in front of the shop. Sokie was helping a customer near one of the refrigerators. Clarissa was taking an order over the phone. Lani was sitting at a small table in the corner of the shop. She waved him over. He couldn't help but glance at Clarissa. She glared at him, rolled her eyes, then continued talking to the customer on the phone.

Lani motioned Malique to sit down. "So, where have you been? I haven't seen you in a long time," Lani said.

"I've been busy with school stuff. What about you?" Malique answered as he sat down. He placed his skateboard under the table along with his bag of bread. He took a sip from his hot chocolate, then put it on top of the table.

"School and shop stuff," Lani said. She grabbed a deck of cards from a plastic container he hadn't noticed before. "Wanna play Go Fish with me?"

He knew she wasn't asking. He sighed.

"Sure. I have to warn you, though. I haven't played in a long time."

"Oh, don't worry, it's not that hard."

Lani shuffled the cards a couple of times then dealt five cards each.

"Okay, since you are visiting, you get to go first, Mali," Lani said.

"Okay, do you have a five?"

Lani grinned, "Nope, go fish."

They continued to play for at least twenty minutes. Finally, Lani won. "So, what did you do to Clarissa?" Lani asked out of the blue.

"What? What do you mean?" Malique asked innocently.

Lani tilted her head, "Come on, Mali! Don't play stupid with me. That's why I came outside. I knew she had just talked to someone, and when I saw you outside--- I knew it had to be you. What did you do to her?"

"Nothing--- I didn't do anything---" now it was his voice that was starting to squeal.

Lani rolled her eyes. "Maybe that's the problem. Look, she obviously likes you, but you're too clueless to see it."

"Why? Why though? Why would she like me? I'm a freak. You see my skin, don't you?"

Lani tilted her head to the side again, concern on her face. She frowned. "What do you mean? What about your skin?"

He sighed. "Look at me, Lani. Don't tell me you haven't noticed my two-tone skin. My face, my arms, my legs--- every part of my body has two tones. Why would she want to hang out with me? People usually try to avoid me. They think they are going to catch some sort of disease or something. I'm not easy on the eyes, you know?"

Lani's eyes widened. "Malique, you're the most handsome guy I've ever met!" She shouted. A little too loudly--- okay, it was deafening because the customers that both Sokie and Clarissa were helping stopped talking and turned to stare at Malique and Lani.

"I'd better go," Malique said, reaching for his skateboard.

Lani's left foot was too fast, though. She placed her foot on his board and scooted it over to her. She grabbed the board and said, "No, Malique. We need to talk. YOU need to talk." She wrapped her arms around the board. Apparently, planning to hold the skateboard hostage.

Malique glanced around the shop, hoping there would be someone who would come to his aid. How could a ten-year-old overtake him? This certainly wasn't helping his self-esteem--- especially--- A ten-year-old girl for crying out loud!

"What do we need to talk about?" He asked, almost whining.

"Well, for one, I had a dream about you."

"Really?"

"Yes, it wasn't the first time. We were on a ship, and there were two guys holding you down." She gripped the skateboard tighter.

"Why were they holding me down?"

"I don't know--- but--- an old woman was telling them what to do. She wanted---"

Malique waited.

"She wanted to see something--- I think she wanted to see your back."

Malique frowned. He started to rub the back of his neck. He was beginning to feel uncomfortable.

"Why?"

"I don't know. Can I see your back?"

"Lani, can I have my skateboard?"

"No, we are still talking," she said stubbornly. "Look, this isn't the first time I had a dream about you. Something strange is happening, and I don't know who else to talk to."

"You have your Aunt Sokie," Malique suggested, desperately.

74

"Yes, but she thinks I'm just making stuff up. She doesn't understand that it's all real. And--- well--- the thing is--- it didn't start happening until I met you. So, I think you have something to do with it."

Malique's skin began to prickle with heat. If he could blush, he was certain he would be blushing right about now.

"Do--- do you ever hear voices?"

Malique took a deep breath in and shook his head, "This is the second time today someone has asked me that."

"So--- is that a yes?" Lani asked. Her eyes were wide.

Malique sighed again, "Yes," he said reluctantly.

"Me too--- It's an old man and a young woman, huh?"

Malique squinted his eyes suspiciously but nodded his head in agreement.

"Why do you think we are hearing them, but no one else is?"

Malique shrugged his shoulders, "I don't know."

A customer left the store then Sokie joined them at the table. "Hey, Malique, it's good to see you again. We haven't seen you in a while. How's everything going for you?"

"Um--- I've been good. What about you?"

"Busy--- Really busy. I guess it's a good thing, right? I might have to hire an extra florist."

Clarissa just finished talking to another customer and walked the customer out. She turned back and joined them at the table. Malique looked up and into her eyes. He saw sadness there. The sadness he caused. He swallowed. "Um--- do you mind if I talk to Clarissa for a minute? Outside? Um--- alone?"

Sokie smiled a little, then said, "Sure." Sokie placed a gentle hand on Lani's shoulder to keep her from getting up. Lani gripped Malique's skateboard tighter.

Clarissa frowned but followed Malique to the front of the store and then outside. It was getting a little chilly. A breeze blew around them as they stood face to face. Clarissa crossed her arms then leaned against the glass window. "So--- talk," she mumbled.

"I didn't mean to hurt you. That's the last thing I ever wanted or want to do. If anything, I was protecting you, C."

She tilted her head to the side and shook her head, "If anything, you were protecting yourself Malique. You got scared. Just admit it."

"Yeah--- yeah--- I was scared. You can be with any guy on campus or any guy in the universe. You don't need me. I'm the freak on campus--- the freak of the city or even state--- you don't need me."

"You don't know what I need. You don't give anyone a chance to get to know you, and you don't try to get to know other people. You are selfish, and you are just plain---" She pushed away from the window and moved away from him. "Just--- mean." She balled her hands up in a fist and stormed back into the shop.

She grabbed her purse and keys, "Sorry, Sokie, I just can't stay here any longer today. I'll be back tomorrow--- when HE isn't here." She stomped off and got into her car.

What was he supposed to do now? He wondered. Girls were so complicated. First, they hound you to talk to them, then when you start to talk to them they storm off. Whatever. Now he was getting cranky. He apologized to her, didn't he? He explained himself, didn't he? What was her problem?

Sokie gestured Malique to come back into the shop soon after Clarissa stormed away. He leaned against the counter with his elbow. He lowered his head in defeat. Lani walked over to stand next to Malique. She was still holding his skateboard. "So--- what's going on between you two?" Sokie asked Malique.

"Well--- she--- I--- when she--- when she came over last week. She was helping me with something and--- and just before she left--- we--- well--- we kissed."

"WHAT??" Lani dropped Malique's skateboard. "Are you crazy??"

Sokie looked at Lani with surprise. "What's the matter, Lani?"

"He's not supposed to kiss Clarissa. We're all like family. You don't kiss family like that! How could you?" Lani stomped off. She went to the back of the store. They heard a slam of a door then the stomping of footsteps going up a flight of stairs—more stomping and slamming in a faraway distance.

Sokie puffed up her cheeks then slowly exhaled. "Well--- I bet this isn't going the way you thought it would, huh?"

Malique shook his head no. "I don't get it. I don't understand why Clarissa kissed me in the first place. I didn't mean to hurt her."

"So, you're saying she kissed you, but you didn't kiss her back?"

"Well--- No--- I mean--- She started it, but--- yes, I kissed her back. It was the first time anyone kissed me before. I never thought someone like her would be interested in me. I don't get it. I mean, look at me, Sokie." He stood up straight, put his arms out, and he spun around.

Sokie eyed him up and down. She smiled. "You're a good looking young man Malique."

"What is wrong with you and Lani??" He asked—his voice squealing again.

"Yes, Malique, you have two-toned skin. There are a lot of multi-racial people who have two-tone skin. Yours just happens to be more pronounced, but still, other people have the same issues that you do. When Lani and I tell you that you are a handsome young man, it's because of who you are inside. It is also because of your eyes. So much about you reminds me of my sister. She had this way of making people look up to her without realizing it. She had a way of having men fight over her too. Believe me--- she never intended to hurt anyone either. She just wanted everyone to be happy. But in the end, she was taken away from me by someone who was so jealous. Oh--- I just can't get into that now, but--- Malique--- You have to stop asking why people love you and want to be around you--- start telling yourself--- you are a good and beautiful person inside and out. You are smart and funny. You have to believe in yourself, Malique. Believe you are here for a purpose, and nothing is by chance--- Follow your heart and believe in yourself." Sokie said so much in such a little amount of time. She reached for her bottled water and took a long swig.

Malique hadn't said anything. He was letting her words sink into his heart. His foster mom had told him something similar a few years ago but somehow hearing it again, but from Sokie, he started to believe the words--- maybe if two women he cared about said the same thing--- perhaps it meant it was true. Maybe he wasn't such a bad person--- perhaps he wasn't a freak after all.

There was the sound of a door shutting, then light footsteps approaching. Lani returned to tap Malique on the shoulder. "Do you plan on kissing Clarissa again?"

"I--- I don't know--- it's not like I planned on kissing her the first time. And for the record, she kissed me first."

"Okay, well--- you have to promise not to keep secrets from me. Do you promise?" Lani stuck her pinky out to him.

"I--- fine." He stuck his pinky out, and they interloped their pinkies and shook on it.

"Good, so now you can tell me what she was helping you with."

"I needed to borrow her computer to research a professor online. My mom had her laptop, so I didn't have any other computer to use. Clarissa just showed up on my doorstep, and she just happened to have her laptop with her."

"Nothing is by chance," Lani said, repeating what Sokie had said only a moment before.

"Anyway, that's it. Okay?"

"You're telling me everything?" Lani asked suspiciously.

"Yes," he lied. He didn't want to have to explain about his birth mother and Professor Chapman. He just wanted his skateboard and to go home.

Lani clenched her jaw and had a stubborn look in her eye. "You're not telling me everything--- We aren't going to figure this all out until you tell me everything---"

Sokie shook her head, "Sorry, Malique. You'll have to excuse Lani. She's been having bad dreams, and her imagination is running away with her." Sokie said, glancing at a small digital clock on the counter. "Lani, why don't you go upstairs and watch television? Your favorite show is about to come on." She walked over to Lani and gave her a gentle nudge on both of her shoulders, guiding her back towards the stairs at the back of the store.

"Fine, but just letting you both know--- this isn't over. Nope--- we have lots to talk about," Lani insisted over her shoulder, almost out of breath.

Malique took that as his cue to leave. "Thank you for everything, Sokie. I'm going to go now."

"Okay, Malique. Don't make yourself a stranger to us, okay? Come by soon."

He nodded before grabbing his board and skating off.

Of course, on his way home, he kept thinking of Clarissa. He needed to talk to her, but he just didn't know how. He said all the wrong things whenever she was around, and if he thought he was saying all the right things, she would utterly misunderstand and take it absolutely the wrong way. He wished there was some way that he could get all of his feeling out without her interrupting or him panicking--- then he started thinking--- wait. She had given him her email address. So maybe, if Sasha would let him borrow her laptop tonight, he'd be able to express all that he genuinely wanted to say to her in an email. Yes, that's what he would do. He would send her an email. Or not--- not yet.

CHAPTER SEVEN

Sasha allowed Malique to borrow her laptop. He was sitting in his room, at his desk, staring at the screen for the longest time. He kept watching the cursor flash over and over again. Finally, he decided to stop worrying and just start typing. He just typed whatever popped in his head to convey his heart to Clarissa.

Malique finally unfolded the piece of paper that he always kept in his pocket wherever he went. It was the one Clarissa had given him with her phone number and email address. He typed in her email address then began to write.

Hi Clarissa,

Well, you gave me your email address, and I thought well--- maybe I should use it to explain myself to you. You're right. I don't have any social skills. I am not really a people person. Or rather, most people don't want to have anything to do with me. They see my skin and think that I have some sort of disease that they can catch or something. The truth is, I don't know why I am the way that I am. So, when someone wants to be around me, my gut instinct is that it's some sort of joke, or they just need something from me and don't want to be around me.

If you are hanging out with me as some sort of social class experiment or some sort of popular kids joke or something--- It needs to end now. I won't judge you. I understand.

Malique stared at the screen then re-read what he had just typed. Is that truly what he wanted to say? He felt he had more to say, but couldn't find the right words. After staring at the screen for a few minutes, he decided that he would send it.

Less than a minute later, he received an instant message from Clarissa.

Clarissa: So, you think that I am using you as an experiment?! Where did that idea come from??

Malique gulped. Rubbed his nose, shrugged his shoulders then typed. *Malique: It's the only reason I could come up with for you wanting to hang out with me.*

Clarissa: You are ridiculous! I don't know why I am even bothering to argue with you.

Malique: Me, either.

Clarissa: Oh, quit the sob story and self-pitying act, okay? Let's agree to pretend the kiss ever happened and move on, okay?

Malique knew he would never forget the kiss. It was an amazing kiss! But, if he wanted to keep the peace with Clarissa, he thought it best to agree.

Malique: Okay.

Clarissa: Let's talk about something else.

Malique: Okay.

Clarissa: So, what did you find out about the professor? Or what did he want to tell you?

Malique: Not much, but he wants to meet again. It turns out that he was in love with my mom. But he says that since my mom knew he was a player, she wouldn't go out with him--- or that she just knew him too well.

Clarissa: Hmmm--- Did he say why he thinks your sister is still alive?

Malique: We didn't even get to her. I think we were both too emotional or something. But, hopefully, soon we can meet again.

Clarissa: Next time you meet with him, let me go with you. Maybe you both need someone who can kind of guide you both--- lead you in the right direction for the conversation. It's not like you are the most talkative and outgoing person. The professor probably has his own agenda. We need to figure out what he honestly wants, and we need to get the information that you want and need.

Malique: Yep, I want to find my sister. I want to know more about my mom. I don't remember a lot. Oh, but I remember her making banana nut bread, and we would argue over who was getting the last piece.

Clarissa: Cute.

Malique: Stop it.

Clarissa: Why?

Malique: Nothing about me is cute.

Clarissa: Will you knock it off already? There are lots of things about you that are cute, and you just need to be brave enough to embrace it. Your eyes, the way you speak. You think before you talk--- you care.

Malique: Knock it off.

Clarissa: Okay. Fine. So--- are you going to stop avoiding me now? Are you going to hang out with me at school and after now?

Malique's mouth moved to the left side, and he took a deep breath, thinking about it. He missed Clarissa. He didn't want to avoid her anymore.

Malique: Yes, I will stop avoiding you now.

Clarissa: Okay, see you on Monday.

Malique: Okay. Bye.

Clarissa: Bye.

Malique shut down Sasha's computer and felt so much better than he did when he first turned it on.

There was a light tap on his door, then the door opened. "Everything okay?" Sasha asked as she entered his room and sat on his bed. He turned his chair around to face her. He put his elbows on his knees.

"Yep, just finished talking to Clarissa."

Sasha smiled. "So, you two are okay now?"

"I guess so."

"You looked pretty upset when you asked to borrow my laptop. What's going on?"

Malique debated whether or not to tell her everything that's been going on. He doubted she would want to know about the voices or the pain he felt across his skin, but he could tell her about the kiss with Clarissa and the meeting with the professor. "Well, Clarissa and I kissed, and afterward, I just avoided her."

Sasha's eyebrows raised from surprise. "When did this happen?"

"A couple of weeks ago, when you took the boys to their game."

"Hmmm--- I thought you were acting a little wackier than usual," she grinned.

Malique rolled his eyes.

"Ahh--- Teen love--- Nothing like it."

"Stop it," Malique said. He massaged his temples with his hands as if trying to rub away a headache.

"Just teasing Mali," she said, patting his left knee gently.

"I know--- I was avoiding her for a while because I just didn't know how to act. I didn't know what was expected of me. Then her ex-boyfriend threatened me. I kept telling myself I wasn't avoiding her because of him, but maybe a part of me was. I'm just tired of fighting. I'm tired of people bugging me. I just want to be left alone, but---"

"Too many people love you, Mali. You can't hide. I know that it's hard to be different. I mean, I was the only Native American in my school for a long time, and I was teased and harassed, but times have changed a lot. I know that you stand out, but let that work for you, not against you."

He hadn't thought of Sasha having problems when she was in school. She was so smart and tough. He looked at her and asked, "Really, you were teased? You're the coolest person I know."

"Yes, everyone gets teased for one reason or another. You just have to decide how you are going to react. Sometimes ignoring the idiot's works, but sometimes it just eggs them on to do worse or more. Sometimes, you just have to fight. It's hard. But, you will make it through." Sasha leaned back a little, still staring at Malique. "So, is there anything else going on?"

Now was the time to tell her about the professor. He bit the right corner of his bottom lip then explained about the professor. Sasha leaned forward; this time, her elbows were resting on her knees. "It seems a lot happened the day I took the boys to the game. Maybe I shouldn't leave you alone anymore." She said half-joking and half-serious.

"I'm fine, Mom."

Sasha half-smiled. "It's a lot to take in. I mean, I know you want to know more about your real mom. I don't blame you for wanting to meet with Professor Chapman. But, you said he said he thinks your sister is still alive?"

Malique scratched his head, "Yep, that's what he said."

Sasha rubbed her chin. "I tried to get more information about her after you arrived, but the social workers told me she passed away in the car accident. But, I supposed it could be possible I wasn't given all the information."

Malique nodded in agreement.

"Can you promise me something, Mali?"

He looked at her.

"Don't hide anything from me. Okay? I'm here to help you. I'm not your enemy, okay?" She asked. He could see the hurt in her eyes.

He said in a low whisper, "Okay. Sorry, I didn't mean to hurt you."

"I'm not hurt that you want to find out more about your family. I fully understand. I'm just hurt that you hid it from me."

85

Malique nodded.

"So, do you know when you will meet with him again? Do you want me to go with you?"

Malique shook his head to say no. "I'm not sure when we will meet again. Clarissa said she would go with me next time, though."

"Okay, good. I don't want you to meet with him alone, okay. Either have Clarissa or me go with you--- And--- when am I going to meet Clarissa?" She asked with a smile.

"Oh, I--- we aren't--- I---"

"I--- I--- I---" Sasha teased, "Malique, it's okay. Whenever you're ready to introduce me to her is fine with me. She sounds like a very special girl."

Malique nodded in agreement. "She is. She's beautiful."

Sasha rose from the bed, then stuck her right hand out. "Okay, well, you're done with my laptop, right?"

He closed the lid to the laptop then handed it to her. "Yep, thank you for letting me use it."

"I'll see if I can get you your own soon. Maybe for your birthday, okay?"

Malique's eyes widened from shock and delight, "Really? Can we afford it?"

Sasha smiled. "I will figure it out--- it's not for you to worry about. You will need it more now for school and college." She emphasized the word college. Malique groaned.

"Speaking of college. Have you met with your school counselor lately?"

Malique groaned again. "Not lately."

"Okay, I will call the school on Monday and talk to them. We need you to start taking more college prep classes. I think it's time for you to stop hiding and pretending you're remedial."

Malique started massaging his temples again, "Do I have to?"

"Absolutely," she was near the door now, "it's my motherly duty." She grinned and walked out of his room.

"Great," Malique said to his now empty room, then plopped on his bed, "more to worry about."

Malique was on his bed, staring up at the ceiling. He wondered and imagined if he could make his mind go blank. There had been too much to think up about. Suddenly, an older male voice said, "It's time for you to find her. She needs you, and you need her. She will help you read the map."

Malique sat up and looked around. "What?" He asked loudly.

"Find her," the voice said again. It was so clear and familiar.

"Who are you? Where are you? Why can't I see you?" Malique's eyes were wide and glossy. He still frantically looked around his room.

"You will know soon enough."

Malique's skin tightened and felt hot with prickly heat as if a billion needles were poking at his skin. He jumped from the bed and closed his door. He stripped off all his clothes and glanced down at his arms. The dark tones of his skin turned a bright red while the lighter tones seemed to turn white. He wanted to scream, but he didn't want to alarm anyone else in the house. He broke into a sweat. His throat burned. He needed water. Malique frantically glanced around his room to see if he had a bottle of water anywhere. As he turned, he felt extremely dizzy. The corners of his eyes turned foggy, and then entirely white overtook his vision. He collapsed and passed out.

He was in a cloud, walking in what seemed to be in midair. Everything around him was cool, and he felt comforted. A woman was walking towards him. She was so familiar--- so--- beautiful: caramel skin, petite, curly brown hair, and golden eyes. "Mom," he whispered.

"Yes, Malique. I've missed you so much," she said. She wrapped her arms around him and enveloped him in a hug. She didn't seem to mind; he was absolutely naked. Surprisingly, he was not embarrassed but held her for as long as she allowed him to. Finally, they let go of each other.

"We don't have much time," his mom explained, rushed. "You have to find your sister. You will need to work together to find the way to the ship. Get to the pebble before they do."

Malique frowned, "What are you talking about?"

"I wish I could explain it all to you, but there isn't enough time. Tell Evan. He'll figure it out. You will need to go to New Orleans."

"Where is she? Can't you tell me where she is? Why New Orleans?"

"Don't you remember your sister's name?"

"What?"

His mom looked disappointed. "You have to remember on your own. It's part of the spell. I shouldn't have told you that either. I have to go--- Just talk to Evan. Be safe, and remember--- you are never alone." She held his face with both of her hands and said, "Nothing happens by chance." She kissed Malique on the forehead and walked away. She disappeared into a cloud.

"Mom!" Malique shouted, but the whiteness around him seemed to break up into dots of blackness--- black dots all around him, then his head began to throb. "Mom!" Malique shouted with desperation. He felt his body flop around like a fish. His head banged against something, and his knee rammed against something hard. His body began to relax, but his head began to hurt even more. Malique rubbed his eyes then slowly opened them. He looked around himself. He was in his room, but everything was blurry. He blinked again, hoping to clear his vision. His skin no longer burned. He realized he was naked and wondered what in the world had just happened to him.

He carefully rose to his feet and went to his dresser. He pulled out a fresh t-shirt and boxer shorts. He put them on, then went to the kitchen for water. He thought of taking Tylenol or something for the headache but thought maybe all he needed was sleep. He drank a full glass of water, gulping it down and feeling much better but still achy. He wondered if perhaps he had a seizure, but there was no real way of knowing without someone being there to tell him. He glanced down at his right knee. There was a small gash. He guessed he hit a part of the bedpost with it. He reached for a small zip lock sandwich bag and put some ice in it. He sat at the kitchen table and placed the ice on his knee.

He felt sadness in his heart from missing his mother. He felt her. It wasn't a dream. He was certain of it. She smelled of coconut, lime, and cookies. He moved the ice around in small circles over his knee. The ice was melting. His knee was feeling better already. Malique tried to remember what she'd said. She wanted him to remember his sister's name. He frowned. What was wrong with him? Why couldn't he remember? He glanced at the clock in the kitchen. It was eleven fifteen at night. He wondered if the professor was still awake. He also wondered if Clarissa was awake. He needed to talk to someone.

Malique went back into his room to find the piece of paper that had Clarissa's phone number and email address. It was on his desk from when he was emailing and instant messaging her. He glanced at it and made his decision. He had to talk to someone, and she would be willing to listen and wouldn't be mad at him for calling late.

He walked back into the kitchen and picked up the phone. He said a tiny prayer that she wouldn't be mad and that it wasn't a mistake to call her then punched in her number.

CHAPTER EIGHT

An older male answered the phone on the third ring, "Jones residence."

Malique wondered if the person that answered was either Clarissa's dad or maybe a butler. Hmmm--- did she have a butler? It's highly possible since she had a nanny and a housekeeper. "Hi--- Um--- Is Clarissa awake?"

"Whom shall I say is calling?"

"Oh, um--- A friend from school."

"It's rather late, don't you think?"

"Yes, it's important. But--- If she is sleeping--- I can talk to her tomorrow or Monday."

"Well, you are in luck. She just happens to be standing right next to me. One moment," the man said. Malique could hear the shuffling and exchange of the phone being passed to her. He could hear her mumbling something, the man said something back to her, but Malique couldn't understand what they were saying. It sounded garbled and muffled. He guessed someone was covering up the mouthpiece.

Finally, Clarissa said into the phone, "Hello."

"Hi Clarissa, sorry for calling you so late. I just really needed to speak to someone."

"Why? Are you okay?" He could hear the genuine concern in her voice.

"Yes--- Well--- No--- I don't know. Do you have time to talk?"

"My dad wants me to go to bed soon because he's making me go with him to an early mass tomorrow before he goes to work. Don't you think it's a little hypocritical to force someone to go to church, then turn around and work on the Lord's Day?"

"Why can't he work on a Sunday?"

Clarissa breathed a heavy sigh. "It's like a commandment or something. It's like--- like--- a massive no-no to work on Sundays. You're supposed to relax and pray and relax and pray--- spend time with family," Clarissa explained with bitterness evident in her voice.

"Oh," Malique said.

"Anyway, enough about me--- what's up? Why'd you call me?"

He decided to tell Clarissa everything that just happened to him. When he finished explaining, Clarissa said softly, "Maybe it really was a dream. Maybe you had a seizure. You should let Sasha know tomorrow morning. She will probably want you to see a doctor."

"So, basically, you're saying you don't believe me. You think I'm crazy and need to see a shrink."

"Well, no, I just think that with the talk from Professor Chapman, you started to miss your mom. I think it's your brain's way of bringing her back to you for a little while."

"But it was so real, Clarissa. She hugged me, and I felt it. She told me she missed me."

"I'm sure she does. But, I still think you should tell Sasha or, at the very least, tell Professor Chapman."

He was angry that she wasn't more supportive. Upset that she didn't believe him. Mad that she was essentially admitting that she thought he was crazy. How could he hang out with someone who thought he was crazy? He couldn't. He wouldn't allow himself to set himself up for heartache. "Look, I'll let you go now. Maybe I'll see you around campus. Go to bed. At least you get to spend some time with your parents--- even if it's just for a little while." He felt his throat tighten involuntarily, and the intense burning sensation in the back of his throat; unshed tears that he would not allow to form. He hung up the phone without giving Clarissa a chance to speak.

He wandered back into his room, turned out the light then laid down on the bed. In the morning, he would call the professor and arrange for another meeting. In the meantime, he stared into the blackness and replayed all the words his mother had spoken. She had asked him if he remembered his sister's name. He hadn't thought of it in years, but now that she might be alive, his mind drew up a blank. Why couldn't he remember? It would seem to be an automatic thing--- like a person should know their sibling's name. It wasn't like he was a baby at the time of the accident. He was five years old. He should know his sister's name. He kept thinking back--- racking his brain and yelling silently at his mind for being so useless and idiotic. He remembered a "T" somewhere. Her name must have begun with a T. Teacup? No--- that sounds like a dog's name or something. Maybe that's what his mom used to call her---. *Yes,* he thought--- his mom used to call his sister "Teacup" because she was so little.

The next morning, Malique called Professor Chapman and left a message on his voicemail to call him back. In the meantime, Malique played video games with his brothers. Melanie was at one of her friend's house, giving each other manicures and pedicures. Later in the afternoon, while he was eating ham, lettuce, and tomato sandwiches with his brothers, in the kitchen, Professor Chapman called him back. They agreed to meet each other the following Saturday at the coffee shop again. He wasn't sure if he was going to allow Clarissa to go with him to meet the professor. Maybe he would mention it to her at some point during the week.

On Monday, Malique went to the first three classes of the day in a mechanical blur. When the lunch bell rang, he figured he would go to the library as usual. He just thought if Clarissa seriously wanted to see him, she would just go to the library and talk to him there. Otherwise, he wasn't going to go out of his way to seek her out. She managed to make him doubt himself on so many levels he hoped she decided just to leave him alone.

But of course, less than two minutes after he took a seat at his cubicle in a hidden corner of the library, Clarissa showed up. She gently tapped the imitation oak cubicles and whispered. "Hi Mali, thought I'd find you here. I brought us both a sack lunch. Do you like ham and pepper jack cheese with a little bit of mustard and some mayo on wheat? I also packed us some potato chips and apple juice."

He gave her a little smile. "Sure," he said resignedly.

She pulled a chair from the cubicle to the right of him and scooted it close to him.

"So, why are you here with me instead of your regular lunch crew?"

"That's one reason why I'm here. I don't feel like being surrounded by a bunch of hoopla. I just want some peace and quiet."

Malique nodded from understanding. Clarissa passed Malique one of the brown paper lunch bags. His name was on the bag, written in what must have been a black Sharpie pen. She had also drawn a smiley face. He paused to admire the artwork and smiled. He glanced at her lunch bag to see if she had written her name on it. She had--- she also had a flower. In the center of the flower was a happy face. "Creative," he said, pointing to her lunch bag.

She smiled. "I know it's silly, but it's something I've always done ever since pre-school. My nanny would make me pack my lunch the night before, and I had to write my name on the bag, then we would stick it in the frig until it was time to leave for school in the morning. It always makes me smile to see a smiley face or a flower."

"Hey, it's cool. Kinda girly and foo-foo--- but cool."

"Foo-foo? Did you seriously just say foo-foo?"

"It's a word."

"Foo-foo is such a foo-foo word though--- you shouldn't use words like foo-foo because then you start to sound foo-foo." She giggled.

Someone in a cubicle close to them said, "Shhh---"

"Keep your voice down, C," Malique whispered harshly.

Clarissa laughed but said, "Okay."

He finally opened his lunch bag and pulled out the sandwich. He unwrapped it then took an enormous bite. He chewed his first bite. Lettuce, tomatoes, and pickles were also on the sandwich. He groaned from satisfaction. He swallowed then said, "Thank you, Clarissa. It's delicious."

"You're welcome."

"I talked to Professor Chapman yesterday," he said before taking another bite of his sandwich.

"You did? Did you tell him what happened to you on Saturday night?" Clarissa asked in a loud whisper leaning closer towards Malique with her elbows on her knees. She took a bite of her sandwich and chewed while she waited for Malique to respond.

Malique was still chewing but was examining Clarissa's hair. Today she wore her hair in a single French braid with the braid tossed over her right shoulder. She was wearing a brown halter top and form-fitting blue jeans. Large silver hoop earrings dangled from her ears. Suddenly Clarissa waved her right hand in front of him. "Are you ever going to answer my question?" She asked, evidently impatient.

"Oh, yes--- well--- no. I didn't tell him anything about Saturday. He sounded as if he were in a rush, and I figured it was something that could wait until we meet in person."

Clarissa nodded in agreement, "Okay, I can understand that. Did you tell Sasha, at least?"

94

"Clarissa, I only told you. It's not something I want a bunch of people to know about. I already stand out because of my skin. I don't need to stand out because of my brain. I am starting to think maybe it all was a dream, or maybe I did have a seizure. How would I know if I had a seizure anyway?"

"MRI or CT-Scan, I would imagine?"

"What the heck is an MRI or CT-scan?

"An MRI is that big tube thing that doctors or rather technicians slide patients into--- they strap the patient down and tell the patient not to move for like twenty minutes; then they take images of the brain. They check waves and stuff. The CT-scan looks kind like a giant donut. They slide you thru it, but it's quick. It also takes an image of your brain, but I guess it isn't as complex as the MRI."

"Huh--- I don't think Sasha or social services will pay for me to get either one of those. They would send me to another shrink in a heartbeat, though." He finished off his sandwich then opened the bag of potato chips. He reached inside the bag of chips and grabbed the largest chip in the bag. "So why do you know so much about MRIs and CT-scans?"

"Biology, health, and science class. Didn't you learn about them too?"

"I guess I don't pay enough attention."

"So anyway, what did your mom say to you?"

"She asked me if I remembered my sister's name, and I realized that I didn't. Isn't that weird? I mean, I never realized that I didn't remember her name. I remember her. She was so little. Little hands and toes. She was the same complexion as my mom. She had caramel skin and hazel eyes. She had a whole lot of hair on her head--- super curly. She looked so much like my mom, just a miniature version. We didn't even get a chance to have stupid fights--- I feel like the world's worst brother because I can't remember her name."

"She was only a few months old Mali, and you were only five. You were in a horrible accident too. Give yourself a break sometimes. Geez," Clarissa said softly, placing her right hand on his left forearm.

Malique felt butterflies in his stomach from her touch. He wished he could hug her now but didn't want to risk another kiss. They were supposed to be just friends now, right? As friends, there would be no pressure or awkwardness.

"Thanks, C." Malique gave her a half-smile.

"It's kind of strange how so much has happened since you walked into the flower shop, huh?"

"Yeah, it is. Lani mentioned that too. She said ever since we met, she's been having these weird dreams."

Just then, the warning bell rang that lunchtime was over, and they had only a few minutes to pack up, go to their lockers, and the next class.

"Hmmm--- She didn't mention any weird dreams to me. I'll have to ask her about it. Anyway, we'd better go. I'll walk with you to your locker."

He nodded in agreement.

CHAPTER NINE

On Saturday, Clarissa tooted her horn on her Beetle parked in Malique's driveway. Malique grabbed his skateboard, gave Sasha a quick kiss on the cheek, and rushed outside before Clarissa found another reason to toot her horn. He didn't need to make any of the neighbors mad at him for Clarissa's obnoxiousness.

"Let's get this party started Mali, come on. Step on it!" She yelled from the driver's seat with the top down. It was a sunny day in Southern California. Beach City was beautiful today. He could never imagine living anywhere else. He hopped in the car and strapped himself in with the seatbelt. She zig-zagged her way through traffic and got to the coffee shop at 9:45 AM.

"Did you, by chance, have coffee already this morning?"

"Ab-so-lute-ly! I can't get the day started without some good ole' coffee."

"You know we are meeting the professor here? At a coffee house?" Malique asked with a little smirk.

Clarissa shoved his left shoulder playfully. He laughed then got out of the car. They walked the few feet to the coffee house. He held the door open for her. She skipped in. "Geesh, you're so perky."

"I love coffee!" Clarissa said, "Let's get in line."

She grabbed his hand before he could stop her. She dragged him into the line. "So, what do you want to drink?"

"Um---"

"You're dragging--- hmmm--- I think you should get a double espresso mocha latte," Clarissa suggested.

"Clarissa, I don't drink coffee."

"Pssst--- Today will be the day of firsts for you," she said with a smile. She was still holding his hand as she ordered two double espresso mocha lattes and two colossal chocolate chip cookies.

"Oh," they heard a voice behind them, just as Clarissa was paying for their drinks and cookies. They both turned around to see Professor Chapman behind them. "You already ordered?" He sounded disappointed.

"Yes, I insisted on treating him today," Clarissa explained. She extended her right arm and shook Professor Chapman's hand. "It's nice to see you again, Professor."

"Oh, please, call me Evan," he smiled.

"Okay," Clarissa nodded. Clarissa reached for Malique's hand again.

Malique felt relieved, holding Clarissa's hand. It kept him steady instead of feeling uneasy from the professor's sudden appearance. Yes, they were expecting him, and meeting the professor was the whole reason they were here at the coffee shop in the first place. He squeezed her hand gently. She turned her head to gaze into Malique's eyes. She seemed to tell him; *It's going to be okay. Just tell the professor everything*, with her eyes. He blinked.

"Why don't the two of you find a place for us to sit and eat before all the tables are taken up?" The professor suggested.

They found a small round table near the large front window. It was the seat right behind the one where Malique and the professor had sat previously during their first meeting.

They were only sitting for a few short minutes when Clarissa's name was called announcing her order was ready. "I'll get it since you paid for it," Malique said.

"Okay," Clarissa agreed bubbly. Malique shook his head. She did not need any more caffeine today. She probably didn't need any more caffeine for the rest of the year. When Malique returned to the table, the professor was already seated and waiting for his name to be called for his order. "I'm glad you called me. I have to tell you---" the professor ran his right hand through his hair, "I feel as though we are running out of time for finding your sister. I feel as if I've been looking for her forever, even though it's only been less than a year."

Malique nodded in agreement, "I think we need to find her soon, too."

Just then, the professor's name was called to pick up his order.

When he returned and sat down, Clarissa nudged Malique and insisted, "Tell him what happened, Malique. It's the whole reason you called him, right?"

Malique nodded again.

"What happened?" Professor Chapman asked Malique; his eyes were wide with awareness and enthusiasm.

Malique relayed his experience of the tingling, prickly heated skin then the time he spent with his mother in mid-air. The professor was fascinated. "And you say that Mo told you to come to me. She thinks that I would know what this was about?"

Malique nodded once again in agreement.

"Professor," Clarissa started then corrected herself, "I mean, Evan--- Malique doesn't remember his sister's name. Do you think that is unusual? I mean, I explained to him that he has to give himself a break. He was only five years old when the accident happened."

"Oh, Malique, you went through an extremely traumatic experience. I agree with Clarissa, you must give yourself a break," Professor Chapman said before taking a sizeable gulp of his straight black coffee then took a bite of his blueberry muffin.

"So, if you have been searching for her for over a year, then that must mean that you have her birth name? Right?" Clarissa asked

"Oh, yes, I do," Professor Chapman admitted.

Malique waited eagerly for the professor to divulge the name. When it seemed he wasn't going to provide the name unless specifically asked, Malique asked, "So--- what's my sister's name?"

The professor shook his head as if to shake himself out of a haze. "Oh, I'm sorry," he said, blinking his eyes, "I couldn't think for a little while--- Your sister's name is Lanelle Theresa Laveaux."

Malique snapped the fingers on his left hand, "That's it!" He grinned. He felt something familiar stir inside of him.

"Sounds familiar," Clarissa said, tilting her head to the side. She ran her right hand through her hair. "Did the accident happen here in Beach City?" Clarissa asked.

"No, it happened in Los Angeles. I'm not sure where your mom was planning on going or what she was doing. She hadn't spoken to me in a month or so. We had an argument. She was talking about moving to New Orleans to be with your father. I didn't like it. Your father was behaving mighty strangely. He'd spend half the year in New Orleans then half the year with your family."

Malique frowned. "I don't remember spending any time with my dad. So, you're telling me that my father is still alive."

The professor shook his head in disagreement, "Honestly, I don't know. I have a feeling that your mom was on some kind of errand for him at the time of the accident."

"What was my father like?"

"He was very much into History and Art. In fact, that was his major--- double major, I mean. He was---" The professor squinted his eyes while he tried to search for the right words. "He was a collector. He was fascinated by the multi-culture of his ancestors. He was very much into theology too. In fact, he was accused of practicing voodoo. It was not surprising with his last name. He insisted he was not related to the famous Voodoo Queen, Marie Laveau. Still, I did find it interesting by some of the things he would do---" The professor's voice drifted, and both Malique and Clarissa turned to look at each other quizzically.

Clarissa was the one to ask, "Like what? What did he do, Professor?"

The professor shook his head again, blinking his eyes. "Well, one time I was visiting, and I went to the bathroom. I was walking back to the kitchen from the bathroom. As I passed by your room Malique, there was a crack in the door. I could see you were in your crib, you must have been about a year or so old at the time, but your father was standing over your crib with his arms out. His hands were spread out and palms down hovering above you while you were sleeping. He had his eyes closed, but his lips were moving--- he was chanting something repeatedly. I couldn't hear what he was saying--- well--- I don't think he meant for me to see him doing it either."

"He was probably just saying a prayer," Clarissa offered.

"I supposed," the professor said.

Malique thought it was strange. It was interesting to know that his father was ever with him.

"Charles was protective of you and your sister. I know you don't remember him. I think you should know that. Both of your parents loved you very much."

"So, that's his father's name? Charles?"

"Oh, yes," the professor nodded.

Malique took a sip of his coffee for the first time, not from wanting--- just from needing to touch something and just for something to do. There was so much to process. As soon as the coffee touched his tongue, he grimaced. Clarissa saw him shiver then said, "Hey, are you okay, Mali?"

Despite the taste, Malique forced himself to take another sip. "I just wished I could remember more about my family." Then he thought of something. "Do you know if my grandfather is still alive?"

Professor frowned, "I don't know. You're mom never introduced me to him, and I didn't think to research him. She mentioned that he lived in Georgia at one time. I don't know if he still does. We can find out his name and research if you'd like."

Malique nodded in agreement. "I'd like that. I remember him the most." He smiled.

"So, what do you think my mom meant when she said we need to go to New Orleans?"

"I'm not sure. Perhaps to find your father. She probably wants you and your sister to be with him. But why she would think I needed to be there, I'm not sure."

Clarissa gulped down the rest of her coffee then said, "I want to go too."

This time, the professor and Malique looked at each other then at Clarissa. "We didn't say we were going," Malique said

"Right," the professor agreed.

"But--- but we have to," Clarissa insisted. Her eyes were wide and glazed over. "Don't you see? We have to go. Your father is probably there. Maybe even your sister."

"No--- no---" the professor shook his head. "She's here. She's somewhere here in Beach City. She must be using a different last name, but I believe she is here."

"You mean, I've been living in the same city as my sister the entire time."

"I don't know if it's been the entire time, but I have reason to believe she's here in the city now."

"But how? Why--- How do you know?" Clarissa asked the professor. Her arms were crossed, and her eyebrows were meeting each other, creating a scowl.

"It's just this gut feeling that I have. I can't explain it," the professor was frustrated. "Mo and I have always had this connection. I felt it for both of the kids after they were born too. I feel your sister's presence just like I felt yours, Malique."

Clarissa just stared at the professor for a few loud silent seconds.

"I can understand if you don't believe me, but it's true, Malique," the professor said with desperation in his voice.

Malique shrugged his shoulders. "I don't know what to believe anymore."

"I'm curious about something," Clarissa said, uncrossing her arms and leaning her elbows on the small round table. "Do you recall if anyone in Mali's family has the two-toned skin as he does?"

"Clarissa!" Malique shouted, exasperated by the question.

"What? Don't act like you don't want to know."

"I thought you said you didn't care."

"Of course, I care. I meant I don't care that you feel uncomfortable with it. I like the way you are--- you're you--- I just want to know---" She turned back to the professor, "so--- do you?"

The professor scratched the right side of his chin with his right hand and said, "No one else has his complexion. The interesting thing is that I don't recall him being born with two-toned skinned."

Malique and Clarissa's eyebrows raised at that.

"In fact, the last time I saw you was probably before your fifth birthday, and from what I could tell, you had the same skin tone throughout your entire body."

"Hmmm---" Clarissa said.

Malique's mouth dropped open.

"So--- hmm--- do you think something happened during the accident? It's not burnt skin---" Clarissa pushed up Malique's sleeves on his left arm and rotated his arm so the professor could see palm up and palm down--- his upper arm.

"Fascinating---" the professor said, shoving his glasses up his nose.

"Can we get on to another subject, please?" Malique said, snatching his arm back and away from Clarissa's reach.

"So--- how do we find his sister?"

"We could hire a private detective," Malique suggested.

"That's what I was thinking," Professor said.

"I can talk to my foster mom too. She might be able to tell me more or at least tell me where I can start looking."

"Okay, so, do you want to talk to her? I'll hire a private detective next week, and we can meet here again at the same time next Saturday?" The professor suggested.

Clarissa nodded in agreement, "Yes, we will."

Malique felt a little annoyed that Clarissa took it upon herself to answer for him. What if he didn't want to meet with the professor? He did, but that wasn't the point. He'd have to talk to Clarissa later about her bossiness.

The professor rose from his seat, grabbed his coffee and pastry bag. "Okay, this was a very productive meeting this time around. Don't you agree, Malique?"

"Yes," Malique said as he rose from his seat. He grabbed his skateboard and waited as Clarissa grabbed her purse. They all walked out of the coffee shop together. Malique and Clarissa stood on the sidewalk and watched the professor get into his car then drive away in his silver Lexus. They waved as he passed them by in silence.

Clarissa turned to Malique and wordlessly hugged him. Malique had to drop his skateboard to keep her in his arms. The unexpected embrace was welcomed. He inhaled the scent of her shampoo--- coconut and lime, maybe? He wondered. She felt so good in his arms. He felt that warm bubbly feeling in the pit of his stomach. She squeezed him tighter. His heart began to do the unexpected racing. She shifted in his arms. Clarissa turned her head to look up at him.

Their eyes locked on each other. She reached up on her tippy toes and kissed him on the lips. She was about to withdraw from the kiss, but he pulled her closer. He felt the need to keep her next to him. He craved, kissing her the way a man kisses the woman he loves. He didn't know where the feelings were coming from. He didn't think he should have them. But they were here. She was here. He needed her. He was sure that she needed him, but for now--- She was his. He pried her mouth open with his tongue, and she welcomed him.

They both moaned.

"You can stop any day now!"

Both Malique and Clarissa jumped from the familiar voice that appeared out of nowhere. They turned to find Lani standing next to them with her arms crossed, tapping her foot impatiently.

"You promised you wouldn't kiss her like that anymore!" Lani said, giving Malique an angry, annoyed look.

Malique opened his mouth to say something but then closed it.

"Lani---" Clarissa said, covering her heart with her right hand. "You scared us."

"Good," Lani said, her arms still crossed her and tapped her foot. "You shouldn't be kissing him like that. It's going to ruin everything."

"Lani, he's my friend. I can kiss him if I want to."

"You don't kiss friends like that. I'm your friend, and you don't kiss me like that. Give me a break Clarissa. I'm ten years old, not five. You two are going to end up getting in a fight or something, and then I won't be able to be with both of you at the same time. Why can't you both just keep your lips to yourselves?"

Malique still hadn't said anything, but he was still holding Clarissa's hand. So much emotion. So much has happened today, and he didn't want to let Clarissa go. He needed her. He realized that now. She kept the questions going when his mind froze when they were sitting with Professor Chapman.

"You're right, Lani."

"What?" Both Lani and Clarissa asked in surprised unison.

"Friends don't kiss that way. Clarissa is more than a friend to me. So, I think you're just going to have to get used to it."

"Wait--- what?" Clarissa asked, her eyes wide from more surprise.

"I know it's weird. We are still getting to know each other, but there is something more than friendship between us, and I'm not going to fight it anymore." Of course, at the moment, a big part of him wanted to run away as fast as he could, but he wasn't going to let them know that.

"Why can't you two just stop? Why? Why do you two have to make everything complicated?" Lani looked both ways when she saw that the street was clear; she ran across the road to the flower shop. Her curly hair flopped up and down her back as she ran.

"Lani!" Clarissa called after her.

"Let's go talk to her," Malique said, grabbing Clarissa's hand and not letting go as they crossed the street and walked into the flower shop.

Sokie was behind the register counter when they walked in. Lani was rushing to the back of the store. "Lani---" Sokie said, confused.

Malique waved to Sokie then asked, "Hey Sokie, do you mind if I go talk to Lani upstairs?"

"I--- sure---" Sokie agreed. "Clarissa, I'm glad you're here. Can you work today?"

"Sure," Clarissa said to Sokie then turned to Malique, "You go talk to her. I'll help out down here."

CHAPTER TEN

Malique said a small prayer for strength and courage as he walked up the stairs to Sokie's apartment. When he entered the apartment, he found Lani sitting curled up in a ball on the couch. She had her arms around her knees, and her head was down. Her shoulders were shaking. "Lani, do you want to talk about it?" Malique asked gently.

She let out a sob, "No!"

His heart ached for her. He never meant to hurt her. "But---"

"You guys are ruining everything. We have to find the pebble, and you two are too busy kissing and getting all mushy."

"What? What pebble? What are you talking about?"

"Don't you see? Didn't you have the dream last night too?" She asked, looking up at him. Her hazel eyes were overflowing with tears.

"What dream? Tell me." He said, he sat on the couch next to her.

She sniffed. "Can you get me some tissue first?" Her lips were swelling. He vaguely remembered something about his mom. When she cried, her lips would swell, and her face would get splotchy. He wandered around the apartment until he found the bathroom. There was a big box of tissue on the countertop next to the toilet. He grabbed it, pulled out a few pieces of tissue then decided to carry the entire box with him back to Lani. He handed her the tissue then sat down next to her. He put the box on his right knee, which was closest to her.

She grabbed the tissue and blew into it. "Can you get me some water too? There's some bottled water in the fridge. You can have one too if you want some."

Malique gritted his teeth. She was so bossy, just like Melanie. He had the feeling if the two of them ever met, they would become the best of friends but then again--- maybe they would hate each other because they were so much alike. Despite his irritation, he went into the kitchen and took out two bottles of water.

When he walked back into the room, Lani was no longer in a ball, but sitting up straight with both feet firmly on the ground. He opened the bottle of water for her then passed it to her.

"Thank you," she said in a little mumble.

"You're welcome," he gave her a little smile then sat next to her again. She placed the box of tissues on the oak coffee table. "So, tell me about your dream," Malique encouraged her.

"Remember, I told you about the two guys that were holding you down and the crazy lady that wanted to see your back?"

"I think so, yep."

"Well, she wanted a pebble. We need to get to it before she does," Lani explained.

Malique shrugged his shoulders. "I think you just had a bad dream, Lani."

Lani put her face in her hands and shook her head. The curls in her hair shifted side to side as she shook her head. "I can't do this alone. Malique, you have to help me."

"But I don't understand what I need to help you with. What pebble are you talking about?"

"I don't know!" She shouted, sounding tired and fed up.

"Maybe we should talk to Sokie," Malique offered.

She shook her head in disagreement. "She's not going to understand."

"But Lani, I don't even understand." Malique explained. "Look---" he rubbed his temples with each of his index and middle fingers. "It's been a long morning. Why don't we just go downstairs and help Sokie and Clarissa with the flower orders?" He offered, hoping to change the subject.

Lani let out a sigh of resignation, "Fine." She got up, went to the door that led to the stairs, and stomped down the stairs. She refused to make eye contact with Clarissa.

Clarissa watched Lani as she silently grabbed a spool of ribbon and began making bows. Clarissa's mouth tilted to the side, and she gave Malique a questioning gaze. He merely shrugged his shoulders and asked if he could do anything to help.

"Well, I was just asking Clarissa if she would mind making a few deliveries for me. You can help her with that if you'd like," Sokie offered.

"Sure, sounds good," Malique agreed.

Lani immediately ended the silent treatment by asking loudly, "I wanna go. Can I go too?"

Sokie looked from Malique to Clarissa and back to Malique. "Um--- no--- I don't think that is a good idea, Lani. Clarissa is driving her Beetle, and they won't have enough room for you and all the flowers too." Not to mention Clarissa unquestionably shouldn't be driving in the first place, but no one said that little weighty detail.

Lani stood up quickly, causing the chair she was sitting in to tilt backward and crash to the ground loudly. She then threw the spool of ribbon across the room, almost hitting one of the glass refrigerator doors that held red roses. "I can't do anything!" She turned to stomp up the stairs.

Sokie immediately followed her calling out, "Lanelle Theresa Laveaux, get back here this instant!"

Malique felt his heart ram into his chest. He turned to find Clarissa staring at him with her mouth and eyes wide open from equal shock and disbelief. "Oh, my---" she pointed to the stairs and at the backs of Sokie and Lani.

"She--- She's my sister. She has to be," he said, stunned. "What--- what--- how---"

"Then--- oh--- Sokie--- she's your aunt---" Clarissa said in a whisper.

Malique sat down at the table where Lani had been only seconds before. He was trying to process this new information. This day was too much. He didn't know what to do. "You have to tell them--- Mali--- You have to go up there and tell them right now," Clarissa tugged on his arm, trying to get him to stand up. She somehow managed to get him to his feet. He was rubbing the back of his neck when they heard the stomping of feet coming back down the stairs and stomping their way back to the shop. Sokie was holding Lani by the collar of her shirt with her right hand while her left hand was on her hips. "Now, Lani, apologize."

Lani crossed her arms, "I'm not sorry. So I'm not apologizing."

"I am counting to three, and if you don't apologize, you will have no video games or television for two weeks. Do you understand? You do not throw chairs and things in this store. You don't do that period. Do you understand?"

Lani's lips wouldn't budge.

Sokie started counting, "One, two---"

"Okay, okay--- I'm sorry," Lani said. Sokie finally let go of Lani's collar. "It's just not fair that they get to do everything together. I am always here. I am always stuck here at the shop and don't get to go anywhere."

"Um--- can I ask you something?" Clarissa said, interrupting their spat.

Sokie nodded in agreement.

"I know I've known you both for a long time, but---" she cleared her throat then asked, "What's Lani's full name again?"

"What?" Sokie asked with a confused look on her face.

"You called her Lanelle Theresa Laveaux," Malique explained.

Lani rolled her eyes, "She always calls me by my full name when she's ultra super mad at me. It's so annoying."

"I just want to make sure you understand before I get to you, you are in serious trouble young lady," Sokie explained with her hands on her hips.

"So--- that's her name. Really?" Clarissa asked. She began to jump up and down.

"You're acting weirder than usual, C. What's going on?" Lani asked.

"Malique, you need to tell them," Clarissa urged.

"My last name is Laveaux. I think Lani is my sister," Malique said quietly.

Sokie covered her mouth with both hands and gasped.

"Wait--- What??" Lani asked with wide eyes. Her posture was straight and attentive with her hands on her hips, waiting impatiently for a clearer explanation.

"But that's impossible," Sokie said. "You told me you lived with your mom, sister, and twin brothers."

"Yes, my foster family," he explained.

Sokie sat down, dazed. "Why didn't you explain that?"

"It just never came up. I mean, it's not something that I usually have to explain to people."

Sokie nodded.

"So, what's your mom's name?" Lani asked.

"My birth mom was Monique Laveaux. She was married to Charles. I don't know her maiden name, though," Malique admitted.

Sokie gasped again. Tears were forming in her eyes. She rose from the chair and walked over to Malique. "I couldn't find you. I looked, and I couldn't find you." She embraced him in a hug, swaying back and forth as she held him tightly.

He held her tightly, with his eyes closed. His throat was constricted from unshed tears.

"Eeeee---" They heard a high pitched squeal of delight coming from Lani. She was jumping up and down. "I knew it! I knew it!!" She rushed over to Malique and Sokie and joined in their hug. All three of them formed a circle of hugs and tears of joy.

Clarissa rushed over to all of them and planted herself behind Malique and wrapped her arms around his waist, holding on tightly.

They were in the circle of hugs for several minutes. Finally, Sokie cleared her throat and said, "Okay, we have to talk. We have so much catching up to do. Do you think your foster mom will allow you to spend the night?"

"Oh--- Please--- Please, Mali, ask her. We could cook s'mores tonight and stay up talking--- please." Clarissa chimed in.

"Yeah, let's make s'mores--- I have a brother!!" Lani jumped up and down, did a little dance then jumped up and down again.

Malique didn't know what to say. He was flustered. He needed to talk to Sasha about his father and grandfather, but yet--- perhaps Sokie would know more. He felt torn. He needed to be there for Sasha and Melanie and his brothers, but a big part of him wanted to stay here at the shop with Sokie, Lani, and Clarissa.

"I don't think I can spend the night, but I will spend as much time as I can with you both."

"You have to tell Sokie about the professor Mali," Clarissa encouraged.

Sokie frowned, "Professor? What professor?"

"Did you know Evan Chapman?"

Sokie rolled her eyes. "I dated Evan. He was such a womanizing pig. He and Mo were best friends in college. They were like this," Sokie explained, holding her hand up with her index and middle fingers crossed. "They were inseparable. He always had a crush on her, but she would never give him a chance because she knew he was just full of himself." Despite her bitter words, she actually smiled an enormous smile, exposing dimples in both of her cheeks. "I haven't thought about the knucklehead in years." Malique thought he saw a twinkle in Sokie's eyes.

"Well, he's a professor now and---" Clarissa excitedly explained but was interrupted by Sokie's disbelief.

"Evan's a professor?" She asked in disbelief.

"Yep," Malique answered.

"How did he find you?" She asked.

"Not sure exactly. I just know that he looked at the police report from the car crash. He told me he believed Lani was still alive."

"Why didn't you tell me you were my brother?" Lani asked, confused.

"I couldn't remember your name. Mom used to call you Teacup all the time. I guess after the accident I forgot a lot of stuff--- like names and places. But I met with Professor Chapman earlier today, and he told me your name," Malique explained and looked at Sokie. "Maybe you should meet my foster mom and---"

"I know--- maybe we should all meet with Sasha and Professor Chapman. Maybe we can all figure out what happened on the day of the accident," Clarissa interrupted and suggested eagerly.

Sokie nodded in agreement.

"But," Clarissa glanced at the orders on a table ready to be delivered, "I think Mali and I need to make the deliveries before we start getting calls asking why they haven't been delivered yet."

Sokie sighed, "Yes, absolutely right."

"Ah, but I want to spend time with my new brother."

"And you will--- We have some responsibilities to take care of first," Sokie explained to Lani, then turned to Clarissa and Malique, "Drive careful. See you both soon."

113

Malique was quiet as Clarissa took charge and drove her Beetle to all the necessary delivery stops. There were six deliveries in total, but they had to stop at the shop again to pick up another seven more deliveries. Clarissa surprisingly gifted Malique with silence. He was grateful. He needed time to let all of the newfound information pertaining to his family to sink in.

When Malique finally arrived home, Sasha was sitting at the kitchen table, sipping chamomile tea and eating graham crackers at the kitchen table. The rest of the house was dark and quiet. "Well, hello, son," she said softly with a smile, "I feel like I never see you anymore. What have you been up to today?"

Malique put his skateboard by the front door and sat at the table across from Sasha. He sighed, "I don't know where to begin."

"Uh, oh. It sounds like you had an exhausting day."

"I guess you could say that," he agreed.

Sasha stood up, reached into a top cabinet, and pulled out a coffee mug. She reached for the tea kettle, poured some water, and grabbed a teabag. She placed the cup and tea bag in front of Malique. "Have some tea, and let's talk."

He told Sasha everything that happened during the day. When he was finished, he noticed all of his tea was gone. He didn't remember drinking any of it. He felt so relaxed, though now that he told Sasha everything.

"Wow," was the only word Sasha was able to speak after all of what Malique knew was revealed to her.

"Clarissa and Sokie think we should all meet with Professor Chapman. They think that if all of us meet, we might be able to fill in the gaps. Like, what happened to my grandfather and father? Are they still alive? If so, where are they? If not, what happened to them? How did they die? Where were they the day of the accident? Do or did they know about the accident? Do they know that my birth mom is dead?"

Sasha put her hands up, signaling him to stop or slow down. She finally found her voice and said, "Hold on, Mali--- everything is moving so fast that I can't think straight." She took a bite of another graham cracker and another sip of tea. (It was her third cup since Malique had sat down.) "Yes, I agree. I think it would be a great idea for all of us to meet. I don't think you should be meeting with Professor Chapman alone."

"I had Clarissa with me."

"Yes, I know--- I just think you should have another adult with you."

"Oh," Malique's mouth twisted to the side.

"So, when are you supposed to meet with him again?"

"Most likely, next Saturday at the coffee shop again."

"I have an even better idea. Why not meet here on Saturday instead? If it's not raining, we can have a barbeque. If it rains, then I can just whip up something for all of us to eat inside. How does that sound?"

Malique smiled, "I like it. Thanks, Mom."

Sasha reached out and grabbed his hands. "I love you, Malique. I don't care that we aren't blood. You are my son, as far as I am concerned. Do you understand?" Her eyes were glistening.

He squeezed her hand and nodded. "Yes, I understand, Mom."

"Well, I think we should both go to bed."

The next morning, Malique called Professor Chapman and left a voice mail message inviting him over to Sasha's house on Saturday to meet with everyone. He then called Sokie and Clarissa to invite them, as well. He decided to spend the Sunday with Melanie and the twins. They spent

the day playing video games, arguing, and an impromptu
game of soccer in the back yard.

Malique and Clarissa spent time together during lunchtime
in the library talking about the upcoming Saturday and
what the future might hold. On Friday afternoon, they were
holding hands as they were exiting the library. Suddenly,
Malique tripped. His backpack flew off his shoulders, and
he was sprawled spread-eagle under a tree on the quad. The
wind knocked out of him, momentarily. "Why did you do
that, Erik?" Clarissa shouted at the burly senior standing a
few feet away from Malique.

Erik had dark spiked hair that stood six inches straight
up with the help of hair gel, but his sides were nearly bald.
He crossed his arms and said in a deep voice with a scowl
on his face. "Why do you think C? Huh? You were
supposed to go out with me, but you changed your mind.
No one sees you anymore because of this guy."

Malique took a deep breath. Finally, able to breathe
without pain, he sat up. Took another deep breath then got
to his feet. He cracked his knuckles. His skin felt prickly
and began to burn. "Erik, you don't even know me. Why
did you trip me?"

Erik shook his head, "What are you? Deaf? I just said
why. You are keeping C from all of her friends. It's not
right for you to shelter her. Just because you don't like
people doesn't mean that you have to hold C prisoner or
turn her into you. You know what I mean?" Erik looked
genuinely concerned at Clarissa.

Erik raised his hands up, "Look, I have no beef with
either of you. I just worry. I miss you, C. It's OK if you
want to see this guy, but don't close out everyone else who
cares about you too."

Clarissa opened her mouth to say something, but no
words came out.

"Look, we all have to get to class. I'm sorry for tripping you, but at the same time, I'm not. At least, I didn't sucker punch you. Gotta go."

Malique picked up his backpack, cleared his throat, then looked at Clarissa. "Maybe he's right."

"Don't start Mali," Clarissa said with a simple warning. "Let's get to class."

CHAPTER ELEVEN

Clarissa arrived at Malique's house on Saturday afternoon, full of energy and enthusiasm. Melanie and Sasha greeted her at the front door. His brothers were in the living room playing video games with no intention of getting up to say hello to anyone. Sasha threatened the twins shortly after Clarissa's arrival to use their manners and greet her. They both walked to the kitchen where they were all sitting and grumbled, "Hi Clarissa," in unison.

"Hi," she replied. The boys turned right back around and went back to playing their video games.

Melanie, on the other hand, sat next to Clarissa at the kitchen table. "Malique has never introduced us to a girl before. You must be important to him."

"Mel--- really? Did you have to say that?" Malique asked, embarrassed.

Sasha giggled.

"Mom, can't you make her go to her room or something?" Malique whined, glancing at Sasha.

Sasha just giggled again.

"Guess that means I can stay," Melanie said wickedly.

"So, what's the plan today?" Clarissa asked.

Sasha sat at the table. "Well, I was thinking of making spaghetti for dinner for everyone. Maybe a salad and garlic bread."

Clarissa nodded in agreement, "That sounds good. What about a dessert or snacks beforehand?"

"Oh--- I didn't think about that," Melanie admitted.

"Clarissa and I can make cookies or cupcakes or something," Melanie volunteered.

Clarissa nodded. "Okay, I love to bake."

Melanie bounced excitedly in her seat then asked, "What time is everyone coming over?"

Clarissa answered, "My guess is around six-thirty. Sokie is closing the shop a little early today so that they can come."

"Oh, I hope it didn't cause them any trouble. Maybe I should tell them seven-thirty?" Sasha asked.

"Oh, no, trust me--- Sokie is excited and eager to meet you. She would be here right now if she could afford it. She and Lani will be here at six-thirty. Trust me," Clarissa said with a grin.

Melanie used a chair to reach into the top cabinet above the refrigerator. She grabbed two cookbooks and dropped them on the table. She handed one of the cookbooks to Clarissa while she kept the other one. "Here, you look through the baking recipes in this one, and I'll look through the other one."

"Hopefully, we have all the ingredients for whatever you two decide," Sasha mentioned.

"Oh, no worries if you don't," Clarissa said matter-of-factly, "I got paid yesterday so I can take Mel with me to the store to buy whatever we might need."

"Oh," Sasha said, surprised. "Okay, thanks."

"You're welcome. I want to help any way I can," Clarissa explained.

The phone rang. Melanie rushed to pick it up on its second ring. "Mali, it's Professor Chapman." She handed him the cordless phone, where he was sitting next to Clarissa at the table.

"Hi," Malique said into the phone.

"Hi Malique, I'm sorry, but I won't be able to make it tonight. I have to go to a conference in Atlanta. I just found out about it a few minutes ago," Professor Chapman's voice sounded full of regret.

"Oh," Malique said disappointedly.

"I want to meet with everyone as soon as I get back. It should only be a couple of days. I will call you as soon as I get back, and we can arrange something. Look--- I'll take everyone out to dinner. It will be my treat," he suggested urgently.

"I--- okay---" Malique said resignedly.

"I really am sorry. Please don't cancel the dinner tonight just because of me. Go ahead and meet with everyone. It will be beneficial for you."

Malique felt a twinge of annoyance, wondering why the Professor would think that he would cancel everything just because the professor wasn't going to attend. He started to believe Sokie was right when she said the professor was self-absorbed.

"Okay," was all that Malique could think of to say.

"I'll call you as soon as I get back."

"Okay."

The professor disconnected the call before Malique could say anything else, not that he had anything else to say but still.

Malique scowled.

"Who was that? What's the matter?" Sasha asked.

Malique pressed the end call button and placed the phone on the table. "Professor Chapman won't be able to make it tonight. He has some sort of conference in Atlanta that he didn't know about."

Clarissa rubbed Malique's back, "Oh, bummer. I'm sorry, Mali."

Malique shrugged his shoulders. "It's okay. He'll let us know as soon as he's back and said that he would treat us all to dinner."

"Hmm---" Sasha said with a smirk.

Later that evening, Sokie and Lani arrived. Lani was holding a bag of Oreo's and a gigantic smile. Her hair was down, and she was decked out in a pair of blue jeans and a simple white t-shirt. Sokie was in blue jeans and a magenta

120

t-shirt with silver hoop earrings. Sokie's hair was in a neat ponytail.

Sasha and Melanie took turns hugging each of them then ushered them both inside. This time the twins were sitting at the table and said, "Hi Sokie and Lani," together. They each waved. Sokie and Lani waved back. Clarissa moved away from the kitchen table to give Sokie and Lani a hug too.

Malique had just finished taking a quick shower and entered the kitchen. "Hi, Aunt Sokie, hey sis," he said with a grin. Sokie's eyes watered, and Lani jumped up and down excitedly.

"Hi nephew," Sokie said as she embraced him in a hug and kissed him on the cheek.

"Hello brother," Lani giggled and gave him a giant hug as soon as he was done hugging Sokie.

Malique rubbed his hands together, "So I guess you've already figured out who's who--- but just to be polite. This is my mom Sasha, my sister Melanie, my brother's Adam, and Rick." He pointed to each of them. "You already know C--- Mom, and sis," he glanced at Sasha and Melanie, "This is my Aunt Sokie and my sister Lani."

Clarissa grinned as Malique nervously made the formal introductions. She knew it was hard for him to be in the spotlight. This meant a lot to him, and he was handling himself well. She felt a little bit of pride swell inside of her.

"I'm so happy to meet you finally. I know it's only been a week since we all found out this wonderful news, but it's felt like an eternity. I wanted to meet you all since the moment we found out," Sokie said to everyone seated at the table.

"I feel the same way," Sasha admitted. "Unfortunately, Professor Chapman had to cancel. He has an unexpected conference to attend in Atlanta."

"Hmm---" Sokie said, sounding suspicious.

"That's what Sasha said," Clarissa said, intrigued.

"I'll just say, I'm not surprised he canceled," Sokie explained vaguely.

"Well, he said he would let us know once he's back in town and will treat us all to dinner," Malique said in the professor's defense.

"Hmmm---," Sokie said again.

"Well," Sasha said, clapping her hands once, "dinner is ready. The place settings have been set thanks to the twins. Why don't we all grab a plate, dish what appeals to you and let's eat."

Fifteen minutes later, they were all sitting around the table. They were all quiet as they were eating. Finally, the twins finished first then asked to be excused from the table. They wanted to continue playing their video games. Melanie wanted to stay with everyone else in the kitchen.

Clarissa was the first to ask the question that was on everyone one's mind, "So tell us what you know about the accident," she spoke to everyone at the table, no one specific.

Sokie answered, "I was in Louisiana at the time it happened. I was informed my sister's car was sideswiped. Mali wholly vanished from the scene of the accident, at least that's what the officers and social services told me. Lani's car seat was thrown from the car and was missing for a few hours, but later, they found her a few yards away near a tree. She was still strapped in her car seat and not a scratch on her."

Sasha frowned, "Interesting--- it's the opposite of what the officers and social services told me. They found Mali immediately. Rushed him to the hospital, but Lani vanished from the scene."

"So--- someone lied. It had to be an officer or someone from social services," Clarissa said.

"I knew Mali was still alive," Lani announced.

"What do you mean?" Sasha asked.

"In my dreams--- I knew he was alive. I could feel him. I can't explain it. I didn't know what he looked like, but I knew he was alive."

"Oh, honey, we talked about this before. It was just your hopes. You wanted him to be alive."

"No," Lani said, slamming her fist to the table. "I told you she wouldn't understand," Lani almost shouted, looking at Malique.

"What does she mean?" Sasha asked Malique.

Malique explained, "Well, Lani said she's been having dreams about me ever since we met--- when I ran into the flower shop. She said that men and a crazy woman were chasing after us. The crazy old woman wants to see my back---and Lani says we need to find a pebble before they do."

Sasha frowned.

"It's all child's play," Sokie explained.

"No," Sasha shook her head, "No--- it's more than that." Melanie was still sitting quietly, listening at the kitchen table.

Lani looked at Sasha then to Melanie with hope-filled eyes.

Sasha sighed, "I'm Native American. I believe what she has experienced are visions. It's a warning. We need to find out why these two were deliberately separated. Why would someone murder their mom? What happened that day and before that day?"

Sokie blinked. "But--- it was an accident---" Her eyes began to fill with unshed tears. "Why would anyone want to kill my sister?"

"That's what we need to find out," Clarissa said.

Malique was quiet for a while. Finally, he said, "I had some dreams, and I've heard voices. I haven't wanted to say anything because I didn't want anyone to think I was more of a freak than I already am."

Sasha shook her head in disbelief, "You are not a freak son! Stop thinking that way."

"You make me so angry when you talk about yourself that way," Clarissa said.

"Yeah, knock it off, Mali," both Lani and Melanie said with their arms crossed.

"Are you going to tell them about the seizure?" Clarissa asked.

"What? What seizure?" Sasha asked with concern in her eyes.

"I don't honestly know if that's what happened. I just know that my skin felt like it was on fire, and I think I passed out. But when I came to, my knee was hurting real bad--- and my whole body was sore."

"Hmmm---" Sokie said. Sasha and Sokie exchanged glances.

"Can I see your back, Mali?" Lani asked softly.

Malique looked at her, then frowned. When he looked around the table, everyone was staring at him. They all wanted to see his back, but none of them were going to ask the question. "Fine," he said irritated.

He stood up. He looked over at Clarissa with pleading eyes, "Don't be afraid, okay? You know that my skin is two-toned, but you have no idea what you are about to see. I understand if you don't want to see me anymore after you see. Okay? Don't worry about hurting my feelings or anything? Okay, promise?"

Clarissa wanted to argue with him. She tried to deny prejudice but knew there was no point in arguing--- the only way to prove Malique wrong would be by viewing his back and then staying by his side.

Malique began to unbutton the pressed white cotton long-sleeved dress shirt he was wearing for this special occasion. He wore a dress tank top underneath that he pulled up over his head. Everyone was silent as they stared at him. He closed his eyes, then turned around so everyone

124

could see his back. Immediately, sharp patterns and textures came into view from his shoulders all the way down past his lower back beyond the tips of his black dress slacks.

"Oh---," Sokie said breathlessly.

"Oh my gosh---" Lani said as parts of his skin glowed, a vague golden narrow stream appeared to run down his back.

Sasha gasped.

"It's a map!" Clarissa exclaimed.

As Clarissa said those words, Malique's skin prickled with heat. The hair rose on his arms, and then there was a bright yellow glow emitting off his back. The stream became crisper and sharper. Images became more apparent to Lani. Malique groaned then said, "Tsss--- Owwwww---." He shrugged his shoulders then arched his back.

Lani scooted back from the table and slowly approached Malique. She slowly lifted both her hands, palms facing Malique, "Breathe Mali--- Slow breaths in--- slow breaths out."

As Lani got closer and closer to him, his back began to cool. The glow subsided. Lani placed both palms on each of his shoulders. Malique momentarily arched his back again, puffing his chest out. Then his entire body relaxed. The glow was gone entirely. The images blurred then faded.

Sasha stood and handed Malique his tank top undershirt. He pulled it over him, then grabbed his dress shirt. He slipped the shirt back on then started buttoning it back up. He couldn't make eye contact with anyone. Malique felt embarrassed as if he just proved to everyone just what a giant freak show he indeed was.

Clarissa was sitting at the table silently, awestruck.

Lani turned to Sokie, then looked at Sasha and said, "We have to find the pebble before they do."

"What pebble?" Sokie interrupted, confused.

"I don't know," Lani admitted, "I just know that the old lady and the two men with her are looking for it. They are bad people, and I just know we have to find it before they do. I believe the map on Malique's back will lead us to it."

"Woe---" Clarissa said in a whisper.

"I don't have a map on my back," Malique argued.

"Dude, have you ever really seen your back?" Clarissa asked.

Malique made a face like she was crazy, "Of course I have---"

"Really? You've seen your back? Kind of hard, don't you think? Even in folding mirrors, you can't see your back that well," Clarissa argued.

"Pstt---" Malique spit out.

"You have a map on your back--- and it glows. What's up with that? And why was it moving? What the heck?" Clarissa asked excitedly, waving her hands every which way.

"How did you get a map on your back?" Sokie asked.

"I was born like this--- how should I know?"

"No," Sokie said, shaking her head adamantly. "You weren't born like that. You had smooth single-toned skin. In fact, you were the same shade as me. I use to visit you all the time. This---" She insisted, getting up and pointing to his back, "this must have happened after the accident."

Sasha swallowed.

"Who can we talk to?" Sokie asked Sasha.

"Most definitely not the police or social services," Sasha said. Her eyes were glossy as if she were about to cry and in shock.

"The professor---" Clarissa said, snapping her fingers. "He was closest to his mom. He might know what she was doing. He might know who she was involved with---"

"Well, Mo's husband was working on a theology research paper for his doctorate. He went to France for a

126

while and was supposed to come back, but Mo hadn't heard from him in a week before the accident. I talked to her on the phone almost daily. She was worried that something happened to him."

"Did you talk to her on the day of the accident?" Clarissa asked. Clarissa's eyes were wide, and she started to chew on her nails.

Lani smacked Clarissa's hand to stop her from chewing on her nails.

Sokie shook her head to say no. "I left her a message that morning, but she never returned my call."

"Did she mention where she was going?" Malique finally managed to speak.

Sokie closed her eyes and took a deep breath. "Let me think," she said softly. There was pain etched across Sokie's face. She frowned. A small vein appeared on the right side of her forehead. Her eyes moved back and forth behind her eyelids. She took a slow breath in and then a slow breath out. "I told her not to go. I told her to wait for me. I would go with her."

"Go where?" Clarissa asked.

Sokie opened her eyes. "To France. She wanted to be with your father."

"So she must have been on her way to the airport--- maybe?" Sasha asked.

"I think so."

"We need to get our hands on the police report," Clarissa said. She was about to raise her hand again to chew on more nails, but Lani slapped her hand again.

"Aren't police reports open to the public?" Malique asked.

"No, not necessarily," Clarissa said.

"How do you know?" Malique asked.

"Well, you know how I mentioned my parents are lawyers? Well, my dad is actually a district attorney, and my mom is a judge," Clarissa explained.

Malique's mouth dropped open.

"Now you know why I never see them," Clarissa said bitterly.

"Oh," Sokie said, "I knew your family was well off but had no idea."

"Well, do you think your parents would be able to look into the accident?" Malique asked.

"I guess it couldn't hurt to ask."

Sasha let out a heavy sigh. Everyone turned to look at her. "I just hope it doesn't cause any waves. I don't want to lose the kids."

"What do you mean?" Clarissa asked.

"Social services have a way of turning and twisting words around, then removing kids without quite knowing what they are doing. They mean well, but it doesn't always mean they do the right thing," Sasha said with a worried expression on her face.

"I'm fifteen. Why would they try to remove me now? I thought the last time we met with social services, and they said I could pretty much count on remaining here unless something happened or someone wanted to adopt me suddenly."

"Yes, but if we make waves with the wrong person--- they can easily take you or the twins. It's not like I've adopted you all."

Sokie nodded in agreement.

"Well, maybe I can just ask if I can see the report or ask if they know anything about it."

Malique nodded in agreement. "I think we have to start somewhere, and that is probably the best place to start."

"Wait, why don't we wait until we all talk to Evan first? He mentioned he saw the report, right?" Sasha asked, looking at Malique.

"Yes, he did."

Sasha lifted her hands with her palms up, "So, I vote to wait until we talk to Evan next weekend."

"If he doesn't have enough information, then Clarissa will go to her parents," Sokie said.

Clarissa nodded in agreement, "Okay."

Lani rubbed her temples then grumbled, "Too much grown-up conversation--- are we having dessert or not?"

Malique felt somewhat relieved by the change of subject. It appeared he wasn't the only one. Sasha waltzed to the freezer and took out a container of mint chocolate chip ice cream while Melanie grabbed a package of Oreo cookies.

CHAPTER TWELVE

The following week seemed to drag on. Malique was anxious to meet with Professor Chapman again but had not heard from him since the previous weekend when he called to say he was in Atlanta. On Wednesday, Malique was sitting on a bench near the library, lost in thought, thinking of his mom and wondering where she had planned on going the day of the accident when he saw Clarissa skipping towards him. It was a sunny clear day with a cool breeze. Clarissa was so beautiful. He still didn't understand why she was with him. But there she was skipping with a massive smile on her face. Her dimples were exposed only for him. She sat next to him, bouncing around as she did so, her backpack fell to the ground in front of her feet. "Hey, want to go to the Memorial Carnival this weekend? It's supposed to be awesome. Lots of rides, popcorn, cotton candy--- fireworks tribute to our fallen soldiers---"

How could he say no to someone so amazing? "Sure," he said.

"So, I take it you still haven't heard anything back from the Professor yet?"

Malique shook his head to say no. His afro moved along with him.

Erik passed by and said, "Hey, Clamali! Good to see you both out in the sun for a change."

Clarissa laughed.

Malique frowned. "Clamali?? What is that supposed to mean?"

"Oh--- don't worry about it. The girls were clowning around in Chemistry, and they thought they were cute when they combined our names."

Malique laughed. "I don't think it's a good idea. It sounds like a horrible disease."

130

Clarissa laughed again, "I agree, but I don't think we have a say in the matter. It's already all around the school by now."

"You are a disease, you wacko---" someone said in passing. The comment deflated Malique's mood drastically.

Clarissa placed her right hand on Malique's left and said, "Don't, okay? Just ignore him. He's not either of our friends. He's a stranger that we don't need to know. Let it go, okay?"

Malique clenched his fist. He wanted to chase down the guy and jump him, pound him a few times with his fist. He was tired. He was tired of the wisecracks, tired of hiding his skin--- tired of everyone at the school except Clarissa.

"You sure you want to hang out in public at a carnival with me this weekend? Folks might think I'm the main attraction."

"Knock it off already! We are going to the carnival and on a real date, and it's going to be great," Clarissa said as she stood up. She grabbed her backpack off the ground. "Look, I've gotta get to my next class. I promised someone we could go over flashcards before our pre-final exam. I hope you cheer up and call me later." She planted a kiss on his cheek.

He immediately felt warmth fill his chest from her kiss. Malique frowned, "Oh, I won't see you after school today?"

Clarissa shook her head and said, "No, I have to spend some time with the girls today since Sokie doesn't need me at the shop. Erik is right. I've been avoiding my friends too much. But call me later. Okay?"

Malique felt his stomach cramp. He suddenly felt a million and one miles away from Clarissa. It was strange--- one minute he was on cloud nine with her, and the next, he was on one side of the universe, and she was on the other.

Malique glanced at the library. He wanted to escape, but it was beautiful outside. The bench was in the shade, and only a few people were passing. He grabbed an apple out of his backpack and his literature book. He decided to stay right where he was and enjoy his solitude sitting on the edge of the wide-open high school campus.

Later that night, Professor Chapman called, "Hi Malique!" The professor shouted in his ear with way too much enthusiasm.

"Hi Professor," Malique said, switching the phone to his other ear so he could rub the one that was ringing from the shout.

"Oh, how many times do I have to tell you--- you--- call me Evan, okay? So--- so--- how is Sokie? Ah, I miss her. So beautiful. Is she still beautiful? Her legs--- they are caramel and chocolate all wrapped up in one---, and they--- they go on for miles and miles--- so--- so beautiful."

Malique thought he was slurring quite a bit. "Are you drunk?" Malique asked.

The professor chuckled, "I hope so. It's been a while, but I'm guessing a few shots of tequila would get a person at least a little tipsy. But I--- I don't know--- I can't seem to feel my feet. If I remember right--- That--- That isn't a good thing--- do you think?"

"Well--- I don't know. I've never gotten drunk."

"What? Oh--- when I was your age--- I--- I--- Oh--- Wait--- No. I can't tell you what I did--- Mo would never speak to me again--- I can't---"

"What?" Malique wasn't sure he heard the professor right.

"Oh--- no--- nothing--- look--- my son. We all must go to--- to dinner. This Friday--- My treat--- Hold on. I need another drink." There was a long pause. Malique thought he heard the slamming of a glass on a countertop.

"Did you just take another shot?" Malique asked, frowning.

"Absolutely. I only wish Sokie or Mo were here with me--- ah--- I miss Mo--- God knows I miss her---" Malique heard a sob come from the professor. He heard sniffing, then the professor coughed. It sounded as if he were trying to cough up a lung.

Finally, the professor returned to the phone. "I need to throw these things away--- Malique--- son--- don't smoke--- it's awful."

"You're smoking!" Malique shouted. Sasha walked into the kitchen just then in her nightgown.

"Who's smoking?" Sasha asked.

Malique explained, "It's the professor. He's drinking and smoking--- he's drunk off his butt."

Sasha frowned. "Where is he? Does he need a ride home?"

"Oh, no---" The professor shouted. "Tell your mom that I can hear her--- I'm OK. I'm at the bar down from my home--- I'm not as bad as I sound. I just can't feel my feet."

"He says he's at the bar near his home, and he can't feel his feet."

"Oh, he's going to be in pain in the morning. Does he have someone who will walk him home?"

"Oh, no need!" The professor shouted again. "I'm sleeping with the bartender tonight. She'll take good care of me---"

Malique smacked his forehead then shook his head. "Too much information Evan--- too much information."

"We're friends with benefits--- I'm talking about the bartender and me--- Sokie would never agree to such a thing---" The professor said and laughed wickedly. "Look, I--- What--- Wait--- What did I call you for? Oh, yes, Sondra--- Give me another--- Will you? It's been an emotional roller coaster the past month or so---" The professor put Malique on hold again--- again, Malique could hear the slamming of another shot glass hitting a countertop.

"Is he okay?" Sasha asked, holding a box of chamomile tea.

"He says he's going to stay with the bartender tonight."

Sasha shook her head disapprovingly but said, "Good, at least he won't be alone--- the idiot."

The professor was back on the phone. "This Friday at the new Italian restaurant. It's a little way down from the flo--- flo--- floooower shhhsshhop. Meet me there at sssseeven at night. Okkkay? Tell--- Tell--- Evvverryone." Then, click. The call was disconnected.

Malique stared at the phone. "Well, that was interesting," he said to Sasha.

"Would you like some tea and talk about it?"

"Sure,"

The tea kettle whistled moments later, and Sasha poured them each a cup of water. He told her about meeting with the professor on Friday. "Hmm--- let's see if he even remembers your conversation on Friday. You might want to call him tomorrow evening to remind him." Malique laughed but agreed. They chatted a little longer about the twins and Melanie while sipping their tea. Finally, when all their tea was gone, Sasha announced, "Well, I am going to bed. I will see you in the morning. Love you, son," Sasha rose from her seat and kissed Malique on his forehead.

"Love you too, Mom."

Malique glanced at the clock on the stove. It was almost ten p.m. He wondered if it was too late to call Clarissa. He picked up the phone and was about to dial her number when the phone rang. He glanced at the caller ID and saw that it was her. "Hi C," he said with a grin, "I was just thinking if it was too late to call you."

"See that; we are on the same wavelength--- we were thinking of calling each other at the same time."

"Cheezy---" Malique laughed.

Clarissa giggled, "Yep, that was cheesy. So what's up?"

"Evan called me. He wants all of us to meet him at the new Italian restaurant this Friday for dinner.

"Cool," Clarissa said, "my mom and dad went there a couple of weeks ago. They said it was excellent."

Sokie and Lani arrived at the restaurant a few seconds after Malique, Sasha, Melanie, and Clarissa arrived. They all sat in the waiting area, waiting for the professor to arrive. He rushed through the glass doors five minutes later. He wore a humongous grin on his face. His big blue eyes immediately landed on Sokie. Sokie held her breath for a moment, then covered her heart with her right hand. Finally, she let out a heavy sigh. "Big blue---" she said, barely audible then rose to her feet.

She outstretched her arms and embraced Evan with a hug. He closed his eyes and held her tight, rocking her side to side. When they let each other go, Sokie dabbed at her eyes and cleared her throat. "So--- Mali tells me you're a professor now?" She asked in disbelief.

Evan scratched his head with his right hand but stood a little taller. "Yes, I am," he admitted proudly. "I teach history at Los Angeles University."

"Impressive," Sokie grinned.

"Well, I figured since I majored in History in college, I might as well use my degree and all."

Sokie nodded.

Sasha interrupted their reunion by standing next to Malique and reaching out to her right hand to introduce herself to the professor, "Hi Evan, I'm Sasha. Mali's mom."

Evan blinked. "Oh, yes, hi--- sorry--- didn't mean to be rude. Sokie and I go way back. Nice to finally meet you. How are you?"

"I'm fine. Thank you. I hope you don't mind, but I put the reservation in my name. The table should be ready for us shortly," Sasha said.

Evan waved his hand, "Oh, no--- no worries. Thank you. Glad you thought of making a reservation. I didn't think it would be this busy. But then again, in this town, whenever a new restaurant opens, it becomes the main attraction for a year or so."

"So--- who are these two beautiful young ladies accompanying us tonight?" Evan asked, gesturing towards Lani and Melanie.

Lani stood up with her right hand, outstretched, "I'm Mali's sister, Lani. And this is his sister Melanie--- but we call her Mel." Lani motioned Melanie to rise from her chair and stand next to her. Melanie joined in with welcoming the professor.

"Pleased to meet you, Professor," Melanie said, shaking his hand firmly.

"Wow, you two are the most polite teenagers I've ever met."

"That's because they aren't quite teenagers yet," Malique said. "Lani is ten, and Mel is twelve."

Evan nodded.

Just then, a hostess in black slacks and black button-down top said, "Sasha, party of seven?"

"Good timing," Evan said, "I'm ravished. Shall we?" He outstretched his right arm gesturing everyone to follow the hostess. The hostess led everyone down a short narrow hall into a vast dining room, to a darkened booth the far right corner of the hall. As everyone slid into the booth, the professor opted to sit at the end of the table. Lani, Mel, and Sasha sat on one side while Sokie, Malique, and Clarissa sat on the other.

136

The hostess handed each of them a menu. "Welcome to Romanos. Your waitress will be here shortly to take your orders. Enjoy." She smiled and walked away.

"Well, first, I want to apologize for missing the first meeting last week. I wasn't aware of the conference until the very last minute."

"Oh, I understand--- things happen." Sasha said nonchalantly.

"What was the conference about?" Sokie asked, with elbows on the table and hands folded, her knuckles supporting her chin. Her eyes squinted at Evan suspiciously

"I--- what? I mean--- excuse me?" Evan asked, flustered.

"What was the conference about?"

"Well--- history," Evan said, still flustered.

"Really? They have History Conferences in Atlanta?"

"Yes," Evan said, not convincingly.

"And the University insisted you attend?"

"Yes," Evan answered, now appearing annoyed.

Malique glanced at Clarissa questioningly; she only shrugged her shoulders as if to say- how should I know? Malique shrugged his shoulder back at her to say the same.

Sasha cleared her throat, "Anyway, can I ask why it took you so long to look for and find Malique? And if you were so close to Monique and knew Sokie--- Why didn't you try contacting Sokie in the first place?"

"Well," Evan looked into Sokie's eyes, "I did. I called her many times and left messages, but she never returned my calls."

Sokie held a guilty expression on her face. She nodded in agreement. "At the time, Evan was the last person I wanted to see or talk to."

"Why? Why Sokie? You know I lo---"

Sokie held up her hands to stop Evan from saying anything further, "Don't--- not now."

137

Evan shook his head in defeat then said, "Well--- I adored your sister. She was my best friend. Why couldn't you talk to me? Why couldn't you have called me? I would have wanted to see her. I would have wanted to see her one last time and give her a proper good-bye. Kiss her on the forehead," Evan's eyes glistened as he spoke.

"Well, that wouldn't have happened anyway. A little after the crash, the car exploded. Her body was gone."

Clarissa's jaw dropped. Malique and Lani stared at each other in disbelief.

Sasha and Melanie gasped at the same time.

"But--- but how did the kids get out?" Evan asked in disbelief. A tear rolling down his cheek. He grabbed a napkin from the table and wiped the tear away.

Sokie shook her head, troubled. "I don't know. I thought Malique died with his mom, and I was just lucky that Lani survived."

Sasha's eyes narrowed, and she rubbed the back of her neck. "The whole accident doesn't sound right. Why would the car explode? Was a diesel truck involved? Social services led me to believe that Lani passed away. They also made me believe there was no other living relative in the area. All this time, we've all been living only a few miles from each other. Why haven't we run into each other sooner?"

Lani said in a low voice, "It was the old woman. She cast a spell."

Malique asked, "What? What old woman? What spell?"

Sokie interrupted, "Lani has had dreams of an old woman. Every so often, she wakes up in the middle of the night, screaming. She'd yell out, "Fire! Get out!" I would have to wake her up and stay with her until she went back to sleep."

"Don't you see? Don't you get it, Aunt Sokie?" Lani said, her eyes wide and her voice shaking. "The old woman is behind it all. She wants the pebble. For some reason, she needed Mali and me to be apart."

"Old woman?" Evan asked.

"Yes, she's little but powerful. She has two guys who work for her. She comes in my dreams and threatens me. She wants the pebble."

"Pebble?" Ethan asked, eyes wide. "The pebble--- it can't be--- it can't be true."

Clarissa cleared her throat when the waitress appeared at the table with a pen and pad in her hands. "Oh, we haven't even looked at the menu," Clarissa told the waitress.

"Can you give us a minute or so?" Sasha asked.

The waitress nodded then turned to tend to another table. Each of them grabbed a menu and decided what they wanted. The waitress soon returned, and each of them placed their orders. Lani and Melanie each ordered spaghetti with meatballs. Sasha order shrimp fettuccini with garlic Alfredo sauce. Sokie ordered a single roasted garlic and chicken pizza. Evan grinned childishly and ordered the same as Sokie. Malique and Clarissa each ordered lasagna.

The waitress walked away momentarily then returned with a basket of garlic bread then disappeared again.

"So, what is it about the pebble?" Clarissa asked the professor.

"Well, it's interesting actually," Evan said before taking a sip of water. He cleared his throat, scratched his forehead, then explained, "That was one of the main reasons your father was in Europe." Evan glance at Malique and then Lani.

"What do you mean?" Malique asked.

"He was researching his theology paper, but he was also in search of this pebble. He didn't know what it looked like but had reason to believe that it was in Europe. The last I heard he was in France. He told me it was believed that only one person was meant to hold the pebble. And when that person holds it, they suddenly gain all of the knowledge of the universe. I mean, they know--- everything. How it was truly created, what really is out there, why we all exist--- all knowledge is held within the pebble---"

"That's the most ridiculous thing I've ever heard," Sokie said, shaking her head. "I knew my brother in law was out of his mind."

"But, it's a myth, just a story, right?" Clarissa asked.

"Well, that's what Charles wanted to find out. He wanted to know more about it."

"Who started the myth or story?" Malique asked.

"Charles said he first heard the tale when he went to New Orleans to visit family."

"So, is it some kind of voodoo thing?" Clarissa asked.

"I don't think so. I really don't have a lot of information on it."

"Do you think that the map on Mali's back leads to the pebble?" Lani asked.

The professor sat back in his seat as if he were just struck by something. Then he blinked his eyes rapidly. He held his breath for a moment, then finally let it out slowly. "What--- what are you talking about?"

"Well--- it looks like the zebra stripes on my skin is a map--- according to them," Malique gestured to everyone seated at the booth, "I have a map on my back that glows with running water--- so if you're thirsty, you can drink---"

"Knock it off, Mali!" Clarissa growled. "This is real. We need to know what's going on."

Lani frowned. "Don't joke about your gift Mali. You will end up cursing yourself," Lani said in a low voice, but everyone heard.

Malique swallowed. "But why? Why me?"

"You know why. We both do," Lani said firmly.

Malique shook his head in denial.

"Charles had once told me that he was Creole royalty. I always thought he was joking, and he would laugh every time he said it. But, he would do things that made me wonder. I wouldn't call it voodoo, and it wasn't magic. I don't know what it was. Like the time I saw him praying over your crib Malique. He had his hands out, and it looked as if a golden light was emitting from his hands, and it was surrounding your sleeping body."

"My dad--- my--- you mean, my dad cast a spell on me? Did he cause this?" Malique asked in disbelief, pointing to his skin.

"No--- I think he was protecting you. But, I always thought I imagined it because I had a few drinks the day I was visiting," Evan explained.

Sokie nodded in agreement, "There was something peculiar about Charles. There were a few times when I would see him do something that I thought I imagined it too, but then there would be a flash, and I couldn't remember what he just did. I thought I was losing my mind. Is he some kind of voodoo master?"

"I wouldn't call it voodoo---" Evan said.

"Then what is it?" Sasha asked.

"The old woman practices voodoo, but she also does something else---" Lani shook her head, frustration evident by her facial expression, then admitted, "I don't know what it is. I just know she's evil."

Malique felt tingly all over. His skin began to prickle with heat, and his mouth began to feel dry. "Isn't voodoo bad enough?" Malique asked goosebumps tingled across his skin.

Evan shook his head in disagreement, "Not all who practice voodoo use it for bad. In fact, many who now practice it are Christian and---"

Sokie frowned and interrupted, "Drink some water Mali." Everyone turned to look at Malique. He looked a little pale.

Lani sat up straight. Lani reached out to touch Malique's hand and told him to take a sip of water just as Sokie had suggested. At the touch of Lani's hand, his skin began to cool.

Clarissa blinked, "They have some sort of connection," she explained to the professor. "The other day, when we all first met. Mali showed us his back. It glowed, and it was undeniably a map on his back with what I'm guessing was a river or stream with water. I mean, you could see the water flow across his back. The more vivid the map became, Mali appeared to be in pain. He arched his back and started to moan. But when Lani touched him, he calmed down, then the map kind of disappeared."

Just then, the waitress reappeared with their food orders. They ate in silence due to the time needed to digest their revelations.

CHAPTER THIRTEEN

The Memorial Day Carnival kicked off to a spectacular weekend of sunshine in Beach City, California. The temperature was at a comfortable low eighties. The sky was clear. The pier was packed with local vendors with booths lined up next to each other. There were sidewalk entertainers from musicians to magicians. Several movies and television celebrities who lived in the city made appearances and enjoyed the carnival, as well. There were several ticket booths set up for folks to purchase ride bracelets and food tickets. Several armed forces appeared in full uniform.

Malique arrived a little after noon to find Clarissa working at a game booth. There were several tiny bowls of beta fish and other bowls with goldfish lined up on a portable table. Clarissa's eyes brightened from the sight of Malique. She grinned, exposing her dimples and perfect teeth. She used her right hand to push her hair over her right shoulder. "Hey Mali, are you going to try to win a fish for your sisters?"

Malique rolled his eyes and sighed. "I can't believe I have two sisters. The sad thing is they are both pushy and stubborn."

Clarissa laughed. "So, how did the sleepover go?"

After the dinner, Mel invited Lani over for a sleepover. The two were up way past midnight giggling, talking, playing video games at one point, then more giggling and talking. "Too well. I know they stayed up past midnight. I went to bed at midnight but woke up a few times in the middle of the night from their giggles."

Clarissa giggled, "They must have had fun. Are they coming to the carnival?"

"Yes, Aunt Sokie said she would meet Mel here tonight after the shop closes to pick up Lani."

Changing the subject, Clarissa asked, "So--- come on--- win a couple of fish so you can give one to Mel and one to Lani."

"How much is it to play?"

"A dollar for four ping pong balls. All you need is to get one in a bowl, and you win the fish the ball lands in. It's simple."

"Yeah, sure it is." Malique reached into his back pocket of his denim shorts and pulled out his wallet. Sasha had given him some money before he left that morning. He handed her a dollar. She gave him four ping pong balls.

"So, the ping pong balls don't harm the fish at all?" Malique asked suspiciously.

"Nope. It's not like the ball will hit the fish. The bowls have a lot of water. They're fine."

"Okay, wish me luck," he said.

"Good luck," Clarissa said before kissing him on the cheek.

Malique moved as close as possible to the edge of the booth then leaned over.

"Hey, no cheating!" Clarissa yelled.

"How's it cheating?" Malique frowned.

Clarissa pointed to a sign hanging over the middle of the booth. It read, "No leaning over the booth. A genuine effort of tossing the ball into the bowl must be made."

"Seriously?" Malique groaned.

Clarissa crossed her arms. "Rules are rules."

Malique stood up straight. He repositioned one of the balls into his left hand then tossed it lightly. The ball hit the edge of the front of the table, not even hitting any of the bowls.

"Well, that's just pathetic," Clarissa teased.

Malique squinted his eyes at her, grabbed another ball with his left hand, aimed the ball for a beta fish then tossed

144

the ball. The ball hit the rim of the glass, ricocheted off two other glasses then landed on the grass next to the table. Clarissa laughed.

"Hey, I have two more."

"Yes, you do."

He aimed for the same beta fish; this time, the ball landed in the dish. Clarissa jumped up and down. "Yay! You just won one of your sisters a fish--- now you just need one more."

"Great--- no pressure," Malique said under his breath. He aimed for a goldfish this time, but the ball ricocheted again.

"Guess you're just going to have to keep playing until you win another fish," Clarissa said.

Malique ended up spending an extra six dollars until he finally won a goldfish. Clarissa kissed him on the lips. "I'm so proud of you. You're such a good big brother."

"Thanks--- so can the fish stay here until we leave tonight? Or do I have to take them now."

"They can stay here. I'll just tell the lady who will be covering the next shift to hold them for us."

"Okay, sounds good." Malique was about to ask her when her shift was over when out of nowhere; he felt something extremely hard and fast ram up against his right cheek, followed by another swift blow to his head. Malique's head immediately felt dazed, and things were fuzzy.

Clarissa shouted something, and Malique saw a vision of what he thought of as Clarissa hopping over the game booth and jumping on someone's back but couldn't remember anything after that.

Malique's head pounded, his right cheek was on fire, and for some reason, the right side of his lip felt swollen, and he thought he tasted blood. He blinked his eyes and wondered where he was. "He's awake," someone said.

He felt something cold on his cheek. He lifted his right hand and realized it was an ice pack. Malique blinked a few times. He realized he was in an unfamiliar room. It was small, and he was lying on what felt like a cot.

"Oh, thank God," Sasha said.

"What--- what happened?"

"Well, some guy sucker-punched you a few times before you had a chance to realize what was happening. He hit you pretty hard because you were knocked out. He said you had it coming for taking his money?" Clarissa explained.

Malique rolled his eyes. "Cheater--- I beat him fair and square at a skateboarding competition a few weeks ago, and he refused to pay me. So I just grabbed it out of his hands when he was flaunting it in front of me."

"I told you not to bet anymore, Mali! You see what happens when you gamble. It wasn't a competition--- not a real one--- It was a bet, wasn't it?" Malique turned to see who was speaking. It was Sasha. The disappointment was in her eyes and voice.

"I---I---" Malique's head hurt too much.

"Well, don't worry, the jerk won't be walking for a few weeks. Clarissa used Tae Kwon Do or something. She beat the mess out of him." Sasha said.

He glanced over at Clarissa, who was standing in the corner. She shrugged her shoulders as if it were nothing. Malique raised his eyebrows from surprise.

"I used to take karate for a few years. My parents insisted."

Changing the subject, Malique asked as he sat up, "Where am I?"

"The piers first aid and nurse room," Sasha explained. "A few guys helped Clarissa carry you here, and she called me right away."

"We need to take you to the ER. Are you okay to walk?" Clarissa asked.

"I'm fine," Malique insisted. He attempted to rise to his feet when he suddenly felt nauseous and dizzy. He immediately sat back down on the cot.

"No, you're not," both Sasha and Clarissa said in unison.

"I'm taking you to the hospital. Clarissa will you be okay with the kids while I take him? Just don't give them too much sugar. I would like for them to go to bed at a fairly decent time tonight. They were up way too late last night."

Just then, Sokie, Lani, and Mel walked into the room. "So, what happened?" Sokie asked, her hand gently touched Malique's chin as she examined his face.

Clarissa explained it to her.

"Was that the same guy that was chasing you the first day you ran into my flower shop?" Sokie asked.

Malique reluctantly admitted to it.

"He gambles," Sasha explained to Sokie. "He just blew it too. I was going to order him a laptop on my next payday, but now he's grounded."

"Ah man---" Malique said with a groan. Suddenly, he felt like he was going to throw up his breakfast and snacks from earlier in the day.

"Ah man---" Clarissa said shortly after Malique, "Does that mean I won't be able to see him either?"

Sokie sighed then suggested to Sasha, "I think he can see her but only at your house or at my house. I don't think he should be allowed to skateboard for a week or two, though."

"What?" Malique frowned in disbelief. "How am I going to get to school then? Dang, I only have a couple of weeks left. You're both acting like I was the one who hit an innocent kid. I'm the victim!" Just then, Malique grabbed his stomach.

Clarissa rushed for the wastebasket then handed it to him. "Here, use this if you're going to throw up."

"Why wasn't an ambulance called?" Sokie asked, worried. "And the police?"

"Because we don't trust the police or social services. But, he needs to go to the ER now," Sasha said. "Sokie, do you mind helping Clarissa watch all of the kids until we get back from the ER?"

"I'd love to," Sokie said. "After all, you had a houseful last night. Thank you for inviting Lani over. She doesn't have a lot of sleep over opportunities."

"Um--- Where are the twins?" Clarissa asked.

"Oh, they wanted to ride the Ferris wheel. I'm sure they are planning to go on the spinning rainbow ride next. They usually go on a bunch of spinning rides after the Ferris wheel until they threw up. Why--- I have no clue. It's probably because they are boys, and boys do stupid stuff."

"Yep, like gamble and get beat up," Lani said, tapping her foot with her arms crossed, staring at Malique.

"Will you guys knock it off? I'm not a gambler. I did it one time--- and that was just because Ricardo was such an arrogant as---"

"Hey," Sokie held up her right hand, with her index finger extended, pointing at him as if it were a deadly weapon. "Don't you dare curse! Do you understand me?"

Malique wanted to cry. His head hurt, and no one gave him any sympathy or a hug. He just wanted to go home and go to sleep.

"Look, we can all talk about this later. I need to take him to the ER in case he has something more than a concussion. As if a concussion isn't bad enough---"

An hour later, the emergency room doctor diagnosed Malique, "He has a concussion. He can take a couple of Tylenol for the headache. He needs to rest. Let him stay up a few more hours. But when he does go to sleep, wake him up every couple of hours or so through the night. We don't want him to slip into a coma," the doctor explained.

"Thank you, doctor."

The doctor nodded, walked to the door with his computer tablet tucked under his arm. "So, you say he was hit by someone at the carnival?"

"Yes," Sasha said.

"You sure you don't want me to call the police."

"No, no police," Malique interrupted.

"No, it's okay. It was a kid from his school. It was just a misunderstanding," Sasha explained. The doctor nodded and walked out of the room.

"Okay, let's get you home," Sasha looped her arm around his right arm then made the journey to the parking lot.

"I thought we were going back to the carnival," Malique whined.

"I'm going back to the carnival, but you are going home. You need to rest."

"But didn't you hear the doctor. He said I should stay up for a few more hours."

They finally reached Sasha's tan SUV. She clicked a button on a remote from her key chain, and there was a chirp from the deactivation of the car alarm. "Fine," Sasha said, "you can come with me to the carnival, but we aren't staying long. We are picking up the kids then going straight home."

As they were buckling themselves in, Sasha's cell phone rang. She answered it on its first ring. "Hi Sokie---" She paused then said, "He will be fine. He has a concussion-like, I thought. But we will meet you at the carnival to pick up the kids right now---" Another pause--- "Oh--- that would be great. Sure, if it isn't too much trouble for you--- Okay, see you soon. Thanks." Sasha ended the call and placed her cell phone in her purse.

"What's going on?" Malique asked.

"Everyone will meet us at the house. The girls will ride with Clarissa. The twins are riding with Sokie."

Malique wasn't sure he liked Clarissa driving the girls home. She didn't have her license yet but didn't want to reveal that bit of information to Sasha, however. He was relieved they were going straight home instead, but that wasn't something that he was willing to admit to Sasha either. He was still feeling queasy, and his head hurt way too much. He couldn't wait to get home to take a Tylenol and rest.

He still couldn't believe Ricardo managed to sucker punch him. The guy could hold a grudge. He wished he could have seen what Clarissa did to him. He leaned his head back against the headrest and closed his eyes.

Clarissa jumped over the game booth and elbowed Ricardo in the nose just as Malique watched himself collapse, knocked unconscious. Clarissa then quickly placed Ricardo in a tight headlock and asked harshly, "Who do you think you are? Huh? Why did you do that to my boyfriend?"

Ricardo was reaching up with his hands trying to pull himself away from her. "He had it coming. He stole money from me!" Ricardo was squeezing and tugging at Clarissa's forearms. She maneuvered his body with one quick motion with her right arm, which caused Ricardo to land on his back, knocking the wind out of him. Ricardo remained on the ground with his hand grasping his chest, trying to catch air into his lungs. His eyes were tightly shut. Clarissa placed her right flip flop covered foot on Ricardo's chest, pressing down hard on his hand and chest at the same time. "Now, tell me the truth! Why did you do that?" She shouted.

He took a couple of quick, painful breaths. "Fine---" he coughed. "We had a bet. I lost but wasn't going to pay him. Okay--- But he took the money anyway."

"So he simply recovered what was due to him. Right?"

Ricardo was quite still trying to breathe.

"Right?" Clarissa asked again, applying a little more pressure to Ricardo's chest.

"Yes. Fine--- It was his."

"Now, I'm going to let you go on the condition that you leave Malique and me alone. I don't want to see your face around me or my boyfriend ever again. If I do--- Let's just say you don't want to deal with me when I'm angry--- Got it?"

Ricardo nodded in agreement.

She lifted her foot off of him. "Now, get up and leave jerk!"

Clarissa turned away from Ricardo and knelt next to Malique. She patted his right cheek gently, whispering his name, "Malique, wake up--- Mali--- come on--- you've got to wake up."

Malique remained motionless on the ground. A crowd had gathered around the game booth. Someone asked if they should call 9-1-1. Clarissa shouted, "No." She reached into her back pocket, and Malique could see that she was dialing Sasha's number.

Now, Malique felt someone tugging on his left side of his trench coat. He could hear his name being called in the distance. "Malique, honey--- Mali---" more tugging on the trench coat. "Son--- wake up!" Sasha finally shouted with her voice full of panic.

"Huh?" Malique blinked his eyes.

"We are home now. Do you need help getting out of the car, or are you okay?"

Malique blinked. He glanced around and remembered he was in Sasha's car. They arrived home from the ER. He had a concussion. "I---" he reached for the handle on the passenger's side door. "I think I'm okay."

"Do me a favor--- don't go to sleep again for a few hours, okay?" Sasha said as she unbuckled herself and then unbuckled Malique. "You were kind of hard to wake up just now, and you were only asleep for a couple of minutes."

"I was asleep?" He asked. "It was so real."

"What was?"

"I--- I--- oh--- never mind---" He climbed out of the SUV then followed Sasha into the house. He sat on the sofa, watching the news with Sasha while they waited for Sokie and Clarissa to show up with the rest of the kids.

They only needed to wait five minutes when they heard the jingling of keys while the doorknob to the front door turned. Melanie had used her house key. Lani and Melanie rushed to Malique's side, and each of them embraced him with hugs and kisses. Clarissa was right behind them. "We were worried about you."

"Me too," Sokie admitted.

"We heard you got beat up, bro. Are you okay?" One of the twins asked in a loud, raspy voice.

"He's not okay. He has a concussion boys," Sasha answered before Malique could come up with a reply of his own.

"I'm staying here tonight," Clarissa said.

Sokie and Sasha looked at each other, trying to gauge each other's thoughts.

Sasha sighed. "Call both of your parents first. If both of them agree, then it's okay with me."

Clarissa immediately pulled out her cellphone from her big bulky purse and called each of her parents. She walked into the family room to talk privately.

"So, you have to wake him up every few hours tonight?" Sokie asked.

"Yes," Sasha said, "he was hard to wake up just now when he dozed from the ER in the car."

Sokie rubbed Malique's back. "Well, your lip should look back to normal in about a week. I don't know about your eye. The guy knocked you around pretty quickly.

Should we have him stay home from school for a few days?" Sokie suggested glancing at Sasha.

"I was thinking the same---" Sasha began.

"No, I'm going to school. Its year-end and finals are coming up. I don't want to miss anything," Malique said, raising his hands to stop the two women from discussing his life any further. "I know you both care about me, but you really can't protect me all the time. I need to go to school. I'm used to standing out in crowds rather than blending in--- I'll be okay."

"Well," Sokie said hesitantly, "if you change your mind, you are more than welcome to stay with me at the flower shop for a few days while school is in session."

"Good thing tomorrow is Sunday. You'll have a full day to rest. Tonight, I don't think any of us are going to get much sleep."

Just then, Clarissa reappeared with her right hand extended, handing her cellphone to Sasha, "I already talked to my dad. He said it's okay with him if it's okay with my mom. So I called my mom. My mom wants to talk to you to make sure it's truly okay for me to stay the night and that I won't be left alone in a room with a hormonal teenage boy." She rolled her eyes as she passed the phone to Sasha.

Sokie and Sasha both grinned. Sasha reached for the phone and said, "Hi, this is Sasha, Malique's mom." She walked into the same room Clarissa was in moments ago talking into the phone.

"Can I ask you something?" Malique asked Clarissa.

"Sure, what's up?"

"How did you beat up Ricardo?"

"Ricardo? That's the jerk's name?"

"Yes."

Clarissa licked her lips then said, "Well, it all happened so fast, so I don't remember the exact details, but at one point he was in a headlock, then the next thing I know I had him on the ground with my foot to his chest."

153

Malique blinked. How could he have seen it all in a dream? How could he have remembered something when he was momentarily knocked unconscious? Malique frowned.

"What? Why? What's the matter?"

"It's strange--- But---" Malique rubbed the back of his neck with his right hand. "I saw the whole thing."

"How? You were knocked out."

"On my way back home from the ER, I saw it in a dream," Malique explained.

"Hmm---" Clarissa licked her lips as she was thinking for a moment, "maybe you heard everything around you while you were knocked out, so your subconscious replayed it to you in your head."

"I don't know--- it's weird, though. It was like I was watching the whole thing again, but while it was happening."

"Hmmm---" Clarissa mumbled.

"Your mom used to do the same thing," Sokie said. "When we were little, if something bad happened to me, she would know exactly what happened to me even though she wasn't there. She would completely freak me out."

Malique looked at his aunt with amazement. It was still a shock to him that he was finally with actual family who could tell him more about his mother and other relatives. "Do you have the same ability?" Malique asked Sokie.

"No," Sokie said sadly. "I do have this feeling, though. I could never explain it. I always had this feeling in my body when something bad was about to happen to my sister. It would make me feel anxious and jittery. Even though we were miles apart, the day of the accident, I was restless. I knew something wasn't right."

Just then, Sasha walked back into the room. "Your mom is okay with you spending the night. You can sleep on the sofa bed." Sasha handed Clarissa back her cellphone.

"Can I spend the night too?" Lani asked.

"No," Malique said, a little too quickly.

Lani's mouth dropped, and her eyes glistened.

"I'm sorry, Lani. I don't mean to hurt your feelings, but I know you and Mel will just talk and giggle all night, and I won't get any sleep. Or you will want to talk all night. I just can't deal with you two partying it up all night."

Surprisingly both Mel and Lani laughed and high fived each other. "Yep, we would be partying all night," they said in unison.

Clarissa shook her head.

CHAPTER FOURTEEN

Sasha had woken Malique up three times during the night with a flashlight in hand to check his pupils. When she was certain he would be okay, she finally went to sleep herself and didn't wake until there was a pounding on her front door at eleven o'clock in the morning. Clarissa was dressed and sitting at the kitchen table, eating a sandwich. Sasha's hair was scrambled atop her head, and there were bags under her eyes as she dragged her feet to the front door. "What on earth could be so important?" She scratched her belly. Not caring that she was answering the door in only an enormous t-shirt and mismatched socks on her feet. "What professor?" She shouted after looking through the peek hole then opened the door.

"What happened to you?" Evan asked Sasha with his eyes wide.

"What didn't happen--- you mean--- Sleep. I need sleep," Sasha explained.

Clarissa stood next to Sasha. "What brings you here, Professor?"

"I was researching some information on the pebble of knowledge, and I found that we must get Malique and Lani to New Orleans as soon as possible."

"What?" Sasha asked yawning.

"Why?" Clarissa asked, wide-eyed.

"May I come in?"

Sasha opened the door wider so that he could enter the house. She closed and locked the door as Clarissa and Evan made their way to the kitchen table. Sasha dragged her feet and followed them, glimpsing into the family room. The twins were already in the family room, playing video games. Melanie was sitting on the love seat reading. It appeared everyone except for Malique and Sasha got sleep.

156

Clarissa was in the process of making a sandwich for the professor. Sasha was amazed at how easily Clarissa made herself at home.

"So, why do you feel my son and Lani need to go to New Orleans?"

"Well, apparently, the pebble of knowledge can only be used by royalty and can only be used on June 21st. Based on the research I've done, it looks like the pebble should be in New Orleans. It will take some time to find it since it is only the size of a pebble. So the sooner we get there, the better chances we have of finding it in time."

"What royalty? What does the pebble do? What are you talking about?" Clarissa asked with her eyebrows scrunched together and a heavy frown on her lips.

The professor removed his glasses and wiped the sweat off his face with his right hand. "I know it all sounds strange, but with everything that's been happening, it all makes sense. I'd like to go to New Orleans and meet with this woman who owns a voodoo shop. She would have more information. But if Malique and Lani are the royalty that I think they are--- then they can use the pebble or perhaps destroy it."

"Why destroy it?" Clarissa asked.

"So evil won't possess it," Sasha said evenly.

"Oh," Clarissa said.

Malique entered the kitchen, wearing a tank top and shorts. Everyone stared at him. It was the first time he let his arms be exposed, and his feet were bare. "He does have a map on his back, doesn't he?" Evan asked.

"Yes," Clarissa said in a whisper.

Evan grinned.

Sasha frowned.

Malique yawned and scratched his head. His afro was lopsided, and his breath was atrocious. Clarissa scrunched her nose. "Malique, turn around, go to the bathroom and please--- Brush your teeth--- Maybe use some mouthwash. Then come back--- Please--- Pretty please."

Malique nodded his head in agreement and lazily turned around and went to the bathroom and did as suggested. Sasha shook her head. "Interesting. He would have given me an argument." Suddenly Sasha realized she hadn't brushed her teeth and looked down at herself. She sighed. "Please excuse me for a moment. I need to brush my teeth too--- and change. I will be right back."

Clarissa handed the professor a sandwich on a saucer, then sat down and resumed eating her sandwich. They ate in silence as they waited for Sasha and Malique to return.

Malique returned in his usual shorts, flannel shirt worn over a black t-shirt, and military boots. His hair was damp and pulled back into a ponytail. Clarissa smiled, "Hey, I like the new look Mali."

He grinned and said, "Thanks."

Sasha appeared moments later. Her hair was damp also but loose. She wore jeans and a plain white t-shirt. "So, you believe Malique and Lani need to go to New Orleans?"

"Absolutely," Evan said.

"Wait--- what? Why?" Malique asked, completely confused. The professor explained all that he had already said to Sasha and Clarissa.

Malique stared at the professor for a few moments in silence, sitting at the kitchen table. He was holding Clarissa's hand in his lap. They sat close together while Sasha and Evan sat across from them.

"I know it's probably a lot to take in."

Malique let go of Clarissa's hand for a moment to hold both of his hands up in a gesture to stop the professor from speaking any further. "Hold up--- This has been a crazy few weeks, okay? I find out my sister is alive and has been living only a few blocks away from me this whole entire time with my aunt. I am told I have a map imprinted on my body. My father was some kind of voodoo who dooey

158

witch crafting warlock whatever, and now I'm just supposed to fly off to New Orleans for a rock?"

"It's not a rock--- it's a pebble."

"What's the difference?" Malique asked with frustration.

"A rock is bigger and would be easier to find," Sasha said.

"So that little bit of information makes things a little more difficult, don't you think?"

"Not when we have the map to find it," Evan said with a grin.

"Why are you smiling? Why do you look like a little boy about to open a magnificent present on Christmas morning?" Sasha asked. She crossed her arms and rubbed her forearms as if to warm them up somehow.

"Are you cold?" Clarissa asked Sasha.

"I'm afraid. I don't like this. This whole thing isn't good. I feel fear," Sasha whispered.

"Unfortunately, I don't think we have a choice," Evan said.

"What do you mean?" Clarissa asked.

Just then, there was pounding on the front door. Malique got up to answer the door. Lani and Sokie entered the house. Lani rushed into Malique's arms with tears streaming down her face. "I had an awful dream Mali--- you were--- you---" Malique continued to hug his sister.

"Calm down, sis. Shh--- Breathe--- It's okay. I'm here. See--- I'm okay." His heartfelt, full, and love poured out of him. He felt his eyes water but would not allow the tears to fall. He missed her so much, the enormity of the years lost between them struck him at that moment.

When Lani's tears and breathing were finally under control, she let him go and looked up at him, "Hey, you called me sis," she said with a small smile.

"Well, that's what I used to call you when you were a baby."

She nodded.

"So, what was your dream about?" Evan asked from the kitchen table.

Sokie and Lani followed Malique into the kitchen.

Lani cleared her throat; she remained standing while the others sat at the table. She explained, "The three of us were in some kind of tunnel, and suddenly there was a blast of light and Malique was lying on the ground in a puddle, and he wasn't breathing. We couldn't wake him up."

"Oh, baby, I tried to explain you were probably just having a bad dream because of that guy who attacked him yesterday. As you can see, he's fine," Sokie insisted.

Sasha gasped and put her hands to her mouth.

"What's the matter?" Sokie asked Sasha.

Sasha shook her head. "Don't you see? Don't you see what's happening?"

Clarissa and Sokie exchanged looks that said- no, they didn't understand or see what was happening.

"Lani and Mali are having visions. Mali can see the past while Lani can see the future."

"I know what Mali thinks, too," Lani admitted.

"Wait--- what?" Clarissa said, her eyes wide from disbelief. Malique looked just as surprised as Clarissa.

"You can read my mind?" Malique asked Lani, she nodded.

The professor rose from his seat and began to pace the kitchen floor. "Can I see the map on your back, Malique?"

Malique stiffened in his seat. Clarissa reached for Malique's right hand and held it in both of her hands.

Lani asked protectively, "Why? Why do you need to see it?"

"Because if I'm right--- it may be a map of underground tunnels in New Orleans."

"It causes my brother immense pain when he exposes the map to others," Lani said with both of her hands balled up into fists.

160

"Sokie, if you agree--- I think the professor should see it," Sasha said.

Sokie nodded in agreement.

Malique frowned but rose from his seat. He took a deep breath, then slid off his flannel shirt, handed it to the professor. He lifted his arms to peel off the black t-shirt. He turned so that his back was facing the professor. Lani quickly stood close to Malique. She reached up and placed her right hand on his right shoulder. "Keep taking deep breaths," Lani instructed.

Malique nodded in agreement.

The professor tilted his head to the side while examining Malique's back. "It just looks like a birthmark to me," Evan said disappointedly.

"It's because Lani is controlling it. She's only allowing you to see what she wants you to see," Sokie said, matter of factly.

Clarissa's mouth was open, and her eyes were wide.

"I agree," Sasha said in a whisper. "Lani, slowly let go of Mali's shoulder."

"No," Lani insisted. "I don't want him to feel any pain."

Malique shook his head, "It's okay sis. The professor needs to see. We all need to know what all of this means."

Lani bit her lip and swallowed, "Okay," she said in a low whisper. She slowly let go of his shoulder but closed her eyes.

As she let go, Malique's back began to glow a bright yellow. Malique arched his back as images started to protrude ever so slightly. The professor's eyes widened, and he tilted his head again. "Well, I'll be da---"

"Evan--- no cursing---" Sokie stopped him.

"Come see Sokie--- see the flowing river--- It's the Mississippi River."

Malique arched his back further and groaned as his skin prickled with the feeling of fire.

Lani reached out and grabbed each of his shoulders, and looked up to Malique. "Mali, open your eyes. Breathe," she said calmly.

Malique's groaning subsided, and he opened his eyes to look into Lani's.

Do you trust the professor? Malique heard Lani's voice in his head.

Yes--- I think so. Do you? Malique asked.

I don't know. But I don't think we have a choice.

"So, what now?" Clarissa asked. "Are we all going to New Orleans now or what?"

Sasha immediately shook her head in disagreement. "No--- no--- we can't go."

"All of us don't need to go. I can take them," the professor volunteered.

"Not without me, you aren't," Sokie stood to stand in the middle of the kitchen next to Malique and Lani with her arms crossed.

"Where's New Orleans?" Lani asked.

"It's in Louisiana. Much of our family is from there," Sokie explained.

"I don't want to go," Malique said, stubbornly. "Nothing is there for me. Everything I need is here in Beach City."

The professor shook his head in disagreement. "That isn't true. You have to go. It's your destiny."

Lani shifted from foot to foot nervously.

"Can you give us time to think and talk about it? We can't just hop on a plane and go--- School is almost over. Summer vacation will begin in a couple of weeks. At least give us until the end of school to figure out what we are going to do."

The professor ran his right hand through his hair, then scratched the right side of his jaw. "That will have to do--- but understand, we won't have much time. We need to find the pebble by June 21st."

The professor handed Malique his flannel shirt and t-shirt back. Malique quickly pulled the t-shirt on then tugged the flannel shirt back on.

Later that evening, Malique and Clarissa sat on the couch alone, snuggled close to each other. "I don't want you to go, Malique."

"I don't want to go. But I get the feeling that Lani and I have to. I don't think it's optional. Something is there in New Orleans, and it's calling or demanding Lani, and I to be there. I understand if this is all too weird for you and you don't want to be with me anymore---"

She punched him on the arm. "I thought I told you to stop it. I am not leaving you. I need you too much."

"But why? Why do you need me?"

"I feel safe with you, okay? Everyone else I know only hangs out with me because they think I can give them something. Because of my parents or because of money--- or just popularity. It's all so stupid. I just--- I just feel free with you, Mali. I feel happy when I'm around you."

He sighed. He still didn't understand why she was with him.

"Really? You feel safe around me? I have a map on my back that glows. I have to find a pebble before some evil crazy old lady finds it--- my sister has the power to control me and the power to read my thoughts--- And you feel safe around me?? I don't even feel safe around me--- And I can't get away from me," he laughed, shaking his head.

"But you're protective---"

"No--- no," he shook his head vigorously in disagreement, "You--- YOU are protective. I mean, you are the one who kicked Ricardo's butt while I was passed out on the ground."

Clarissa laughed. "So--- maybe our roles are reversed a little bit. You're the lady, and I'm the man," Clarissa suggested with a laugh.

Malique reached for one of Sasha's embroidered throw pillows and gently knocked Clarissa with it. "Oh--- No--- I wouldn't go that far," Malique said. Clarissa grabbed another pillow and began to beat Malique with it. The pillow fight continued until finally, Malique successfully managed to yank the pillow out of Clarissa's hand. He managed to nudge her onto her back. She attempted to wrestle with him, but he grabbed her wrists and pulled them above her head. They were both laughing, but the laughing subsided as their lips were only inches apart from each other.

"I get the feeling that you can easily pry yourself out of this, but I'm going to pretend you can't," Malique said in a low voice. He slowly moved in closer to kiss her.

"Oh--- no--- uh--- uh---" Sasha said from behind the couch.

Both Clarissa and Malique immediately jumped to their feet.

"We--- I--- Ummm---" Clarissa stuttered.

Malique's heart was racing. He shifted his shorts.

"Thank you for visiting this weekend, Clarissa, but I think it's time for you to go home. You both have school tomorrow."

Clarissa fidgeted with her hands, her eyes still wide. "I--- Ummm---"

"We weren't doing anything, Mom," Malique said defensively, not wanting Clarissa to go.

"I---"

"Really?" Sasha said, crossing her arms. "If that were true, then why do you both look guilty, and Miss Talkative is suddenly at a loss for words." Sasha tilted her head to the side and smirked.

"Come on, Mom--- does she have to go?"

"I like you, Clarissa, but I don't want to become a grandmother yet. Besides, I think it is time for you to go home. You both have school tomorrow."

Clarissa nodded in agreement. Her cheeks were still flushed from embarrassment. She grabbed her purse and pulled out her car keys.

Malique grunted. "I'll walk you out."

"Okay, thanks."

Sasha watched the two of them walk out the front door. She shouted just before Malique closed the door, "And don't take more than five minutes!" She shook her head.

CHAPTER FIFTEEN

The halls were cluttered with paper and other debris as it was every year on the last day of school at Beach City High School. Lockers were slamming shut; teenagers were running off the campus, eager to start their summer vacations. Clarissa, however, sat on a bench pouting. Malique sat next to her. "Lani and I will be back before you know it."

Clarissa sat stiffly, clutching her purse. Her hair pulled back in a lazy ponytail. She stared down at her sandal covered feet and French manicured toes. "I just have an extremely terrible feeling about this. I don't think you should go--- I mean--- do you believe you can trust the Professor? You just met him."

"I just met you, and I trust you."

"But that's different, and you know it."

Malique cleared his throat. He was afraid to go too, but he didn't want Clarissa or any of the others to know. He needed to put on a brave face and embrace his destiny. He hadn't told Clarissa, but the other night while he was sleeping, he heard a voice that sounded very much like his grandfather's explaining that it was time for him to go. He needed to discover the truth since his grandfather couldn't tell him for fear of the consequences. Before reuniting with his sister, he would have ignored the voice, but considering all that has happened. He knew from his gut he had to listen to the voice, especially since his grandfather's voice sounded so full of urgency.

"Malique---" Clarissa said in a whisper.

"Yeah, I know--- it is different," he whispered, reaching for her hand with his right hand.

"Can I ask you something?" Clarissa asked.

"Of course."

She cleared her throat then said, "Well, I've been thinking--- remember how you had the vision of the past--- about what happened after Ricardo attacked you on Memorial Day?"

Malique nodded his head to say yes.

"Well--- why can't you do that for the day of the accident? With your mom and Lani?"

Malique blinked his eyes.

"I mean--- you blacked out the day Ricardo attacked you, and you said you blacked out the day the accident happened."

Malique stared out--- his eyes glazed.

"Malique?"

He had dreams of the accident. They all were the same. Why didn't he think of that before? He mentioned them to the therapist he was forced to visit, but she had dismissed them as wishful dreams or flashes of memories. He had ultimately convinced himself that it was just plain and simple dreams--- More like nightmares than dreams.

"Malique?" Clarissa asked again. This time she let go of his hand and began to rub his back with her left hand. "Are you okay?"

Malique nodded, "Yes, I just--- for the longest time, I thought that they were just nightmares, but--- now that you mentioned it. Maybe it was what happened."

Clarissa lifted her eyebrows in shock. "I didn't think you would agree with me," she admitted. "You've been fighting me the past couple of weeks."

"I know---" he admitted. "Honestly, I am not jumping for joy to go on this crazy hunt for a pebble, but I have to go--- you understand, right?"

She frowned but mumbled, "Yeah, I guess so."

They held each other for a little while, then Clarissa asked, "So, what kind of nightmares were you having?"

Malique let her go and rested his elbows on his knees. He looked down at his hands and explained, "Well, after

167

our car was struck, there was a bright light. My mom was moaning. She was still alive. I could see that my sister's car seat was still in the car, but she was quiet. She wasn't crying. I couldn't see her face, so I didn't know if she was alive or not. There was another flash of light, and then my mom vanished--- I---"

"She just vanished?" Clarissa asked.

Malique licked his lips, then said, "Yep."

Clarissa narrowed her eyes. "Malique--- do you think there is a chance---"

"She may still be alive?"

"Do you?" Clarissa asked.

Malique shrugged his shoulders. "If she is alive, why didn't she come for Lani and me?"

"Maybe because she can't. Maybe she's being held against her will."

"But why? None of this makes any sense."

Clarissa began to wrap her index finger around a loose strand of hair that fell out of her ponytail. "The map on your back doesn't make sense. You being separated from your sister up until now doesn't make sense--- Wait--- didn't Sokie say you didn't have the multi-tone skin when you were a baby or when she last saw you when you were like--- what five or something?"

Malique nodded in agreement.

"What if you didn't have it until the time of the crash--- the light--- or something--- the bright light--- there must have been a spell or something---"

"Something---" Malique whispered.

"You have to go--- you have to go with the Professor and find out what all of this means."

When Malique arrived at home, Melanie and the twins were waiting for him on the couch. He noticed a banner hanging above the entranceway to the family room. It had

Mardi Gras masks along with purple, yellow, and green streamers and confetti. It read, "Have a safe trip. We will miss you!"

The twins shuffled around the couch to stand near Malique. They were looking down at their feet; their faces were pouting. Mel, on the other hand, rushed to embrace him in a tight hug. "Do you really have to go, Mali?"

He sniffed but held her tight too. "Yep."

"Promise to be careful and promise to come back?"

"Yep. I promise."

"You aren't crossing your fingers, are you?"

He thought about it but said, "No."

"Boys, check behind his back. Is Mali crossing his fingers? Or eyes?"

Malique managed a laugh, "What? You don't trust me."

"Sometimes yes, sometimes no," Mel managed a little laugh.

The boys checked his hands and eyes anyway. One of them announced, "He's not crossing his fingers or eyes, Mel."

"Okay," she said. This time her voice was muffled because her face was buried into his chest. They hugged for another minute in silence. Finally, Malique let her go. Mel wiped her eyes with the back of the t-shirt sleeve.

Malique outstretched his arms to the twins. "Come on, guys, give me a bro hug."

The twins embraced Malique together for a much shorter group hug than the one Melanie provided. Just as they released from the hug, Sasha walked through the front door.

"I didn't think I would ever get off of work, geesh! We were so crazy busy. Ah, Mel, boys--- Ahh--- The banner and streamers look great. Great job!"

Malique thought Sasha was behaving a little more perkily than she usually did, which could only mean that she was trying to put on a brave face. Malique thought she was probably just as afraid as he was. He guessed she didn't want to make the other kids worry.

"I'm ordering pizza. For dessert, we have ice cream and cookies. I will even let you all drink soda today."

"Awesome," one of the twins said in a raspy voice.

Melanie was still pouting.

"Mom, can I go with them?" Melanie asked. She had asked the same question daily at least once for the past few weeks ever since finding out that Lani and Sokie were going with Malique and the professor.

Sasha rolled her eyes. "You know the answer."

"But why? Why?"

"I told you the reasons why already. We don't have enough money. You also don't need to step your foot into other people's business. And--- just because someone else is doing something, it doesn't mean that you have a right or should do it too." Sasha said, exasperated. "Now--- what did I do with my phone? Can someone give me the house phone? I want to order a pizza. I'm hungry."

Mel stomped off down the hallway and into her room, slamming the door shut. One of the twins handed Sasha the house phone.

While Sasha ordered the pizza, Malique joined the twins in the family room to play some video games with them. "Did you finish your packing Mali? You're flight leaves at midnight. You will want to leave at nine o'clock for traffic and check-in."

Malique groaned. "I don't even have a suitcase," he said, not taking his eyes away from the video game he had been playing. His hands held tightly to the game remote control.

"Yes, you do," Sasha said with a grin.

He finally took his eyes away from the video game to look at Sasha. "Mom, what did you do?"

"I stopped at Target and got you a suitcase that has rollers. So you can pack as much as you want and wheel it around without having to carry it."

"Mom, I can carry a suitcase," Malique said defensively.

"I didn't say you couldn't," Sasha explained. "I just wanted you to have the option of using wheels if you needed to."

While Malique was waiting for Sokie, Lani, and the professor to arrive, he dozed off for a few minutes on the couch. He heard someone whisper his name. When he tried to open his eyes, he couldn't. His heart rate increased, and panic began to seep its way throughout his blood. "Malique Laveaux," the voice of an elderly woman said crisply, "I know you can hear me. I want you to know that I know you are now seeking the pebble. I will find you first--- then you and your sister can lead me to it. It's rightfully mine, and I will have it. Understand me. You have been warned." She said sharply.

Malique continued to struggle with opening his eyes, "Whatever you do, grandson--- Don't let her have it."

Malique still could not open his eyes. He wanted to see if he could see his grandfather. He wanted to see him at least one more time. He didn't even know what happened to him. He supposed he could ask Sokie about him. Then he wondered if his grandfather from his mother's side or his father's side. When he was younger, he never thought to ask. He guessed his father's side because his mother didn't resemble his grandfather at all.

"Where are you?" Malique asked as he still struggled to open his eyes.

"In you--- in your heart always," his grandfather's voice began to fade away.

Malique didn't want him to leave.

171

"Don't go---" Malique begged. His eyes filled with tears, then his eyelids fluttered open.

He felt exhausted. His forehead glistened with sweat. He looked around him then realized he was still home. "Are you okay, Mali?" Melanie asked, plopping down on the couch next to him. "Lani just called. They are on their way."

"Kids, get your shoes on. We will be leaving for the airport soon."

"Are you sure you don't want us just to take a shuttle?" Malique asked. He was ignoring Melanie's question. He was not okay, but he didn't want to admit it, nor did he want to talk about what he just experienced.

A few seconds later, there was a knock on the door. "Malique!" Lani called out as she continued to knock on the door.

When Melanie opened the door, Lani rushed in and hugged Malique. "I heard her--- I heard what she said."

"How??"

"Remember, I told you when you are under stress, I can hear your thoughts," Lani explained.

Professor Evans and Sokie rushed inside. "Lani, what is going on?" Sokie asked, catching her breath.

Lani let go of Malique and turned to face her aunt and the professor. "Mali was falling asleep, and he heard the voice of the crazy old lady. She threatened us. She said she knows we are looking for the pebble, and she will find us. She plans to use us to get to the pebble," she explained.

"Calm down," Sokie said calmly, "breathe. It's okay." Sokie reached out for Lani to embrace her in a hug.

"Is that true?" Professor Evans asked Malique, his blue eyes wide. "Did the crazy old woman threaten you?"

"Yep," Malique said simply. "Are we still going to New Orleans?"

"Absolutely. We have to," Professor Evans said, his voice was full of determination.

Sasha entered the room holder, her purse, and car keys. "Are you ready to go? We will take the van. Everyone will be comfortable---" She glanced around the room and saw Lani clinging to Sokie for dear life, the determined Professor and her baffled son. "What just happened? What did I miss?"

"The mean old lady threatened us," Lani explained, finally letting go of Sokie.

"Mean?" Professor Evans asked. "You didn't say she was mean, Lani. You only said she was crazy. But now she is mean and crazy? Or is she one or the other--- If it is one or the other--- which one?" He gave Sokie a wink in hopes to lighten the tense situation.

"She's evil!" Lani shouted. "I don't think we should go."

"Lani," Sokie said gently. "We talked about this. We have to go. We have to find out the truth, and you are the one who told us about the pebble. You know that we need to find it before this woman does. We have too many people depending on us--- of course, not many people even know about the pebble, but that is beside the point.

Just then, the house phone rang. One of the twins answered it.

Sasha threw up her hands in defeat. "We need to go--- we don't have time for phone calls."

"Mali, the phone is for you. It's Clarissa," the twin said.

Malique took a deep breath then reached for the phone. "Hey C. We are just about to leave."

"I thought so. I just wanted to hear your voice one more time before you leave. Have a safe trip. Call me when you can."

"Okay." He cleared his throat, then said, "I'll call you as soon as I can. Talk to you soon."

"Bye," she said in a barely audible whisper.

Sasha tapped her foot. "Okay, everyone pile into the SUV--- let's go."

CHAPTER SIXTEEN

Fortunately for Malique, Lani had slept during the majority of the flight to Dallas, Texas. They switched planes then flew into New Orleans, Louisiana. They arrived a little after six in the morning. After they deplaned and claimed their luggage, they searched for the rental car company. As they stepped outside, Lani squealed, "Omigosh! Why is the air so heavy?? Ew. No one told me about this. Omigosh!" Malique was walking behind her so he could only see the back of her head. He was pretty sure she was making a face. He imagined her face squelched up the way she looked when she was a baby and was about to cry. He laughed from the memory.

Lani stopped walking for a moment, turned and squinted her eyes at Malique. "This isn't funny. This--- this is far from funny."

He only laughed a little harder. He nodded, "Yes, it is."

"Come, children--- the faster we walk, the faster we get our car," Sokie said, not turning but kept walking following a sign that pointed rental cars to the right.

The professor was following Sokie and was talking on his cellphone.

"It's so hot!" Lani whined. "How could it be cloudy and so hot? It doesn't make any sense."

"It's called humidity sis," Malique explained.

"Well, I don't like it.

"You don't have to like it, Lani--- just gotta deal with it."

"I don't want to," she mumbled.

Fortunately, they didn't have to wait long for a car. "Okay, I just called the hotel, and our rooms are ready."

"Really, so early?" Sokie asked in surprise.

"Yes, I have connections at the Ritz," he winked at her. "Stop winking at me, Evan--- I don't like it."

An hour later, they arrived at the Ritz Carlton on Canal Street. Both Lani and Malique stood in the lobby with their mouths wide open. White marble surrounding them, a dazzling expanse that triggered thoughts of wealth and privilege. "Don't think that I am impressed by all the material glitter Evan," Sokie whispered for Evan's ears only. "I forgave you a long time ago, but I have no intention of picking up where we left off decades ago."

"Hey, it wasn't decades ago---" Evan stammered. "It was only one decade and a half--- maybe less. I don't think Malique was born when we broke up Sokes."

Sokie lifted her index finger in warning, "Oh, no, you don't--- don't you dare call me that--- ever."

"Well--- ouch--- That truly hurt."

"Enough of this--- go check us in since you have amazing connections," Sokie grumbled bitterly.

"Fine, why don't you wait with the kids over there on the sofa? I'll be back in a moment," Evan said, annoyed, pointing to an elegant off white sofa with gold trim. Sokie nodded in agreement and guided the kids to sit with her as they waited for Evan.

Evan returned fifteen minutes later, holding two sets of hotel keys. We have a double bedroom. Sokie sat staring at him without blinking. Evan returned the stare evenly.

"So, what about your room?" Sokie asked.

"What do you mean?"

"The kids and I have the double bedroom, right?"

"Right," Evan said through clenched his teeth.

"So, where is your room?"

"Sokie, we only have one room. There are two beds for crying out loud!"

Malique and Lani stared at the two adults arguing.

They did date each other, huh? Malique heard Lani's question clearly in his head.

Yep. I guess so.

Do you think they still love each other? Lani asked.

Possibly. But I think the professor hurt Aunt Sokie pretty severely. I don't think she will ever give him another chance.

I think your right. Lani replied.

"Well, I hope you don't think for a second that I am sharing a bed with you," Sokie stood from the sofa and crossed her arms. "That mistake will never happen again."

Um--- Malique--- do something. They are starting to talk about stuff that I don't want to know about. And look--- people are beginning to watch us.

Malique sighed heavily. *Fine, okay.*

Malique stood up and stepped between the two adults. "Aunt Sokie, you can share a bed with Lani, and the professor and I will bunk together."

Sokie clenched her teeth. "Fine."

"Fine," Evan said.

Their room was made of neutral tones of browns, beige, white, and some gold. The beds were king-sized with a simple nightstand between them. A flat-screen television with video game controllers. "Swag!" Malique exclaimed excitedly.

"Awesome!" Lani exclaimed.

"Awesome, I understand--- but swag??" Evan asked, glancing at Sokie.

"It means it's cool, Evan--- Geesh--- and you call yourself a professor," Sokie said.

Evan rolled his eyes.

"I've never been to such an amazing place!" Malique said.

177

"You've been to several charming hotels Mali. You just don't remember. Your mom and I took you to Disney World and also Disneyland. You were little. We all had so much fun." Sokie smiled.

"Did I go?" Lani asked.

"No, honey--- you didn't. You weren't born yet."

"Well, I don't know about the rest of you, but I'm hungry. Why don't we unpack? Grab something to eat and then do a little sight-seeing? Tomorrow--- we get serious."

They all agreed and began claiming different drawers in the large dresser and closet space.

A couple of hours later, Sokie announced she had a migraine and declared she needed a nap while the others went sight-seeing. Evan happily escaped the hotel with the kids in tow.

Buildings stood aside each other, mostly made of brick, two to three stories high along Bourbon Street. Beautiful black wrought-iron balconies. Most of the stores were painted of earth tone colors of brown, khaki green, or left with the brick exposed. It felt comforting to Malique. In some strange way, he felt a long-awaited sense of coming home. Lani didn't feel the same way when she said, "I don't like it here. This is awful. Every other store sells alcohol or adult shows. I don't like it."

"Ah, Lani, you're right, but you're missing the most important part about New Orleans---" Evan said with a huge smile on his face.

Lani crossed her arms while her eyebrows raised. "And what's that?"

"The music," Malique said before the professor could answer. Malique's eyes were glossed over.

"Yes," Evan said. "Close your eyes Lani." He bent down to look Lani in the eyes and waited for her to close her eyes. "Now, do you hear that?"

A saxophone was playing close by, then a piano and drum began to play. There was something familiar about the tune. She opened her eyes.

She smiled. "Yes, where's it coming from?"

The professor signaled for the two of them to follow him as he crossed the street after looking both ways for cars. They walked about three stores down to a store that had a bright neon sign of yellow, red, and purple, which read, "Live Music Cold Drinks."

Lani rushed up to the professor and grabbed his right hand, pulling hard on it, bending her knees and tugging. Malique was sure if they were walking on dirt rather than brick, Lani would have left skid marks from her effort of trying to stop the professor from going into the store.

"We can't go in there."

"Oh, don't be silly. Why not?"

"They serve alcohol. I'm not allowed."

"Don't be silly. I'm not ordering you any drinks with alcohol. They don't have a sign which excludes kids--- You're fine. This is a part of who you are, Lani. I'm not going to allow you to miss this opportunity to hear music--- jazz music--- real music--- live." There was a vibrancy and excitement evident on the professor's face.

Malique walked around the professor and his sister. He couldn't wait any longer to step inside the restaurant/store. There was one vacant round table. Malique couldn't stop smiling. When he took a seat, a waitress approached him holding a round serving tray with a notepad atop it. "Hi," she smiled brightly, "What can I get you?"

"Just a coke. Thanks." Malique assumed the professor would pay for their drinks and that he would be able to order whatever he wanted since it was the professor's big idea or rather demand that they leave for New Orleans as soon as possible. Malique didn't quite understand why the professor was in such a hurry. They've been mostly site seeing since they arrived.

Finally, Lani and Evan sat next to Malique. Malique was moving his head back and forth to the beat of the music; his right foot was tapping in time of the music also. Soon, the professor was doing the same as Malique, except he was also tapping his left hand on the table after he ordered himself and Lani a Coke also. Lani soon found herself dancing next to the table.

"That's right, Lani--- never waste good music. Get up and dance!" Professor shouted over the music.

The following morning, Evan insisted they go to Café Du Monde on Decatur Street. They arrived to a huge coffee shop that was located on a corner. The patio was enormous, with white and green cloth overhang, which covered several rows of white round table tops. It was crowded with lots of chatter. It made Lani nervous. She didn't like crowds or loud noises. She craved for the quietness of Aunt Sokie's flower shop. "They have the best donuts ever--- except they are called beignets," Evan explained enthusiastically, interrupting Lani's self-pitied thoughts.

"Anyone want coffee? They use chicory. It's the best coffee."

"I'll take your word for it. I don't like coffee." Malique said.

"Me either," Lani said.

Sokie began to tap her foot impatiently. "Can we submit our orders already? Evan? Really?"

"Hey, don't ruin this trip with all of your grumpiness and bitterness. You need to learn patience and learn to enjoy all the pleasures in life. Life goes by way too quickly to just submit an order and be done with it. You are at one of the most famous places in the world. Not to mention your heritage, and you are just on the LA or New York clock where everything is rush, rush, rush. Sokie--- just stop. Okay? Please. Just stop making the mean jabs at me. Stop being rude. Stop being impatient. Just stop---" Evan said pleadingly yet bitterly. "I realize I hurt you. I will never forgive myself for that. We have both moved on--- so just let the past go. Let's submit our orders and have a seat at one of these welcoming tables with all the happy go lucky people sitting around here and just relax awhile. Can we do that?"

Sokie sulked for a moment. She sniffed then bit her lower lip, closing her eyes for a moment. When she opened her eyes, she stopped biting her lip and took a deep breath. "You're right. Absolutely right. Sorry, Evan."

"Apology accepted," Evan said.

"Now, how many beignets am I ordering?"

"May as well order a dozen. If there is any leftover, we can save it for later."

"Okay, and would you like a coffee?" Evan asked Sokie.

"No, thank you. It's way too strong here," Sokie said, pointing to a random customer who was holding a cup of the strong dark liquid.

"You can order with cream and sugar, you know---" Evan suggested. "See, that's what that customer is doing now." He pointed to the same customer she had pointed to.

"What are you? A coffee dealer?" Sokie asked. She managed to giggle a little for the first time since they arrived in New Orleans.

"Ha, ha--- Funny--- Hey--- You cracked a joke for the first time since we got here---" Evan said with a smile, then he pointed his right index finger at Sokie and then to the air. "Progress--- we are making progress." His smile grew bigger.

"Oh--- don't push your luck, professor," Sokie said. "Go submit our order, please. I'm hungry, and it's been years since I had a real beignet." She smiled.

Lani had powder sugar all over her chin and some on her denim shorts. She hadn't noticed as she was too busy eating her second donut.

"So, Aunt Sokie--- if our family is from here, why aren't we staying with them?" Malique asked curiously before he bit into his last beneigh.

Sokie looked sad for a moment, "Well, unfortunately, much of our family moved away after Hurricane Katrina. Everyone is pretty much scattered all over the country. We have relatives in Georgia, Tennessee, Utah, Colorado, and some in California."

"Wow," Lani said, taking a break from eating. "What's in Utah?"

Malique and Evan laughed.

"Beats the heck out of me," Sokie said, shrugging her shoulders. "But we have a family."

"What about my dad's family?" Malique asked.

Sokie shook her head. "Sorry, I didn't know anyone from your father's family. I rarely saw Charles as it was. It seemed as though Charles was always on the go. I never understood why my sister married him. I'm sorry, kids---" Sokie paused for a moment, "I don't mean to talk bad about your father. I just never understood their relationship."

"Me either," Evan confessed.

"Really? You never told me that?"

"Actually," Lani interrupted their conversation, "I think he mentioned it the last time you two were talking about my daddy."

"Oh," was all Sokie could say.

"Well, enough about the past--- we need to start talking about the now---" Evan announced.

Malique took a sip of his hot chocolate, then asked, "Where do we start?"

"Back to Bourbon Street," Evan suggested.

CHAPTER SEVENTEEN

"Why is it so hot??" Lani whined again for what seemed the thousandth time while they were relaxing in their hotel room.

"Oh, suck it up, niece," Sokie said. "I lived in this for the first ten years of my life."

"But look what it does to our hair!" Lani insisted. "My hair was straight this morning, but now look at it. It looks like Malique's afro."

Malique laughed at that. "You know what, Lani--- you're right. Your hair does look like mine--- I wonder why that is--- Hmmm--- oh--- right! Because we are related!" He gave Lani a playful shove.

Lani looked as if she was going to cry.

"Hey, Lani, your natural curls are beautiful," Evan tried to soothe her.

"This isn't curl--- there is no-curl, Professor! This is frizzy and out of control," Lani lifted a strand of hair as an example.

"I tried to tell you this morning, didn't I?" Sokie said impatiently. "You rarely use the flat iron on your hair when we are California, why on earth would you try to use it here in humidville? Did I not tell you to use some hair gel and put your hair in another braid---? You wore it pulled back and in a braid yesterday--- why couldn't you do the same today?"

"Because, according to fashion magazine's you aren't supposed to wear your hair the same two days in a row--- just like you aren't supposed to wear the same clothes two days in a row. You have to switch it up a bit every day," Lani explained as if her explanation was perfectly logical.

"If that is what you want to do, then don't complain to me, Mali or Professor Chapman. Got it."

"Can I get the Brazilian blow out while we are down here then?" Lani asked seriously.

"No!" Both Sokie and Malique replied

Sokie and Malique exchanged looks.

"Why not? And why are you saying no to me, Malique? I wasn't asking you."

"Look, Lani, I just think you have beautiful hair. Why not go natural while you are out here. This is the way our hair was meant to be."

Lani shook her head adamantly.

"Just put gel in your hair, and you will be fine."

"But, won't it just be a Jheri curl?" Evan asked seriously. "That was an eighties thing, right?"

Sokie's lip disappeared, and she clutched her fists.

"I'm wearing my hair naturally now--- are you trying to tell me my hair looks like the Jheri curl?" Sokie asked, offended.

"I--- Um--- I was just--- I," Evan was at a loss for words.

"Look, Professor--- Aunt Sokie--- Stop fighting! All of the bickering and arguing--- it's old. Aunt Sokie, the professor, didn't mean anything bad or wrong by asking the question. He certainly didn't mean to insult you. You are the last person on the planet or maybe the universe that Professor Chapman wants to hurt."

"Sure--- whatever," Sokie said, crossing her arms. She redirected her attention back to Lani. "Go into the bathroom and use the hair gel and brush that are in my cosmetic back. Make sure that you put back anything you use in my bag when you are done."

"Fine," Lani said as she stalked off to the bathroom.

Changing the subject, Malique looked at the professor and asked, "So, what do you hope to find on Bourbon Street."

"Well, there are lots of voodoo shops there, and I thought we could just browse through the shops and see if

185

anything pops up--- any kind of clue, or maybe someone there will recognize you, or perhaps someone can tell us more about the pebble."

Sokie's eyes widened, "Uh--- I--- I don't know if going to a voodoo shop is a good idea. I mean, it's a voodoo shop. We don't want any curses placed on us or anything."

"Aunt Sokie, don't you think I already have one?" Malique asked seriously. "My body is a map. Someone put it there, don't you think? I want to know--- why me? And if the professor is right, we have to find this pebble or rock or whatever by June 21st--- We need to start searching for it."

Sokie bit her lip. "I guess you are right. Lani probably isn't going to like it, though."

"Well, Lani will just have to get over it," Malique said.

"Get over what?" Lani asked, coming out of the bathroom with her hair now slicked back into a ponytail and braid.

Professor Chapman sighed. "We are on our way to Bourbon Street to visit some voodoo shops."

"Oh no, we aren't," Lani argued in a high pitched voice, with one hand on her hip.

Sokie bit her lip again then offered, "How about we go with the guys to Bourbon Street, but while they go into the voodoo shops, we can go into the clothing or gift shops?"

Lani frowned, then looked at Malique and asked, "Are you okay with that? Are you okay with going into a voodoo shop?"

Malique shrugged his shoulders and raised his hands. "We are here to find the rock. So anything that might help, we need to try."

"Pebble," both Lani and Professor Chapman correct.

Malique rolled his eyes.

As they walked along Bourbon Street Lani, and Sokie peeked at a few of the gift shops. One shop had Mardi Gras masks displayed in the window. "Can we go there before we leave today?" Lani asked.

"Sure," Sokie said, wanting to see what other items the store might have, as well.

They walked passed a few more stores when suddenly Evan stopped and pointed to a small store next to a candy store. There was a small sign that advertised voodoo dolls for sale. "We can check this store out if you'd like," Evan directed the question towards Malique.

Malique shrugged his shoulders.

"Aren't you hot in that coat, Mali?" Lani asked, referring to Malique's grey trench coat. "Do you see any of us wearing a jacket? It's got to be a thousand and one degrees out here."

Malique sighed but didn't answer her.

"Lani, leave your brother alone. He's comfortable. Right Malique?" Sokie asked.

"Right." Malique turned back to the Professor. "Let's go check it out."

"Why do you wear the boots anyway? Aren't those military boots?" Lani asked.

"What's your deal Lani?" Malique asked, exasperated. "You never questioned what I wore before why all of a sudden, are you bothered by my clothes?"

They were still standing on the sidewalk outside of the shop.

"Because you wear the same thing day after day after day after day--- I just think you need to change your clothes every day. You can't go through life wearing the same clothes daily. I can see it maybe weekly--- but not every single day."

"Thanks for the fashion tip sis--- Maybe when we get back to California, I will use your advice."

"You're welcome," Lani said.

Malique rolled his eyes. He realized he seemed to be doing that a lot lately. Ever since Lani and Aunt Sokie returned to his life, he has probably rolled his eyes at least twice per day.

Professor Chapman turned and walked toward the shop that displayed the voodoo doll sign. "Let's go, Mali. We've got to start getting to work."

Malique followed the professor inside. The shop's door was painted a dark green with a large window on the top half of the door. When the professor opened the door, a tiny bell clattered against the door announcing their arrival.

"Hello, welcome to Enchanted," a woman with strawberry blond hair and green eyes said from behind a register that was sitting atop a thick glass encasement. The store itself was long and narrow.

"Thank you," Evan said.

"Are you looking for anything in particular?"

"Um--- no, we are just looking around. Thanks," Evan replied.

Malique glanced around the shop. There were shelves of crystal figurines, fairies, and crystal balls. There was a small clothing rack to the right of the store that held what looked like witch costumes. "This looks more like a witch shop than a voodoo shop," Malique said in a whisper to Evan.

"Oh, no--- we are both really," the woman said.

"You advertise voodoo dolls on the sign in the window," Evan mentioned.

"Oh, yes." The woman stepped behind her register and gestured them to follow her to a corner on the left side of the store. She reached for a wicker basket and offered it to Professor Chapman to hold. Malique looked inside the basket and saw approximately ten dolls made of what appeared to be nylons and socks. There was yarn at the top of the heads representing hair, and each of the dolls had two small buttons where he assumed were the eyes. He thought they looked like something either Lani or Melanie would make.

As if reading Malique's thoughts, the professor asked the woman, "So, did you make these yourself?"

"Oh yes," she admitted with a smile. "Do you like them?"

Instead of answering her question, the professor asked, "So what does it take to make a voodoo doll? And do they genuinely work for spells and such?"

"Oh, well, seriously anyone can make a voodoo doll. It just takes sewing skills. But then sometimes people make them out of clay. And yes, they do work. You have to attach something that is directly connected to the person you are putting a spell on to the doll."

"Like what?" Malique asked.

"Well, like hair or a scrap of clothing--- but it would have to be something that they wear a lot of times. Something that is directly linked to them. The person you are putting a spell on would also need to know about the spell for it to work."

"Really?" Malique and Evan asked in unison.

"Yes," she said. "Most of the time, I think it's the person's mind that makes them believe in the spell that makes the spell work. Let's say an old girlfriend is mad at her ex-boyfriend, so she casts a spell of millions of spiders to crawl over him. Well, once the ex finds out about it, suddenly his skin begins to crawl, and he feels like he has a million spiders on him. It doesn't matter whether or not the spiders exist or not--- because ultimately, it just depends on whether or not he believes they are there."

"Interesting," Evan said, scratching the right side of his chin.

"Do you know if there has ever been a spell made that changed a person's skin?"

The woman nodded her head vigorously. "Oh yes, plenty--- usually some sort of rash. Like hives or warts--- chickenpox."

"What about a map?" Evan asked in a whisper.

The woman frowned. "Now that would be strange, wouldn't it? No, I've never heard of that before."

"Do you know of anyone who might have?"

The woman's mouth moved to her left as she stood, thinking for a few moments. "Well, you might try the voodoo shop on the corner," she raised her left hand and gestured to the left side of her store. "She is extremely knowledgeable about voodoo and sorcery. Oh--- but please avoid the shop across the street," she warned.

"The shop across the street?" Malique asked. "Why?"

She whispered. "She's crazy."

Malique and the professor studied each other for a moment.

"Thank you, Mam."

"You're welcome. Please do come back again and have a nice day," she said perkily. The professor handed the basket of dolls back to her.

When they were outside, and the shop door closed behind them, Evan asked, "So what do you think, Malique?"

"Well, Professor, I think we need to go to the shop across the street," Malique replied.

"Precisely what I was thinking," Evan grinned.

"Should we let Aunt Sokie and Lani know?"

"Nah, they are busy looking at girly stuff. They probably forgot all about us," Evan said as he looked both ways before crossing the street. Malique followed him.

"Which shop do you think she was referring to?"

They stood on the sidewalk after crossing the street, looking at the shops in both directions left and right. "The first one we see any signs of voodoo stuff is my vote," Evan said.

190

"Okay," Malique agreed.

They walked passed a couple of shops to the left. One was a bar; the other was an adult shop. The next one, though, had a large window with a black velvet curtain draped across the window from the inside of the shop. The words "Incense and More" was painted on the window in white lettering.

"Let's try this one out, shall we?" Evan asked.

"Sure," Malique agreed.

The door to the shop was solid wood painted black. There was no clanging of a bell to announce their arrival. The shop was narrower than the previous shop they visited. Malique could have easily stretched out his arms and would have been able to touch one side of the store and the other at the same time width wise. On each side of the store were shelves of candles and incense. A few Mardi Gras masks were hanging up against the walls. The walls themselves were painted a dark purple. The ceiling was painted black. The lighting was dim.

"Ahh--- so you have come at last---" an old woman spoke calmly from a corner to the right in the back of the store. She was seated in a folding chair. She was dressed in a white, flowing dress that reached her feet. She had a white scarf covering her hair. What hair that was exposed was gray and curly. It was hard to tell the color of her eyes due to the lighting in the store. As Malique and the professor moved closer to her, Malique guessed they were a light brown or perhaps hazel. Her skin was of caramel complexion, similar to Aunt Sokie's. She remained sitting.

"You'll have to forgive me for not rising at your entrance," she bowed her head at Malique, "It pains me to stand much of the time now."

"It's okay," Malique said, not knowing what else he was supposed to say.

"You were expecting us?" Evan asked eyebrows squelched together.

The woman lifted her head and looked into Malique's eyes. "Yes, I have been waiting for a long time."

"For what? Why?" Malique asked.

"Oh, je suis sur que vous svez deju," she said, her eyes were glossy.

"Huh?" Malique made a face that clearly explained he was clueless what she just said.

"She said she is sure you already know," Evan explained. "She is speaking French."

"Oh--- why?"

The woman shook her head in disappointment and said, "You are supposed to be royalty, but you don't even know your tongue," her words were harsh.

Malique felt as if he were slapped.

"Why does this man know what I say, but you don't?" She asked, reaching for a cane he hadn't noticed before.

"He has been missing for ten years and was just found recently. He doesn't know much about his heritage," Evan tried to defend him.

"Too many of our people have lost our culture. We were people not accepted by any one race. So we created our own culture, our own language in a way. But yet, now--- it's dwindling away." She shook her head from sadness as she slowly lifted herself to a standing position with the aid of her dark wooden cane.

Malique frowned. "I--- I want to know more. I don't want it to dwindle."

The woman waved her left hand dismissively while her right hand gripped the cane handle tightly. "No time for that now. You must find the pebble. But---" She looked around the shop.

The woman must have only been four feet tall, but her speech and spirit superseded any physical height. She gasped, "But where is your sister. She must be here. You cannot do this alone."

"What am I supposed to do?" Malique asked.

"Find the pebble before anyone else! You have to come back to me once you find it! Les jeunes! Tellement stupide!" She shouted, pointing her left index finger at Malique. Malique stared at her finger. Her nails were long, and her fingers were skinny with wrinkly skin. "You cannot leave your sister alone! Find her--- then find the pebble. You must hurry. Time is running out!"

Malique jumped from her last shout. The professor also jumped. The professor appeared just as nervous as Malique. Evan had his hand shoved deep into the pockets of his khaki pants.

"But how are we supposed to find the pebble?" Malique asked in a low whisper.

"You have the map, boy. I cannot tell you anymore. You must find the pebble with your sister. It is the only way. Now go--- to find your sister and then the pebble." She coughed, then took a deep breath. "Then--- come back to me. I will guide you."

Malique frowned.

"Go--- go now!" The woman shouted, pointing to the entrance to her store. Both Malique and Evan jumped. Then they rushed out of the door.

When they reached the sidewalk and closed the door, they stared at each other for a moment. "Geesh, she was mean," Malique said. He glanced down at his own hands and noticed they shook profusely.

Evan nodded in agreement.

"What did she say to me when she was shoving her finger at me and shouting?" Malique asked.

"Basically that you are young and foolish."

"Dang," Malique said, scratching his forehead. "We were in there for less than five minutes, and she just chewed me out and spat me out like a little piece of fat from a juicy steak--- dang!"

Evan laughed. "I never heard that expression before." He laughed some more then said, "But, yeah, I have to agree with you."

"What now?" Malique asked him.

"Well, I guess we need to do what she said and find your sister," Evan said.

Just then, they heard a scream coming from a shop to the right of them. It sounded like it was coming from the store that Lani wanted to go in with the Mardi Gras masks.

CHAPTER EIGHTEEN

Malique and the professor ran to the shop. They opened the door to the shop and found it empty. "Where are they? What happened?" Malique asked, his voice squeaky from fear.

"I--- I don't know."

"Lani! Aunt Sokie! Where are you?" Malique shouted desperately.

"Let's go check if there is a back door," Evan suggested. Malique followed the professor to the back of the shop. There was a curtain in a doorway; they pushed it aside and found a tiny office. There was a narrow back door. The professor pushed it open. There was as a narrow alley. They looked right and left but saw no one in sight.

"Where can they be?" Malique was frantic.

The professor shook his head; sorrow and fear filled his eyes as he looked at Malique.

"Wait, you can talk to Lani telepathically, can't you?"

Malique nodded. He began to call out to her. *Lani!?! Lani?? Where are you? Do you hear me?*

Omigosh! Malique, I'm so afraid.

What happened? Where are you?

I don't know--- Aunt Sokie, and I were trying masks on and clowning around--- then the two big men that I saw in my visions came up behind us. They grabbed us, and now--- I don't know where we are.

Are you in a car or a place or--- give me something--- I don't know--- it's dark.

"Did it work? Is she talking to you?" The professor asked, pinching his bottom lip with his right index finger and thumb. He pushed his glasses further up his nose with his left hand.

"Yes, she said two big guys grabbed them from behind. It was the same guys from her vision."

"Does she know where she is? Is Sokie with her?"

"Sokie is with her, but she doesn't know where she is. She only said its dark."

Is Aunt Sokie still with you?

Yes, but they covered our mouths. I only know she is here because we are sitting next to each other.

Are you tied up?

Yes. I'm so scared, Mali. I don't know what to do.

"What did she say?" The professor asked.

Malique relayed all of what Lani told him. "What should she do? What can we do?" Malique was doing his best not to lose it. He just reunited with his sister and aunt. Now, some crazy old woman was trying to take them away from him again.

"Tell her to try to get rid of whatever is covering their mouths. We need to communicate with Sokie too," Evan said, pleadingly.

Try to remove whatever is covering your mouths.

How?

Malique thought for a moment. Then an idea came to him. *You said Aunt Sokie is sitting next to you, right?*

Yes.

Okay, move closer to her and try rubbing whatever is around your mouth off by using her shoulder.

I don't know Mali. They wrapped it pretty tight.

Did they shove anything in your mouth? Are you teeth clamping down on anything?

No.

Okay, good. Give it a try.

Okay.

There was silence. Malique stared at the professor. They waited.

Mali?

I'm here.

Mali, it worked. I'm helping Aunt Sokie now.

Don't talk loud, okay? Whisper. You don't know if they can hear you or not--- and don't let on that you can communicate with me, okay?

Okay.

When Aunt Sokie's mouth is free, see if you can use your teeth to get your arms and legs free.

Oh, our legs are free already.

Really? Malique was shocked.

"What?? What happened--- you have this shocked expression all over your face--- come on, Malique! You've got to keep me in the loop here," Evan said anxiously.

"Lani said her legs are free. Isn't that strange?"

"I think it shows we have hope. It looks like the guys who kidnapped them are idiots."

Malique grinned.

"Ask her if their hands are tied behind their backs? In front? Are they tied to anything like a chair or anything else?"

Are your hands tied behind you or in front?

In front. Why?

Are they tied to anything?

No. Why?

Malique told the professor.

"Wow--- Amazingly amateurish, don't you think?"

Are you able to use your teeth to untie yourselves?

Hold on--- Aunt Sokie is whispering something to me.

"Well, what's going on now?" Evan asked.

"She's talking to Aunt Sokie."

"Okay, well, let's get out of this alley and back inside the store. Maybe there is a clue where they went," the professor suggested. They walked around the store. The store walls were painted pink, and lots of strings of fluffy feathers surrounded the store. It was such a girly store— lots of masks and some crystal figurines. Malique glanced down on the ground and saw a sizeable muddy footprint. He pointed it out to the professor. "That is one huge print."

Malique nodded. "Yep."

"What's that over there?" The professor asked and pointed to what looked like a business card near the entrance to the store.

Malique walked closer to it, then bent over to pick it up. He examined the card, then shook his head.

"What's wrong?"

"It's a business card to a boat touring company," Malique handed the card to Evan.

"This is all too easy. Don't you think?" Evan asked suspiciously.

Malique bit the inside of his right cheek then said, "It's a setup."

"Yep," Evan agreed.

"So, what do we do now?"

"We fall into the trap, but they don't know that we know it's a trap."

"Or so we think--- What if they know that we know, though?"

"Well, we all want the same thing--- the pebble--- right?"

"Yes, but we want it for different reasons--- well actually, if I had a real say in this whole entire crazy thing--- I wouldn't want anything to do with it."

"But it's your bloodline. It's your responsibility."

"How is that anyway? How in the world am I royalty? Do you realize how crazy all of this sounds?? We are in the United States. We are in a democratic country--- there is no such thing as royalty. Except maybe the first family but come on--- stop with the royalty garbage, okay?"

Mali? Mali--- are you there?

Yes.

Our hands are free. Aunt Sokie thinks this is all too easy. She thinks whoever took us is setting us up for something.

That's exactly what we were thinking.

So, what are we going to do now?

We are going to fall into their trap---, but they won't know that we know it's a trap.

And that is going to help us how??

Honestly, I'm not sure, but I don't think we have any other choice at this point. They want the pebble, and we want the pebble. Maybe we need them just as much as they need us to find it. But hopefully, we will be the first to find it. Tell me something--- does it feel like you're on a boat? Do you smell saltwater or anything?

Yes, I smell saltwater, but I don't think we are on a boat.

Do you hear boats or anything?

I thought I heard a jet ski a little while ago.

How did you get there so fast? We heard you scream, and then you both just vanished.

I don't know. It all happened so fast. We were in the store one minute, then here the next. I think they used some kind of magic or something.

Hang tight. We will find you soon.

"So, do you think we should drive over to this tour boat?" Malique asked Evan.

The professor nodded in agreement, "Yes. It looks like it's near the Riverwalk."

"Oh," Malique said, surprised. "So, you don't think magic was needed to move Lani and Aunt Sokie?" They quickly walked back to the car. The professor began to sweat on his forehead. He took a handkerchief from his back pocket and wiped the sweat away.

"I didn't say that--- I'm not sure what's going on here anymore. It's definitely not anything ordinary," Evan said

199

as he rubbed the back of his neck. It was obvious to Malique that Evan was trying to keep calm and not show his fear. He remained silent until Evan parked the car.

"Do you think it's okay to leave the car here?" Malique asked.

Evan waved his hand dismissively. "I don't know. We just need to find Sokie and Lani--- Let's go."

Malique walked alongside the professor, who led them to turn right down one corner and then left. "Oh, so--- It's a mall," Malique said with a hint of disappointment. Malique stopped for a moment to look at the grand red and blue sign perched on top of the arch of white metal. The sign advertised Riverwalk Marketplace.

"Well, it's a little more than a mall. It's a tourist spot, casino, and as you saw on the business card there," Evan pointed to the card Malique was still clutching in his hand, then continued, "a tour boat that most likely has our Lani and Sokie."

Malique noticed the hint of protectiveness in the professor's voice and in the stiffness of his posture.

"You do care about them, don't you?"

Evan clenched his jaw, "Yes. Absolutely." The professor led Malique up steps to enter the heart of the Riverwalk. He glanced around to see if there was any sign indication of the boat tour company listed on the card, Blue Moon River Tours of the Mississippi. "When I find whoever took them, they should hope they have magic because I will hurt them with my bare hands."

Malique looked the professor up and down. Evan was only a couple inches taller than him. The professor was a bit stockier than Malique. He wondered if the professor ever had an actual fistfight in his life. He doubted it.

"Oh, I can see the doubt in your eyes. But I will have you know, I was on the wrestling team in high school and in college plus I still go to the gym at least twice a week.

Don't let my intellect fool you. I can handle my own and then some."

Malique grinned.

"What about you?"

"I can handle my own too--- As long as they don't attack me from behind when I'm not expecting it."

"Oh, right--- I've wanted to talk to you about that. That was an extremely low blow that kid did to you at the Memorial Day Fair."

"Well, Clarissa came to the rescue that day," Malique admitted.

Malique? Are you there?

Yes. Malique answered Lani. He stopped walking and sat down on a bench. He was signaling the professor to wait.

What's taking you guys so long?

We just spoke a few minutes ago. Geesh.

Well, hurry up. I don't want to be here any longer.

We are on the Riverwalk. Can you give me any clues as to where you are? Anything? Any other sounds or smells?

I hear metal clanging against metal--- kind of like a chain hitting against something else that's metal.

"Lani says she hears metal against metal. She thinks it's a chain hitting something else that's metal."

The professor nodded his hands on his hips. He glanced around the river walk. A few seconds later, he pointed to a flag pole in the distance. There was a metal chain attached to the pole that kept knocking the side of the pole. "Over there. It looks like there is a storage unit," Evan jogged towards the white storage unit. Malique followed.

"Sokie!" Evan called out. He knocked on one of the metal roll-up doors. When Evan didn't hear a response from her, he rushed to the next one. He kept going. By the time he reached the fifth storage unit, they had heard a muffled tap and shout, "In here! Hurry!" It was coming from the next unit over. Then they heard Lani's voice join in, "In here!"

"It's them," Malique said.

There was a metal lock on the door.

"Sokie, do you have a hairpin on you?"

"Yes!"

"Great! Can you try sliding it under the door?

"Okay!" She shouted. They could hear something scraping from the inside of the unit. They saw the tip of the hairpin, but it wasn't long enough to pull it out. Malique lowered to his knees and tried to pry it out with the tips of his chewed up fingertips, but it wasn't working.

"Can you push it any further?" Evan asked.

"It's as far as I can push it. The door is thicker than I thought," Sokie said.

Evan scratched his head, obviously trying to think of something.

Malique?

I'm here.

Put both of your hands on the door. I will too. I want to try something.

Okay. Malique stood up, then spread his hands across the door.

Are your hands on the door now?

Yes.

Okay, close your eyes and imagine the door rising. Concentrate. Okay? On the count of three.

Malique closed his eyes.

1---2---3.

Malique concentrated hard, imagining the door opening. When the door began shaking violently and feeling hot to the touch, Malique jumped back stunned.

The professor shook his head, "No, you guys are doing it all wrong. Don't focus on the door! Focus on the lock!" Evan clenched his teeth.

"How?" Malique asked. Not sure if he was a part of causing the door to shake and heat up at the same time.

"I don't know!" Evan shouted, full of frustration and agitation. "This is all new to me too--- why don't you try holding the lock with both hands, and then you both concentrate at the same time."

"No, that won't work!" Lani shouted from the inside. "We have to be touching the same object. I just know it."

The professor put both hands in the air and shook his head as if he were giving up and began to pace back and forth.

"Okay, keep touching the door, Lani! I will have my left hand on the door and my right hand on the lock. Just keep imagining the lock opening, okay? On the count of three."

"Okay!" Lani shouted back.

Evan took a deep breath, stopped pacing then stared at the lock as Malique was holding it.

Malique closed his eyes the yelled, "1--- 2--- 3!" He imagined the lock melting in his hands. There was a sizzling and popping sound. Then he felt warm liquid dripping from his right hand.

"Did it work?" Lani shouted.

Malique opened his eyes. His eyes grew enormous from shock and disbelief. In his hands was melted metal. The lock no longer on the door. His hand began to smoke. He frantically poured the liquid out of his hands, then wiped his hands on his denim shorts.

The professor stared at him. "How is that even possible?"

Malique shook his head. "I--- Wh--- I---"

"We'll try to figure it out later," Evan said quickly. Evan bent down to grab the handle of the storage unit door that was in the lower center. He rolled the door up. Sokie and Lani rushed into their arms.

"That was too easy---" Lani said proudly.

"Yes, it was," an old woman said behind them. They all turned around to see a woman who was approximately four feet two inches high with long gray wavy hair that reach beyond her butt. She was round and had big blue-gray eyes and light complexion. "I told my boys it was all we needed."

Malique noticed just then that one of the two boys was Ricardo. Malique's jaw clenched. "What are you doing here?" Malique ignored the old lady and glared at Ricardo.

The old woman held her right hand up to silence Ricardo.

"He owes you no explanation. You came to me on your own free will, so now the curse is broken."

"What? What curse, what are you talking about?"

Lani gasped. "The old man tried to tell me---"

"What old man?" Sokie asked.

"Remember I told you about a dream I had. An old man told me not to allow Malique to go to the lady, but I didn't know--- I."

"It's okay, Lani--- how could you know? We will talk about it later," Sokie said.

"I didn't come to you on my own free will. I only came here to rescue my aunt and sister!" Malique moved closer to the woman.

Sokie reached for Malique's arm, but he shook her hand off of him.

"Who are you? What do you want?"

"You may be royalty, but I am your elder, and you will not talk to me in that tone of voice. Your generation has no regard or respect. You don't even know who you are."

"That would be because of people like you. You had something to do with causing my family to vanish out of my life! I can feel it!" Malique balled up his fists and clenched his teeth. A vein began to pop out of his forehead. He imagined picking up the woman then throwing her as far as he could. The woman began to levitate a few inches off the ground. Her eyes widened.

Ricardo and the other burly man next to him rushed to the woman and grabbed each of her shoulders, gently returning her to the ground.

The old woman closed her eyes, then raised her hands. There was a rush of wind, then suddenly Lani collapsed.

Sokie screamed.

"What did you do?" Malique asked angrily.

"Don't play with fire, young man," the woman said. She turned to Ricardo and the other burly man, "Ricardo, Fredrick. Take them to the boat. We must go. We are running out of time."

"What did you do to my sister?" Malique insisted, even as Ricardo placed a firm grip on Malique's shoulder and maneuvered him in such a way that his right arm was bent at an awkward angle behind his back.

"She will be fine as long as you cooperate. She is in a deep sleep and will only waken when I tell her to," the old woman said smugly.

"Not so smart are you, Map Boy," Ricardo said.

The professor squatted down next to Lani, then scooped her up into his arms. Sokie was crying but tried very hard not to show it. "It will all be okay, Sokes. Just keep believing, okay? You have to keep believing it will all be okay," Evan whispered to her as they walked side by side, following the old woman. Malique followed Sokie and Evan. Ricardo and Frederick each had a hand on Malique's shoulders.

"No more talking," the woman said without looking back at them. She continued to wobble in a slow walk toward the docks.

Sokie looked at the professor and nodded, holding her chin up.

They arrived on a small houseboat. "You may lay her here," the old woman was referring to Lani and pointed to a cushioned bench immediately inside the houseboat to the right. The cushions were a bright green vinyl. Evan placed Lani as instructed. They covered her with a crocheted blanket that was perched on the back of the bench. He kissed Lani's forehead.

"This can all be very smooth and quick if you all cooperate. As you know, we must find the pebble before Summer Solstice."

"Ah, I was right then--- June 21st," the professor said with a grin.

"Really? You're really going to brag right now?" Sokie asked in angered disbelief.

"I'm not bragging--- I'm just saying---" Evan began to explain but was cut off by the old woman's shout.

"The talking will cease to exist now!"

The professor opened his mouth to say something, but no words came out. He raised his right hand to his throat and frowned. Sokie then tried to say something, but no sound came out either. Sokie glared at Evan. Evan smirked back at her.

"Who are you?" Malique asked the old woman.

"My name is Rosette Marcos. Ricardo and Frederick are my grandsons. You will respect them during your stay here and while we search for the pebble."

Malique's face reddened. "You knew about her intentions all along, didn't you?"

Ricardo grinned wickedly.

"He has done all that I have asked him to do. To watch you and report back to me."

Malique thought back on the skateboard competition they had. Ricardo was the one who sought Malique out. Ricardo was the one who challenged him to the bet. Ricardo was the one who ran into him at the Memorial Day

Fair. It made sense. Ricardo was eminently just keeping tabs on him this whole time.

"We only have five days to find the pebble."

"And just how do you supposed we find it?"

"Well--- the map, of course," Rosette said with a sparkle in her eye. "Ricardo, Frederick- help Malique take off his ridiculous trench coat and a tank top. I must see his back." Rosette waved her right hand as if it were a fan to cool herself down. "You must be hot in that coat. Why would you wear such a thing in this humidity?"

"You know why," Malique said, his voice shaky.

Ricardo and Frederick each grabbed one side of the coat then peeled it off of him. Ricardo yanked the jacket out of Frederick's hand then tossed it over the boat and into the water. "I always hated that piece of sh---"

"No--- no foul mouth. Stop it now," Rosette warned Ricardo.

"Take off the shirt," Rosette demanded "and turn around."

Malique swallowed hard, knowing that his skin would burn at any moment. His skin already felt prickly with heat just from removing the jacket. He turned around.

Lani, Malique thought desperately, *Lani?? Can you hear me? Please--- Lani--- are you there?? Lani!*

Wha--- What--- owe--- my head--- oww---? What--- I can't open my eyes. What?? Why can't I open my eyes? There was a whimper coming from the bench where Lani was placed.

Shh--- don't make any noise. They don't know we can communicate telepathically.

Who?? What's happening?

I need you to help me--- the old woman and the two bad guys you dreamt about are trying to see the map on my back. Help me.

Oh no!

There was another whimpering sound coming from Lani on the bench, but she was still in a deep sleep.

Sokie sat on the ground next to the bench where Lani was laying then stroked Lani's cheek.

"Spread your arms across the wall. I need to see it clearly and fully."

Malique took another deep breath. His skin prickled more; heat poured down his back. His skin began to glow. A map of the Mississippi River appeared clearly with running water floating across his back. Malique arched his back from the sharpness and intensity of the pain.

Malique imagine my hands on your shoulders. Close your eyes. Breathe--- In--- Out---. Shhhh--- In--- Out--- Shhhh--- The map will subside--- You feel cool--- No more pain--- Breathe--- In--- Out--- Shhh--- Lani continued the breathing rhythm as she did so, Malique's breathing calmed. His body cooled. The glow dissipated. The river stopped flowing on his back.

"What the he---" Frederick started to curse.

"No--- stop it now!" Rosette shouted.

"It isn't meant for your eyes," Malique explained.

The professor had been standing behind Rosette the entire time and had been studying the map. He quickly moved back to where Sokie was sitting but remained standing.

Are you okay now, Mali?

Yes. Thank you.

Where are we?

On a houseboat.

Oh no--- it's all coming true then, huh? All the stuff I saw, it's happening? I can see the future? She whimpered.

Stay calm and sleep, okay?

That's what I was doing before you interrupted me. How can I sleep now when you need me? We have to get off of this boat.

I know. But maybe we need the boat.

208

What do you mean?

I think the pebble is in the Mississippi River.

How would you know when you can't even see your back?

Something weird happened this time. The hotter my skin felt, the more I could visualize the map in my mind.

But your back wasn't of the river the last time we looked at it.

Maybe it changes--- maybe as we get closer or farther away from pebble, it changes--- So we can find it more easily.

Ew--- that's weird.

"What now, Nana?" Ricardo asked Rosette.

The old woman grumbled. "It's too late today to go out. We will all sleep here tonight. In the morning, we will travel up and down the river until I know."

CHAPTER NINETEEN

Ricardo and Frederick took turns keeping watch over Lani, Sokie, Malique, and Evan. It was obvious Evan had something to say to Malique. He tried on several occasions, but each time, no words would come out of his mouth. Malique finally gave up trying to stay awake and decided he might as well sleep while he could. As he drifted off to sleep, he wondered where his father was, who his father was and why people were referring to him as royalty when all his life had been anything but royalty. He wondered who his father's parents were, why he never met them, or at least he couldn't recall ever meeting them. He wondered where his mother was buried. No one ever told him, and he had never thought to ask. His eyes were heavy; his soul was exhausted.

A man who must have been at least six feet five walked into a room surrounded by white walls. He was medium built with a muscular appearance. Something about him looked familiar, but Malique couldn't quite grasp who he was. He had a nearly bald head. Dark brown eyes and a dark complexion. When he grinned in Malique's direction, he exposed perfect white teeth and dark gums. Full lips. Malique felt comforted by his familiar friendly smile. "Bonjour petit-fil," the man said with a smile.

"Hi," Malique said, surprised he understood what the man said. "I'm your grandson?" Malique asked, confused, pointing to himself.

"Oui, vous l'êtes. Je suis le père de ton père," the man explained.

Malique frowned, "How can you be my father's dad when you are only like--- twenty years old or something?"

"Je ne suis pas vivant. Vous m'avez appelé à vous et je vous apparaîtra à mes plus vives temps dans ma vie naturelle. C'est de cette façon que j'ai comparu lorsque j'ai rencontré votre grand-mère. Je suppose que vous m'avez appelé ici parce que vous avez des questions. Qu'est-ce que c'est? Qu'est-ce que vous voulez savoir?"

Malique blinked. Still not understanding why it was that he understood what the man was speaking even though he was speaking in French. From what Malique could tell, the man said he wasn't alive. The man said Malique called him, even though he didn't. He also said that he appeared to Malique in his most vibrant state. He looked the way he did on the day he met his grandmother. So this man believed he was Malique's grandfather somehow. The man wanted to know why Malique called him. "But I didn't call you. I don't know who you are, and I don't have a cell phone or access to any phone, so no--- I didn't call you," Malique sighed as he scratched his head. His hair was pulled back into a tight ponytail. He wondered when he brushed his hair. For the life of him, he couldn't remember. He didn't remember how he got to this white-walled room, either. Malique frowned, "Do you speak any English?"

"Oh, yes, I do. Is that what you prefer?

"Yes, please," Malique said politely when he genuinely just wanted to let out an enraged scream. He was exhausted and just wanted to sleep, but it felt like whenever he tried to sleep, something or someone would disturb his sleep.

Lani suddenly appeared in the room behind Malique. "Hi, Mali!" She said a little too loudly, causing Malique to jump.

Malique grabbed his chest and whined, "Geez Lani! What are you doing here?" He frowned at his sister.

Lani pouted then said, "I thought you would be happy to see me. I'm still in a deep sleep--- or at least my body is, but I figured out how to visit people in their dreams."

Malique rolled his eyes. "Why mine? Why can't you just let me sleep? I'm tired."

"Well, duh Mali--- Your body is tired, and that's why your body is sleeping, but your mind is all over the place. So I thought I'd come to visit you in your dream and help you sort everything out." Lani then pointed to the man standing in the middle of the room. "That's Andre Laveaux. Our grandfather. He always appears young and looks the same way he did when he met our grandmother. He told me before that day he met grandma was the best day of his life."

Andre smiled softly then nodded his head in agreement, "Yes, it was. But we are running out of time. Tell me what you need from me. What do you want to know, Malique?"

"Why does everyone keep telling me we are running out of time? Isn't that part of the problem with life? Everyone is so busy rushing, rushing, rushing with to-do lists--- no one stops and just appreciates all that they have?"

"Why are you talking like the professor?" Lani asked.

Malique rolled his eyes again, "It's not just the professor. It's everything. Was mom rushing when she was driving? Is that why we got into the crash? She was so eager to get to where she was going that she lost control of the car, and we crashed! Our lives changed that day forever. I'm not rushing. I don't think you can go anywhere without my say so Andre. I think you have to stay as long as I need you to stay or until someone or something wakes me up," Malique said with determination.

Andre had a look that said he was impressed by Malique's outburst. "Well done Malique. Well done. I see you are able to express yourself well. It's a good thing."

Lani smiled proudly.

"So, what do you want to know," Andre asked Malique again.

"Did my mom die? Is my father still alive?"

"That--- I cannot answer. I do not know."

"What do you mean you don't know? You don't see them where you are? Shouldn't you know?"

"No," Andre said, simply with no readable expression on his face.

"No?" Malique asked with disbelief.

"No," Andre confirmed.

Malique took a deep breath, then moved on to his next question. "Aunt Sokie told me that I didn't have this--- this map of multiple colored skin when I was born. Is that true?"

Andre nodded, "Yes, it's true."

"Then who put it on me, and why?"

"The woman you met in the voodoo shop put it on you. She did it the day of the accident to protect you," Andre explained calmly.

Malique felt his hands ball into a fist, and he felt his throat burning from unshed tears of anger.

'Why would she do that? How would this--- this protect me?" Malique pointed to his arms and then to his face. "Why all over my body and not just my back?" Malique asked in a shout. His voice was shaky.

"I do not know. You will have to ask her."

"She doesn't even like me. She put me down and made me feel stupid and foolish when all I wanted to do was talk to her. To get answers--- just like now with you."

"I know Malique," Andre said. "I understand."

"Why was I separated from my brother?" Lani asked. "Why couldn't we be together all this time?"

Andre's eyes saddened. "You both have amazing powers alone. Together, you can be dangerous. It was decided a long time ago that you would be raised apart until Malique's sixteenth birthday. The day when Malique is to acquire the pebble. It is up to Malique what he will do with it. He can either hold the pebble and imprint it upon his soul, or he can destroy it. You both need to agree on the decision, but ultimately it is up to Malique."

213

"What do you mean imprint it upon his soul?"

"It can be his for eternity. If he does that, he can rule the world and perhaps the universe. It contains all knowledge--- everything."

Lani's eyes widened. "Why would it be here? Why Mali?"

"Not just Mali--- but you two. It can only be imprinted or destroyed with the two of you together."

"If it's only the two of us, then why is the crazy old woman trying to find it?"

"If you willingly give it to her, to anyone--- it becomes theirs--- they become royalty, and they can decide whether to imprint themselves or to destroy. But she wishes to imprint it."

"I won't give it to her willingly," Malique said.

"There are ways that she can trick you. Just as she tricked you into coming to her willingly."

Malique frowned. "How did I come to her willingly? I didn't know that she even existed, and I didn't want anything to do with her or this for that matter!"

"You can be angry as much as you want, but it will not solve anything. Anger will only destroy you. Don't allow it to build inside of you."

"Tell me, though--- how did I come to her?"

"When you placed your hands on the door to where Sokie and Lani were held, you willingly crossed Rosette's line of exile. By touching the door, you released her."

"But how?"

"The woman who placed the map on your body also placed a protection spell on you. No one could find you until you found Lani just before your sixteenth birthday. Also, no one who wanted to find the stone could approach you without your willingness to allow them to approach you. Because you have such a strong desire for answers, you allowed her into your life. Rosette has been in exile since the accident. Rosette is the one who caused the accident."

Lani gasped.

Malique felt a tear roll down his right cheek. His nostrils flared.

"Don't allow the anger in Malique," Andre said.

"Easy for you to say. You tell me all of this, and I'm just supposed to stand here and take it. Not do anything. Just let the woman who tried to destroy my family now trying to become the ruler of the universe walk away?"

Andre shook his head, "No, that is not what I am saying."

"We have to stop her," Lani said urgently.

"How?"

"Get to the pebble before she does. You have to get it before your birthday."

"But my birthday is in July."

Andre shook his head, "No, it is on June 21st."

Malique shook his head. "I don't know anything, do I?"

"You will know all soon."

Malique felt something shaking him then a voice from far away, but he couldn't understand what the voice was saying. Malique looked at his grandfather. He studied his face trying to embed his image in the recesses of his brain to remain always. "Will I see you again?"

Andre shrugged his shoulders the same way that Malique always shrugged his. This made Malique smile. He embraced his grandfather in a hug. Lani joined the embrace. A tear rolled down her cheek. Malique thought of something else to ask, "How do I wake up, Lani?"

"Do not worry. She will wake up as soon as the pebble is found. As soon as your eyes see it--- She will see it too and awaken."

Lani let out a sigh of relief.

215

Malique felt another shake on his shoulders now. He could feel it more strongly then he felt something cold splash across his face. Malique blinked his eyes and looked around. He was back on the boat. Ricardo was standing over him with an empty water bottle. "What'd you do that for?" Malique asked, wiping his wet face with his hands.

"To wake you up," Ricardo threw the empty water bottle at Malique's head. Malique caught it before it hit him then squinted at Ricardo. He imagined the cylinder containing a heavy brick then quickly threw it back at Ricardo. The bottle hit Ricardo in the abdomen, knocking him backward and landing him on his butt. Malique laughed.

"I can get used to this," Malique mumbled then smirked.

Ricardo coughed, rolled over into a fetal position, and gripped his stomach. Malique stood up.

"What'd you do that for?"

"For throwing away my coat and because you deserved it."

Malique walked across the deck to where Sokie and Evan were sitting. They were at a table and eating what appeared to be bacon, eggs, and biscuits. Each of them was about to take a sip of coffee when they noticed Malique. The professor raised his mug of coffee in greeting.

"Still can't speak?" Malique asked both Sokie and Evan. They each shook their heads to say no, they couldn't. For some reason, this made Malique laugh.

Sokie glared at Malique.

"Well, you have to admit--- you guys brought it on yourselves. You two are constantly arguing, so I have to say--- It's kinda nice. I mean, look at you two now. You are sitting next to each other and eating breakfast. You are even in synchronization. You eat the same things at the same time. You each take a sip of coffee at the same time."

Sokie's eyes widened then she glanced at Evan. Her mouth opened for a moment, then closed. She blinked her eyes rapidly for a moment. Evan grinned.

"I see you are all awake now," Rosette said, coming out of what Malique guessed was the restroom.

"With the exception of my sister," Malique said bitterly.

"She will be awake once I have the pebble where it belongs."

Malique glared at her.

"Eat. You will need your strength," Rosette insisted.

Malique wished he weren't hungry. He didn't want to accept anything Rosette offered him. He didn't trust her, but he didn't have a choice at the moment. "Frederick, serve Malique a breakfast plate."

Frederick grunted but did as he was told. Malique closed his eyes as he picked up the fork. He imagined the food to be clean and healthy. He believed it to be fulfilling and a supply of strength. He opened his eyes and glanced down at his plate. It seemed as if the amount of food doubled. He took a bite of the eggs first and closed his eyes as he chewed. As the meal went down his throat, he felt his spirit start to lift. He felt sparks of energy triggering throughout his body.

Ricardo entered the dining area, still clutching his stomach. "What's with you?" Frederick asked him.

"Nothing," Ricardo denied.

"Ricardo, you know how to drive this boat, right?" Rosette asked.

"Yes," Ricardo said.

Rosette tossed him the keys. Ricardo moved to the upper deck where the controllers were.

Malique turned to Evan and asked in a whisper, "Don't you need a license to drive a boat?"

Evan nodded to say yes.

Sokie made the sign of the cross.

217

Moments later, the boat jerked a few times, then set sail out of the dock and into the river.

"Hey, is this the route that Huck Finn took?" Frederick asked no one in particular. The professor rolled his eyes, then shook his head.

Forty-five minutes later, Rosette asked Malique, "Do you feel anything? Do you sense the pebble at all? Does your skin feel prickly at all?"

"Why would I tell you if I did?" Malique asked bitterly. He hadn't felt anything nor sensed anything except annoyance and frustration. He wanted to knock Rosette off the boat, then punch Ricardo a few more times via water bottle. He didn't know anything about Frederick, so he didn't feel the need to harm him. He got the feeling Frederick was an idiot and would only cause harm to himself.

"Watch how you speak to me," Rosette said.

"Why did you cause my mother to crash?" Malique asked with a glare in his eyes.

Rosette's eyes widened from shock. "Wh--- I---"

"I know that you were the one behind the accident. I want to know why?"

"You should not ask questions about things you do not understand and do not involve you?"

"What do you mean it doesn't involve me?! It was my family."

"Your mother was trying to hide you and your sister away. I think she was trying to meet your father somewhere with you and your sister. I had to stop her."

"Why?"

"Because you and your sister are needed for the pebble to activate. Without you, I cannot take my rightful place."

"You do not have any rightful place when it comes to the pebble."

"And what makes you think you should be the controller of what happens to the pebble?"

"Because everyone who knows about the pebble and has spoken or appeared to me have told me so."

"Appeared to you? You have had visions?" Rosette asked hesitantly.

Malique nodded, not sure if it was something he should have let Rosette know.

"Have you?" Rosette asked again, impatiently.

"It doesn't matter. What happened after the accident?"

Rosette blinked her eyes rapidly. "I was banished from any contact from anyone in your family. The only way I could be in contact with you was if you came to me."

"What would have happened if you came to me?"

"There was a spell. Whenever I tried, I started to suffocate. I could not breathe unless I moved away from you or any member of your family."

"Where were you this entire time?"

"Here, in New Orleans. My grandchildren lived close to you so they would give me updates on what you and your sister were up to."

"So, you knew my sister was alive all these years too?" Malique asked.

"Yes."

"What happened to my mother and father?" Malique felt his heart racing for hope.

"I do not know. There was a flash of light right after the accident, and I somehow appeared here in New Orleans," Rosette said.

"Do you think they might still be alive?"

"I cannot say," Rosette said softly. There was a part of Malique that wondered if Rosette cared about his family. There seemed to be a small trace of concern in her voice and mannerism. It was only momentary, though. Rosette wiped her forehead then said, "Please turn around and let me examine your back."

Malique wondered why she used the word "please" when she had Lani passed out in a coma or deep sleep or

219

whatever she was in as leverage. Instead of asking her and causing an unnecessary argument, fight, or struggle, he simply did as she asked. He turned around and allowed her to examine his back. Since the other day, he had learned to control the map on his own. He closed his eyes and imagined a smooth surface across his back.

But, he hadn't anticipated her touch. When she touched him with her right-hand fingertips, it triggered the map. He arched his back as prickly heat immediately ignited and set his body with a fire sensation. He screamed. Aunt Sokie rushed to Malique's side, but Rosette held up her left hand to stop Sokie from coming any closer. Sokie stood a few feet away from Malique and swallowed hard.

CHAPTER TWENTY

"We are close," Rosette said in a raspy voice.

Malique closed his eyes and pleaded for Lani's help.

I'm here, Mali. Breathe--- Calm--- Breathe--- Smooth, relaxing thoughts---. Breathe.

Malique took deep breaths in and deep breaths out.

"Stop turning it off," Rosette demanded. She poked his back with one of her sharp nails.

Malique arched his back again but was determined to focus. He refused to allow her to be able to see any more of the map. Malique quickly turned to face Rosette. His hands were balled into a fist.

"Don't touch me again," Malique commanded. He glared at Rosette, to add to the warning.

Rosette put her hands down and looked momentarily ashamed then glanced at her feet. She slowly lifted her head.

Sokie moved towards Malique and crossed her arms. "I will not let you near the pebble," Malicue said.

"My, my, my--- Look who has stepped up as the guardian of the pebble. Do you genuinely believe you can stop me when I'm ready to take it from you?"

"Yes," Malique said without flinching. He thought he did a pretty convincing job of making her believe he believed the words he had just spoken. In reality, he was clueless.

Rosette studied him for a few moments then pursed her lips. "We will dock here for a while and see what happens. Either the pebble will come to you, or you will go to it. I will watch you--- Wait and see."

Malique shook his head from annoyance and exhaustion.

Rosette moved back into the houseboat. Sokie wrapped her arms around Malique. Malique welcomed the embrace and hugged her back.

Mali?

Yes, Lani, I'm here.

Clarissa is crying.

Malique's chest ached, and his throat started to burn. He hadn't thought of Clarissa since he'd arrived in New Orleans. Too much was always happening. He didn't even have a chance to call her. An enormous amount of guilt bared down on him. It was crushing him. He wondered if something was wrong with him. Maybe there was a part of him that was broken. He wondered why he hadn't thought of her even for a moment since their flight landed. Did that mean he didn't care about her? He must not be in love with her. But what was love anyway? Everyone he cared about vanished or lied or---

Stop it, Mali.

Clarissa is crying from missing you so much. Stop feeling sorry for yourself.

Why did you tell me about Clarissa? You know I have so much to deal with as it is, and now I have to worry about C?

Do you want me to send Clarissa a message in her dream?

You can do that?

Yes. That's all I've been doing since Rosette knocked me out.

Talk to her. Tell her all that has been going on and let her know I care about her. Don't use the L-word because I just don't think I'm ready to use that word.

Chicken.

Don't start fighting with me now, little sister.

We'll have lots of time to fight when this is all over.

Malique recalled the words Rosette said moments ago, "Either the pebble will come to you, or you will go to the pebble." What did that mean? *Lani, how am I supposed to find the pebble? Rosette mentioned either the pebble would come to me, or I will go to the pebble--- Any ideas?*

No, I don't know Mali.

Malique let out a sigh of resignation. *Okay, well--- go to Clarissa in a dream and tell her all that has been going on. Let her know I am thinking about her, and I care about her.*

Okay. I'll be back soon.

After lunch, Malique grew tired and needed sleep. He found a cushioned bench on the deck of the houseboat and laid down. Malique barely closed his eyes when an old woman's voice entered his head. "Chile, why you layin' down when you should be searchin' and diggin'? Too much depends on you, and you lay? Get off your feet and work."

"Who are you? Where are you? Why are you in my head?" Malique asked crankily.

"You lazy?"

"Show me who you are!" Malique yelled out in the darkness of his head. He wanted to sleep, not more visions or messages. He was tired. He just wanted to go back to Beach City and Sasha's house. He wanted to be normal and nothing special.

"Why you have such negative thoughts. Be proud of being special. Be proud of who you are, Malique Laveaux!"

"How can I be proud?!" He yelled in a squeaky voice. "You say to be proud of who I am, but how can I be proud when I don't know who I am?"

"You have everything inside of you to figure it all out. All you need is the desire, the will--- to figure out who you are. With the desire, you will have the want, not just the need to find out who you are. To find out who you are, you have to seek. You seek--- You will find."

"What?" Malique asked, utterly confused.

"You have to want to know--- your desire to know who you truly are isn't strong. If you gain strength and determination to figure out who you are--- you will find out. Nothing can stop you." The old woman said.

"Who are you? You sound familiar," Malique said.

"Seek Malique, and you will know---"

Malique focused on the voice. It was old and raspy. An image of the woman in the voodoo shop came to mind. "You're the lady from the voodoo shop?"

"Yes."

"Why were you so mean to me when I came to see you with the professor? Why did you cause the accident, and what did you do with or to my mother?"

"Ahh--- you've done some of your homework," the woman said, impressed.

"Not really, more like spirits, dead people--- whatever you prefer to call it--- keep disturbing me when I sleep."

"Interesting. I thought I was the only significant one."

"Ha," Malique said sarcastically. "More like the cranky, mean one."

"Rosette is the cranky, mean one. I'm the good one."

"So you say---"

"Malique, you are wasting too much of my time. I have only come to tell you that you have to want to know who you are. You have to want to know the truth. You have to want to know all in all about the pebble. The strength of your desire will cause you to seek. What you seek, you will find."

Then there was nothing but a harsh, loud silence.

Malique's eyes were still heavy. He kept them closed, not wanting to be on the boat. He wanted to be anywhere but on the boat. He felt angry at the old woman. Who did she think she was? For most of his life, he'd missed his family. He wanted to know more about his heritage and ancestry, but there was no one there who could provide him with any information. Not until recently. He thought about his father. Who was he? What was his father doing? He couldn't have been gone this long just for some research paper. He must have left for some other reason, but what? The pebble.

What does the pebble look like? How does it feel? How big is it? Is it bigger than a grain of salt? Does it have a taste? He was surprised by the last question. It wasn't as though he was planning on eating the pebble. He thought the pebble should be the size of a dime all around. A perfect circle. It should be royal blue with a pearly appearance. Blue was his favorite color. Royal blue since everyone kept referring to him and Lani as royalty. It would be cold to the touch. He wasn't sure why he thought that, but he did.

Malique felt something wet on his feet; then it moved to his hands. Suddenly he felt himself submerged in water. He instinctively held his breath and opened his eyes. He was sinking deep into the water at a high rate of speed. Finally, when he reached the bottom, he looked around. It was shockingly bright and clear surrounding him. He could see approximately twelve feet around him in all directions. On top, a mound of sand was a perfectly round pebble royal blue. His heart raced. His hands shook as he approached the pebble, then raised his hands to pick it up.

Don't use your bare hands Mali! It will burn you.

Lani?

Yes, it's me. Use your sock or something. Don't use your bare hands!

How'd you know?

Stop asking me questions when you know neither of us has the answers. Hurry up! Rosette will be looking for you.

Malique took a deep breath, surprised that he could breathe underwater. Malique took his shoes and socks off. He grabbed one of the socks and used it to grab the pebble. His hands immediately felt ice-cold when his hands enveloped the pebble with the sock. *Are you sure it would burn me, Lani? It feels like it would be cold.*

Mali, you do know that ice can burn, right?

Oh.

He was slightly annoyed that his sister, who was younger than he was, knew that ice could cause a burn when he didn't. He wasn't going to let Lani know that, though.

Now, what do I do?

Come back to the boat.

Will you be awake now?

I think so, but we don't want Rosette to know. I will keep my eyes closed. We don't want her to know that we have the pebble.

I agree. Okay, I'm going back up to the boat. I'm assuming up anyway.

How did you get in the water if you didn't jump?

I just woke up in the water Lani. I didn't do anything.

You must have done something. You can't just appear somewhere without doing something.

I--- I guess--- I was visualizing the pebble--- what I thought it should look like, and then I woke up in the water. It's weird. I can breathe down here. Like--- normal.

Awesome!

Well, I better get back to the boat. I don't want Rosette to catch on.

Malique began to swim up. It seemed as if he were swimming a hundred miles, but it was one hundred feet. When he surfaced, he glanced around, searching for the boat. The sky was clear blue; the sun was overhead. So it was around noon. But how was that possible? When he had fallen asleep, it was a little after two in the afternoon. Was it possible that he had slept for longer than the short nap he thought he was taking? And where was the boat? He used his right hand to wipe off his face, then blinked his eyes a few times. Still, no boat.

In the distance, he saw an island.

What the heck?!

Mali? What's wrong?

I don't know--- I don't see the boat--- I see an island, though.

Where are you? Lani asked in a panic.

I don't know.

Well, swim towards the island.

That's what I was thinking. Malique estimated he was about five hundred feet from the island. He sighed. He'd been through a lot already, but he figured he could handle swimming a few hundred feet. He had to convince himself. He had no other option.

As he was walking up the shore, a tall, dark man in khaki shorts and khaki button-up shirt walked up to help Malique stand up by extending his right hand out to Malique. "Are you okay?" The man asked in an Australian accent.

"I'm not sure," Malique admitted.

"What do you mean? Either you are or aren't--- where are you coming from, mate?"

"Um--- I--- New Orleans," Malique said.

The man put his hands on his hips and laughed.

"What's so funny?"

"How long have you been in the water?" The man asked.

"I think only twenty minutes--- at least that's what it seemed like."

The man laughed again, then shook his head. "That is impossible."

"But--- where am I?" Malique asked, utterly confused.

The man outstretched his arms and smiled a genuine smile, "Welcome to Casper Island."

"What?"

The man put down his arms in disappointment, "I see this was not your intended destination, but I tell you it's the best place on earth, probably the universe. We are a small island community of about six hundred. We see all and know all--- we watch each other's backs here. Don't think you can come here and try to take anything from us," the man looked at Malique with suspicion. "Why are you here, mate?"

"Why are you talking like an Australian?" Malique asked.

The man squinted his eyes. "We are an Australian island. Now answer my question. Why are you here?"

"I don't know," Malique said honestly. He wanted to be alone so that he could think.

"Come with me," the man's former kindness vanished, now there appeared to be hostility and suspicion. The man maneuvered Malique's right arm so that it was twisted behind his back.

"But why? Where are you taking me?"

"To a holding cell. I cannot have an undocumented stranger wandering around the island. You must come with me."

Malique struggled for a moment, but the man's grip was too tight and restraining. Malique remembered the pebble but felt something in his left pocket so relaxed. They reached a bungalow a few moments later. There were three small desks, a concrete floor, and a small holding cell. A short petite blonde woman was sitting at one of the desks wearing a similar uniform as the man. "Who's this?" The woman asked in a deep voice.

"Not sure. He just washed up onshore. No documents. He says he was in New Orleans twenty minutes ago and doesn't know why he is here. Imagine that, on the other side of the world in twenty minutes." The man shook his head in disbelief.

"I will check if there were any boating accidents reported, or missing person," she volunteered. "Make sure he's clean before you put him in the cell."

The man raised his brows. "Oh," he said simply. The man turned to Malique. "I need to pat you down. Mind spreading your arms and legs, please?"

Malique felt as though he was in a twilight zone or something but did as he was asked. His heart raced a bit as the man began to pat him down.

When the man came across his left pocket, he asked Malique to empty his pockets. Malique reached into his pockets and turned them inside out.

"What's that?" The blonde woman asked.

"Looks like a soggy sock to me," the man said.

Malique hoped the man would leave it at that. But of course, the man reached for the sock. "What's inside it? What's it wrapped around?"

Don't let him touch it, Mali! You have to stop him!

I'm trying Lani. Leave me alone. I can't think as it is.

Fine.

Before Malique could stop the man, the man unwrapped the sock and exposed the royal blue pebble. The pebble sparkled. The man stood staring at it mesmerized. "It's so cold even with the sock---, and it's soooo--- sooo beautiful," he said in a whisper.

The woman moved closer to the man's left palm that was only inches away from the man's face to examine it. She had reached for the pebble before Malique realized what she was doing. "Don't---" he said, but it was too late. She had already grabbed the pebble with her bare hands. Immediately, her right hand, which held the pebble glowed red in color, then steam began to emerge from her hands. The woman's eyes widened from pain, and she screamed as she dropped the pebble. She dropped to the floor and curled into a ball, clutching her right hand firmly to her chest. Tears streamed down her face.

The man turned to Malique in disbelief but then rushed to the woman to help her. Malique immediately scrambled to race after the pebble. It was rolling under a desk. He had grabbed the soggy sock before he dropped down to his knees to retrieve the pebble. He was fortunate enough to grab the pebble before it rolled down a water drain pipe. The pebble was now an orange hue until it was placed back into the soggy sock. His heart calmed as soon as the sock covered the pebble.

"What is that?" The woman asked.

Malique shrugged his shoulders, not knowing what to say to either the man or woman. They wouldn't believe him if he told them.

"Keep it away from me. I don't want it on the island," the woman said in a panic. She turned to the man who now had his arm wrapped around her shoulder.

He nodded in agreement, then kissed her forehead, then went back to Malique. "I'll have to hold you here until we get you on the next boat off the island."

Malique shrugged his shoulders but then nodded in agreement. He didn't exactly want to be on the island in the first place. The man locked him up in the holding cell. There was a ceiling fan above the three desks that were twirling around and around. "I'm taking her to see the doctor. I will be back soon," the man explained to Malique.

Malique was in awe. He was on a small island in a holding cell when he should be in New Orleans on a boat. He was amazed that the man and woman left him alone. It was interesting.

He was sitting in the cell for about an hour; his stomach started to rumble from hunger. There was a chanting in the distance. Malique glanced out the window from his cell and saw a group of people walking towards the building. Somehow Malique knew they were coming after him. Perhaps they all knew what the pebble had done to the woman, and now they wanted to harm him. He thought of the woman from the voodoo shop words, "Seek, and you will find."

He closed his eyes, put his hands in his pockets, and imagined the boat in New Orleans. He held the sock covered pebble in his left hand and erased all other thoughts and noises from his head. He focused on the houseboat. He imagined Sokie and Evan sitting at the table eating breakfast. There would be pancakes, sausage, and a tall glass of orange juice. He imagined the smell. He saw Lani lying on the cushioned bench pretending to be asleep. The smell of pancakes and sausage entered Malique's nostrils. He inhaled deeper, appreciating the delicious scent. Malique slowly blinked his eyes open. He found himself sitting at the table on the houseboat with a plate of pancakes and sausage in front of him, along with a tall glass of orange juice.

Sokie's eyes widened in disbelief. Malique noticed her eyes were puffy, there were bags underneath her eyes, and dark circles surrounded them. Evan looked up and jumped in shock when he found Malique sitting at the table.

"As soon as you have any sign or sound from Malique, you let me know---" Rosette was saying as she walked into the kitchen. She stopped when she saw Malique sitting at the table. She gasped. "So, you decided to return after almost 24 hours?" Rosette asked angrily.

"I never left."

"Don't play games with me, Malique," she warned him.

"I'm not. I haven't been anywhere but here," Malique tried to convince himself. He hoped that if he said it aloud, then he would eventually believe it. From the corner of his eye, he saw Lani scratch her nose and then open one eye.

Stop it Lani. She's going to see you. Close your eyes, and stop moving around. Act like you're sleeping!

Geez--- look who came back from an island cranky. Argghghg.

"Ricardo, start the boat. We are going back to New Orleans," Rosette snapped irritably.

"Why?" Ricardo asked.

"I need to go home and grab a few things. We should also get a couple more days of food."

"We only have until tomorrow to find the pebble, though," Frederick said.

Rosette frowned deeply and gave both of her grandson's angry, disgruntled looks.

Ricardo simply raised his hand in surrender then said, "Okay, okay--- whatever you say, Nana,"

Rosette followed Ricardo and Frederick up to the deck. As soon as the three were out of sight, Evan tapped on Malique's shoulder. Evan spread his palms up in a gesture that asked him to explain where he was.

Malique looked from Sokie to Evan then back to Sokie. He grinned then asked, "You love birds still can't talk? Can you?"

Sokie sneered at him. Evan ignored him but kept moving his hands around, demonstrating how impatient he was and wanted to know where he had been.

Malique whispered, "Calm down. That vein popping out of your forehead is about to explode, and we don't want that to happen cause--- well--- that would just be nasty, and I don't want to be the one to clean it up."

Malique could have sworn Evan's eyes were turning red.

"Okay, calm down," Malique glanced around to make sure Rosette or the two hoodlums weren't around then pulled the sock out of his left pocket. He carefully unfolded the sock to expose a tiny bit of the pebble.

Sokie's mouth dropped open while Evan's eyes became wider than Malique had ever seen. Sokie mouthed, "Put that away! Now!"

232

"And--- Lani is okay. She's awake, pretending to sleep," Malique whispered.

Sokie smirked and mouthed, "I know." She pointed to Lani and demonstrated exaggeratedly what Lani has been doing: scratching her nose, hair, feet, opening one eye and then the other, moving arms every which way. Sokie shook her head but laughed.

Evan was chewing on his lip, obviously deep in thought.

"We need to get back to the voodoo shop, don't we?" Malique whispered to Evan.

Evan nodded in agreement.

"Why would Rosette give in so easily? I mean, why didn't she quiz me more about where I have been?" Malique asked Evan suspiciously.

Evan took a deep breath and shook his head to say he didn't know.

I say we just knock out Ricardo and Frederick. Then we zap Rosette or something.

Lani, how are we going to zap Rosette?

I don't know, Lani's voice sounded high pitch in his head. It reminded him of how his mother would say the same three words to his dad at times. Wow, he finally had a memory of his father. Even though it was a short memory, at least it was something.

You don't need to be sad right now, Mali. We all need you to be alert and ready to pounce Rosette as soon as we have a chance.

I'm not going to pounce her.

Why not? She almost killed us. She may or may not have killed our parents. She's evil, Mali! We need to get rid of her!

Wow. Look who woke up all high and mighty.

If I weren't pretending to be under a spell right now, I would be rolling my eyes at you--- You dork.

233

When they were back at the Riverwalk, Ricardo and Frederick escorted them off the boat. Evan carried Lani. Lani did her best to appear limp but jerked a few times when Evan almost lost his balance. Rosette and her grandsons didn't seem to notice.

Let's push the three of them into the locker where they held Aunt Sokie and me. Then we can all go to the voodoo shop together. Concentrate now, Mali. Imagine the three of them locked in the storage unit.

It was hard for Malique to concentrate on imagining Ricardo, Frederick, and Rosette in the storage unit when he was walking along the crowded Riverwalk, but he did it. Though his eyes were open in order to avoid running into anyone or something, he focused and visualized the three pain in the butts locked in the cold, dark, and storage room. He imagined them vanishing from behind him as he walked, then visualize them in the storage room. Only seconds later, they heard a yelp from Rosette, and then the three of them were gone.

Just then, Lani opened her eyes, "Thank God. You can put me down now, Professor."

Sokie and Evan glanced at each other in disbelief.

"Let's hurry and get to somewhere private, so Malique and I can concentrate and focus so the two of you can get your voices back."

Sokie and Evan each nodded in agreement. They held hands as they followed Malique and Lani to a corner on Bourbon Street. Lani reached for Malique's hand, and they both closed their eyes and imagined Evan and Sokie talking to each other in calm, peaceful, united tones. A few moments later, Sokie cleared her throat. Malique and Lani looked up at the same time.

"I think we are okay now," Sokie said with a smile.

"Finally," Evan said with a grin. "Thank you both. You have no idea how much I've missed Sokie's voice."

"Now, let's get back to the voodoo shop," Lani said, eagerly.

CHAPTER TWENTY-ONE

The old woman was sitting in the back, right side of the shop again, on a stool with her walking cane next to her. "So, you've found the pebble?"

"Yes," Lani said to her eagerly.

"And you have brought the princess with you this time. Good."

"I'm not a princess."

"Oh, yes, you are. Princesses and royalty don't always live in extravagant castles, and dress in expensive clothes and wear ridiculously expensive worthless jewelry. You and your brother come from a long line of protectors and healers. Your father's people have been protectors since perhaps the beginning of time. It is an honor to me for you to be in my shop and my presence. For that, I thank you."

"Why are you being so nice to her, and so mean to me?" Malique asked irritably.

"Silence Malique. Vous devez apprendre à parler avec vos aînés avec respect! Vous avez peut-être redevances, mais vous agissez comme un royal douleur dans la cuisse!"

Malique scowled.

"I agree; my brother can be a pain in the butt."

The old woman laughed.

"This is just not right," Malique whined. He shook his head and squinted his eyes.

"I think it's a female to female thing Mali. Don't take it too personally," Evan explained.

"How can I not? Every time I see her, she makes personal attacks on my character."

"Isn't that a big word for you? Character," Lani teased.

"Oh, now look who is fighting and arguing all the time," Evan said.

Malique shook his head again and ignored them all. He took a deep breath, then reached into his pocket and pulled out the sock covered pebble. He placed it on her glass counter display. The old woman trembled when she saw the sock. Her body continued to tremble as she closed her eyes then made the sign of the cross. "I'm not sure it's a good idea to have this in my shop and my presence. So much power should not be here at this time."

"Well, you're the one who told me to bring it to you as soon as I found it," his voice squeaked as he spoke in a high pitch tone of voice. "You said I was taking too long and that I didn't have enough desire to find it. Well, I found it right after you left me the last time and now I don't know what to do with it. If you can't help me, or show me what to do, then you can at least tell me or guide me of what I should do. Because I know you know what I need to do," Malique said, panicked.

The woman sighed, "Okay, we cannot do anything until midnight tonight until it is officially your sixteenth birthday, and summer solstice begins."

"So, what do we do in the meantime?" Evan glanced down at his watch. It was eleven-thirty in the afternoon.

The woman smiled slightly. She reached down for her car keys and purse. "You will come to my home, and I will feed you. We should have a feast and prepare our hearts, minds, bodies, and spirits for midnight. We will need all of our strength and must be on high alert."

Evan rubbed his stomach. "A feast, huh? I can't argue with that."

They all followed the woman to her home, located in Pontchartrain Park. "So, your house made it through Katrina?" Sokie asked as they followed her up the steps.

"No, I had a trailer here while the house was being rebuilt. It took a while, but when you believe in something and know in your heart where you are, is where you are meant to be, it happens. You just gotta hold on tight, be patient, and pray." She turned to look at Malique. "Believe and trust. That's what you've gotta do." She unlocked her door and welcomed them into her home.

They followed her inside her home. "I'll warm up some gumbo for ya'll. Have a seat and relax. I made a big pot yesterday, knowing ya'll would be here."

Thirty minutes later, they were seated around the old woman's dining room table. They had idle chit chat when Malique finally decided it was time to start asking some of the questions he'd wanted to ask her. "You never told us your name, and you never told me why you put the map on me," Malique said just before eating another spoonful of gumbo.

Lani was busy cracking a crab leg and sucking the meat out. Evan and Sokie stopped eating, for a moment, to hear the old woman's response.

"No, I never did, did I?" The old woman said simply. She ate a spoonful of rice and gumbo juice. After she swallowed, she said, "The map was a deterrent. I knew the pebble was in the Indian Ocean, but because of the map on your body, people thought it was here in New Orleans."

"Do you mean this whole time, you knew where the pebble was?" Evan asked, amazed.

The old woman nodded to say yes.

"Then why didn't you just tell us?" Malique asked, frustrated.

"Because of the curse. No one could tell you precisely what you needed to do. Part of the rights to the pebble requires you to find it on your own. If any of the older generations told you precisely where it was, our souls would be burned along with our bodies. It's not something anyone wishes to go through."

"So, why are you talking to me now?" Malique asked.

"Because you have found it all on your own."

Malique moved his mouth to the side, thinking, "So now what do I do with it?"

238

The woman sighed heavily, "That is up to you. You may keep it in your possession until you die, then it goes back to the Indian Ocean. You can activate it, use it to do great good or great evil, and know all there is to know about the universe. Or you can destroy it."

"You said our father's people had been protectors since the beginning of time. Why does the pebble exist then?"

"Your grandfather's father decided to hide it in the Indian Ocean. Not knowing what the future would hold, he wanted his future offsprings to be able to have the choice to use the pebble for good if needed. In case there was a great war. He didn't want to be the one to destroy it. So he cast the spell for it to remain hidden for a hundred years until the male offspring's sixteenth birthday that coincides with the summer solstice."

"So, I just happened to be the lucky one to be born a hundred years later, on June 21st?" Malique shook his head in disbelief. The old woman nodded in agreement.

Evan and Sokie turned to look at each other as if trying to understand each other's thoughts.

The old woman raised her hand to stop Evan and Sokie from speaking. "Whatever Malique and Lani decide it must be a 100% agreed upon decision and one that they each must make on their own. No one may interfere."

"Oh," Sokie said, and then Evan said the same.

"If we kept the pebble but never used it, do we run into the risk of someone else taking it and using it for evil?" Lani asked, thinking of Rosette and any unknown enemies that might be lurking.

"Yes," the woman said simply.

"If we use it for good, do we run the risk of evil intruding?" Malique asked.

"Yes," she said again.

Let's destroy it. Lani thought to Malique.

I agree. It's done enough damage to our lives.

But what if it can do great and wonderful things?

Then it can attract evil things too. I think we should just destroy it and live our lives as normal as possible.

Does that mean we lose our powers? I don't want to lose them? I mean, I don't want to always listen to your thoughts, but I like popping in and out of other people's dreams. It's fun.

Lani, that is just wrong and on the verge of stalking. Malique shook his head. *So wrong on so many levels.*

Ha! She paused for a minute, cracked another crab leg, and sucked more meat out. Juice dripped down her chin. She reached for a napkin, wiped the juice away, and then swallowed. *This is the best gumbo I've ever tasted.*

"Will you two stop doing that?" Sokie asked agitatedly, looking from Malique to Lani and back to Malique again.

"What?" Malique asked innocently.

"Excluding the rest of us from your conversations. It's rude. This is an extremely important decision, and I realize that we aren't supposed to influence your decision one way or the other, but I, at the least, would like to know what you both are thinking and talking about.

The old woman smiled slightly but looked at Malique with interest and anticipation.

"We want to destroy it."

Evan and the old woman nodded in agreement. Sokie just sat there.

Just before midnight, they all gathered in the old woman's living room. Her living room was composed of gray leather L-shaped couch, a glass oval coffee table on top of oak wooden floors. There was no television, but there was a floor to ceiling white bookshelf stocked with hundreds of books. "It will be excruciating Malique. I will not lie to you. If you change your mind during the process, I understand."

Lani's eyes widened. "Can he die?"

"If the pebble fights him, yes."

Sokie shook her head. "Can't they just keep the pebble and hide it?"

"Yes, but it has to be solely Lani and Malique's choice. We cannot influence them."

Lani looked at Malique. *Do you still want to destroy it?*

We have to. I know it in my gut that we are supposed to destroy it.

Okay. Then let's destroy it. Lani took in a deep breath.

"We will destroy it," Malique announced confidently.

Evan nodded in agreement.

"Okay, the three of us will need to form a circle around the two of them. Lani must stand behind Malique and place each of her hands on his shoulders. The three of us will need to hold hands and not let go until Lani tells us to. Do not let go! No matter what. Think of only love. No negative thoughts. Do you understand?" She asked, looking at Sokie and then Evan.

"Yes," Evan and Sokie said together.

"Okay, we have less than a minute to prepare," the old woman said.

Lani stood behind Malique as the old woman instructed her. Sokie, Evan, and the old woman formed a circle around them and held hands. "Okay, Malique, you must hold the pebble with both of your bare hands. The pebble must touch your bare skin. You have to remove the sock."

"But, it will burn him," Lani said.

"You can control the temperature, Lani. Just keep your hands on his shoulders at all times, and do not let go. You understand?"

"Yes," Lani mumbled.

"We must start now. He has to hold it now before midnight."

Malique nervously pulled out the pebble, still wrapped in a sock. He tossed the sock across the room. It landed on the gray leather couch.

He held the pebble briefly with his left hand only.

"Place your right hand next to your left. The pebble must be in both hands," the woman instructed. "Do not drop it."

He did as she said. The pebble began to glow. It felt cold to his hands.

"It is time. Think of love, positive, happy thoughts," she said to Sokie and Evan.

They all closed their eyes except for Malique, who kept his eyes on the pebble. The pebble began to pulsate and glow. The brighter the pebble grew, the more it pulsated, the faster it pulsated, the pebble started to grow. It began to heat up and charged Malique's body with what felt like volts upon volts of electricity. Malique arched his body. His clothes melted off of him. He arched his back; his eyes rolled behind his head. Malique and Lani levitated a couple of feet off of the ground. Lani managed to contain her hold on Malique with as much strength that she could muster. She kept her eyes closed even when she and Malique began spinning in circles with objects flying about them. As if they were the center of a tornado.

Flashes of light and objects continued to swirl around them as all knowledge and secrets of the universe swirled around them. Malique fought it. He rejected the knowledge. He struggled to maintain his hold of the pebble also. His body began to seizure; only the whites of his eyes could be seen. Lani screamed but kept her hands tightly on Malique's shoulders.

The pebble pulsated into the size of a basketball then exploded. A burst of heat, wind, and glittery like substance filled the room. The glittery substance fell upon Lani,

Sokie, Evan, and the old woman. Malique collapsed into a fetal position on the floor.

"Mali?" Lani asked in a shaky voice. "Mali!" She shouted, "Open your eyes! Help."

The other three opened their eyes and glanced down. Lani was crouched over with her right hand on Malique's shoulder. She was crying.

"He will be okay," the old woman said to Lani.

Sokie crouched down next to Lani and stroked Malique's hair. "Are you sure? He's barely breathing."

"The important thing is that he's breathing," Evan said.

"Should we move him?"

"Let me grab a blanket to cover him. He will be cold, although right now, his body is heated."

Sokie felt Malique's forehead. "He's burning up."

"Yes, that is expected," the woman disappeared down the hall. Cabinets were opening and then closing. The old woman came back into the living room, holding a black and purple crocheted blanket. Let's cover him up then move him to the couch. Sokie grabbed the blanket from the old woman then covered her nephew.

Sokie let out a gasp then said, "The map--- It's gone."

The old woman nodded with a smile. "That was also expected."

Evan scratched the back of his head. "I don't believe it."

"Let's move him to the couch," Sokie said. "I'll grab his feet, you grab his head and shoulders," she instructed Evan.

He did as he was told. They placed Malique on the larger of the two couches. Sokie adjusted the blanket so that it completely covered Malique, and only his head was exposed.

Lani was sitting on the smaller couch, her knees up to her chest, crying.

"It's all over, Lani. You both are okay. Why are you crying?"

"Malique was hurt, but I wasn't."

"Ah, yes, but don't you see. He could have died if it weren't for you being there, Lani," the old woman explained.

Lani nodded but continued to cry silently.

"Give her some time. She will be okay," the woman said. "I will make some tea for all of us. We will we wait for Malique to come to," she announced before she disappeared into the kitchen.

Two days later, the old woman gave them a ride to the airport and walked them as far as TSA would allow her to. Malique wore shorts, a tank top, and flip-flops for the first time. "You still haven't told us your name," he said.

The old woman smiled with a tear in her eye. "No, I haven't." She gave each of them a massive hug, and a kiss on each of their foreheads then said, "Be safe. Believe and trust." She gripped her cane tightly with her right hand, raised it slightly then slammed it down to the ground. She disappeared in a puff of smoke. Left behind was a broach of a lily.

Sokie covered her mouth in disbelief.

"What is it?" Lani asked. She knelt to pick up the broach.

"It was my grandmother's. My sister loved it. She wore it all the time and never took it off."

"What does it mean?"

Sokie looked to Evan for guidance. For once, he was speechless.

If you enjoyed reading this book, please leave a review on either Amazon or Goodreads.

I love to hear from my readers. You may email me at gigilumas@att.net.

www.ingramcontent.com/pod-product-compliance
Lightning Source LLC
Chambersburg PA
CBHW070057260626
47160CB00004B/1232